HEREAFTER

KATE BRIAN

HYPERION

LOS ANGELES NEW YORK

alloy**entertainment**
Produced by Alloy Entertainment
1700 Broadway, New York, NY 10019

First Hyperion paperback edition, 2014
10 9 8 7 6 5 4 3 2 1
V475-2873-0-14091
Printed in the United States of America
This book is set in Janson Text
Designed by Liz Dresner

ISBN 978-1-4231-6526-2 (paperback)

Library of Congress Control Number for Hardcover Edition: 2013008009

Visit www.hyperionteens.com

SUSTAINABLE
FORESTRY
INITIATIVE
Certified Chain of Custody
Promoting Sustainable Forestry
www.sfiprogram.org
SFI-01054
The SFI label applies to the text stock

For Matt, who somehow got me through
the last year in one semi-sane piece

THE TRUTH

The morning sun rose over the ocean, streaking beautiful hues of pink and purple and orange across the sky. I sat in the sand with Tristan Parrish, his hand clutching mine, and stared down at his worn leather bracelet while I listened to the sound of his even breathing and the rhythm of the waves rolling onto shore. On any other day, this would have been the most romantic moment of my life. But this was today. And my life was over.

Focus, Rory. Focus and breathe.

"So that night on the highway . . . that wasn't a nightmare," I said slowly. "Me, my father, and my sister . . . we all died."

1

Tristan's clear blue eyes were shot through with pain. The callus on his thumb pressed into my palm. "Yes."

I was numb as I spoke the next few words. "Steven Nell killed us."

"Yes."

His grip on my fingers tightened, and suddenly a sucking void opened up inside my chest. I gasped, clinging to him as a barrage of images assaulted me one after another, like a film projected on a screen. Mr. Nell charging me, his watery eyes wild with hunger. The knife blade buried deep in my stomach. The bloodstain seeping through my shirt. The tree branches gnashing overhead. My last, choked breaths as I slowly slipped away and everything grew cold.

My heart twisted painfully and I bent forward, struggling to breathe.

"I'm so sorry," Tristan said again. "I had to show you the truth."

He squeezed my hand once more, and his gorgeous, chiseled face zipped into focus. If this had been any other day, I would have been obsessing about what he was thinking. Why he was still holding my hand. Whether it meant he liked me as much as I liked him. I'd be worrying over whether my palms were clammy, if I had morning breath, or if my hair was doing that insane frizz thing around my forehead it so loved to do. These were the things a sixteen-year-old girl was *supposed* to be obsessing about. I was not supposed to be obsessing about how I'd died.

Overhead, a fat crow cawed, swooping in and out before settling atop the roof of the white-and-blue beachfront house my family had been living—no, not living . . . *existing*—in since we arrived in Juniper Landing exactly one week ago. We'd been forced to flee our home in Princeton, New Jersey, when my math teacher, a serial killer who'd already killed fourteen other girls, had set his sights on me.

We'd followed the FBI agent's directions to a T, driving through a torrential downpour to our new location, our new identities as the Thayer family in tow. We thought we'd made it safely down to South Carolina, but we hadn't made it at all. Mr. Nell had found us on a lonely stretch of highway and finished what he'd set out to do. He killed my dad, then my sister, Darcy, then me.

Suddenly, I shoved myself up, spraying sand everywhere in my haste.

"Where are you going?" Tristan scrambled to his feet and reached for me, but I flung his hand away, shaking from head to toe.

"I have to tell my sister. I have to tell my dad," I said, my voice thick with tears.

"No. You can't," he said vehemently. "You can't do that."

Tristan got in front of me and blocked my way. Behind

him I could see the windows of my father's room. The room where he slept, oblivious to the fact that his life had ended. That his attempt to protect his daughters by leaving the house we'd grown up in, the house where my mother had lived and died, had failed.

"What? What do you mean, I can't?" I shouted. "They're my family, Tristan."

I tried to step around him, but he grabbed my arm, his grip so tight it sent a shock of alarm through me. I tried to wrench myself away, but suddenly a soft, soothing sensation sprang up inside my wrist and slowly traveled up my arm and into my chest. He clung to me, and my heart stopped slamming against my rib cage. My breathing returned to normal. I felt suddenly, oddly, calm.

I looked into Tristan's pale blue eyes. They were . . . victorious.

A thump of fear obliterated any sense of serenity. I yanked my arm out of his grasp, his fingernails scraping my skin.

"What was that? What did you just do to me?" I demanded, backing away in terror.

His face paled. "Rory—"

"No!" I shouted, betrayal clenching my gut. "You can't just mess with my mind like that! What *are* you?"

Tristan's face turned to stone, and his eyes flicked just past my shoulder. I felt the presence of someone behind me two seconds before I collided with something solid and unyielding. A pair of strong arms closed around me, locking my limbs against my chest and picking me up off the ground, all while Tristan looked on calmly.

I screamed as loudly as I could. The only response was a seagull's cry.

"This hurts me more than it hurts you," a low voice whispered in my ear.

My chest constricted, tighter and tighter, until I couldn't breathe and the world around me went gray. Tristan stepped forward slowly, looking into my eyes, his mouth set in a grim line.

"Why?" I gasped, trying to cling to consciousness. "Why are you doing this to me?"

"I'll explain everything when you wake up," he said gently. "I promise."

Then his handsome face contorted and blurred, and everything went black.

DIFFERENT

I came to on a dusty couch in a room that smelled like mold mixed with beer and sea salt. My chest ached, and my short fingernails had cut painful grooves in my palm. Nearby, someone laughed.

Tentatively I opened one eye and took in my surroundings. I was in a wood-paneled, windowless basement. The room was decorated with green and orange shag rugs, a dim overhead lamp that looked like a sea urchin, and several saggy plaid couches. Milling near a marble bar with ugly, torn-up vinyl stools were about a dozen kids my age, sipping coffee from paper cups and chatting with one another as if my kidnapping was an everyday social event.

I recognized several of them as Juniper Landing locals, year-rounders in what I'd previously assumed was a vacation town. There was Bea McHenry, an athletic redhead, whose wet hair was slicked back into a ponytail, as though she'd just come in from a swim. Kevin Calandro, whose fire tattoo peeked out from under the arm of a dirty white T-shirt, eyed me curiously over the plastic top of his coffee cup. Next to him was Lauren Caldwell, whose black hair was held back by a plaid headband. Two girls and a guy I'd never seen before hovered in the corner, eyeing the rest of the group as if they didn't want to be there.

A door on the far side of the room opened, and Joaquin Marquez, the boy who seemed so intent on breaking my sister's heart, slipped out, followed by Tristan. One of the girls in the corner, a wispy emo chick with a short blond Mohawk, followed him with her eyes, an expression of longing I instantly recognized. It was exactly the way I used to look at Christopher Kane in the halls of Princeton Hills High, back when he was still with Darcy.

Fisher Morton was the last to step out of the back room. He closed and locked the door behind him quickly, then joined the rest of the party, turning his massive shoulders sideways to slip through the tightly knit group.

My lashes fluttered involuntarily. Why had he locked the door?

"You guys, she's awake," Krista Parrish announced, emerging from the crowd in a pink-and-white sundress. Her blond hair, the exact same shade as her brother's, was pulled up in a high ponytail, her blue eyes expertly lined as she frowned sympathetically down at me. Ignoring the pain in my head, I sat up straight, taking in the whole room now. Behind her was a set of stairs leading up. An escape route.

I scrambled to my feet, my heart thumping. "What's going on?" I asked, edging away from them toward the stairs. "Where are we?"

"Don't worry," Krista said gently, putting out a hand as if trying to soothe a rabid dog. "No one is going to hurt you."

"I'm sorry it had to happen this way," Tristan said, the edges of his mouth curving down. I remembered how he'd looked at me right before I'd passed out, and averted my eyes. "We're in the basement of the police station."

"You kidnapped me and brought me to the *cops*?" I blurted.

Mohawk Girl laughed loudly.

"We didn't kidnap you," Joaquin said, rolling his eyes. "We saved you. You and your family."

Krista, Lauren, and Fisher looked at me so earnestly that all the tiny hairs on the back of my neck stood on end. I felt as though I'd suddenly landed in the middle of a cult.

"Well, if I'm not kidnapped, can I . . . leave?" I said, taking another step toward the stairs.

"Sorry." Fisher shook his head.

My heart nose-dived. That was the voice. The voice of the person who'd grabbed me on the beach. I took an instinctive step back and crashed into the wall. My pulse thrummed quickly in my veins.

"Will someone please tell me what's going on?" I demanded.

"We couldn't let you tell your family," Tristan replied.

"Excuse me?" I exhaled sharply. "You tell me we're all dead and expect me not to tell my family?"

"You can't," Tristan repeated. There was all this emotion in his eyes. Longing and pleading. Like he was just trying to help. Like he needed me to understand. But at that moment, I didn't trust it. I couldn't.

"Try to stop me."

I turned toward Fisher and jammed my foot down as hard as I could into his instep. He cursed and doubled over, giving me enough time to dodge past him, grab one of the wooden spindles that lined the stairs, and swing myself around and up the first two steps.

"Rory, no!" Joaquin shouted. Footsteps sounded behind me.

I tripped but hauled myself back up and kept going. I could see the light framing the doorway at the top.

"Stop!" Lauren called out. "Rory, they'll—"

I flung myself forward, reaching for the door.

"If you tell your family, they'll be damned to the Shadowlands!" Krista cried.

"Krista!" someone hissed.

"What? She was leaving!" Krista replied in a whine.

I paused with my fingers on the doorknob. My chest heaved with each breath. *The Shadowlands?* As I turned around, Tristan stepped into view at the bottom of the staircase. I stared down at him, barely able to make out his face in the dim light. Behind him on the wall was an old-fashioned painting of a sunset, the golden glow forming a halo around his head.

"What is the Shadowlands?" I asked.

"Will you please come back down here?" he implored softly.

"Not until you tell me," I insisted. "What's the Shadowlands?"

"Come down and we'll tell you everything," he said, reaching out with one hand. "You're safe here. I promise."

I glanced behind me at the door, but my curiosity got the better of me. Ignoring Tristan's outstretched hand, I edged past him down the stairs and walked to the center of the room, trying to look more confident and in control than I felt. Stone-faced, stoic, shrewd. But inside, everything quivered. Tristan hesitated, clearly thrown that I had passed on the opportunity to touch him. Well, good. He deserved it for letting his friend knock me out.

"Okay," I said. "I'm listening."

"Juniper Landing is an in-between," Joaquin began, crossing his arms over the chest of his formfitting red T-shirt. "A limbo."

"One of many," Bea added.

"It's a place where people go to work through any unfinished business they have from the other world before they move on," Tristan said. "They arrive on the same ferry you did and stay until they're ready. Once they move on, there are two possible destinations. There's the good, which we call the Light."

"And there's the bad," Joaquin put in, a shadow passing over his handsome face. "The Shadowlands."

"Which was why we had to stop you on the beach," Tristan implored. "We couldn't risk your dad and Darcy being sent there."

"And you couldn't think of another way?" I demanded.

Tristan's cheeks turned pink. "I tried, but you kind of called me on it, remember?"

The warmth. The calming warmth. I realized now that

11

I'd felt it twice before—yesterday morning, when I was on the verge of a nervous breakdown about Olive's disappearance, and again last night when I'd started to realize the disturbing truth about Juniper Landing. Both times Tristan had used his touch, his power, whatever it was, to bring me back from the abyss.

"So why bring me here?" I asked. "With all of you?"

"We wanted to tell you about what we do," Krista replied. "We're the ones who usher people to their ultimate destinations."

"We call ourselves Lifers," Lauren said. She held up her arm to show me her leather bracelet, which slipped down almost to her elbow. One quick look around the room revealed that every one of my captors wore one. I'd noticed the bracelets when I first arrived on the island and assumed they signaled some kind of club or secret society. I'd had no idea they meant *this*.

"Lifers," I repeated, feeling an odd sense of déjà vu. I'd heard that word somewhere before. "So you guys decide where people end up?"

They all laughed. Even Tristan.

"Uh, no," Lauren said, placing her coffee cup on the bar. "Do we look like gods?"

"Well, some of us do," Joaquin said, throwing up his hands.

Bea narrowed her amber eyes and shoved him so hard he almost fell over.

"That's *not* what we do," Tristan reiterated. "We simply act as ushers to the next realm. When someone's ready to move on, their Lifer gets a coin," He produced a gold coin from his pocket and held it out to me. It gleamed even in the duskiness of the room. I plucked it from his hand and turned it over in my own palm. It was heavy and thick, blank on one side with a sun on the other.

"We take the visitor up to the bridge, hand them their coin, and send them on their way," Tristan explained. "The coin knows which way they're supposed to go and leads them there."

The bridge. Of course. The events of last night filtered through my brain. Mr. Nell screeching and writhing as Fisher and Kevin tossed him into the back of a pickup truck. Krista getting behind the wheel and speeding off into the fog toward the bridge on the north end of the island. His screams cutting off abruptly and the eerie silence that followed. She'd ushered him to the Shadowlands. Right there in front of me. And I'd had no clue.

I studied the coin. How could this little hunk of metal know where I was destined to spend all eternity? With a sudden flinch, I tossed it back to Tristan. Not that I had any doubts, of course. It wasn't like they were going to ship me off to the bad place, right? Me, my sister, my father . . . we were all destined for the Light. We had to be.

Tristan stared at me, his eyes suddenly sad, and I felt the mood in the room shift, as if everyone had stopped breathing as one.

"Why are you looking at me like that?" I asked Tristan. The others suddenly became very interested in the crappy oceanic art on the walls. "Tristan, why are you telling me all this? If I can't tell my family, then why . . . why can *you* tell *me*?"

Tristan took a deep breath. He closed the distance between us and reached for both of my hands. I instinctively froze, waiting for that odd warmth, but this time, I felt nothing. Nothing other than the pounding of my heart.

"You know how you've felt all along that something was different about the island?" he asked.

My head went weightless. "Yes," I replied.

"And you asked why you remembered Olive and the musician from the park after they were gone, while Darcy didn't?" he said.

I blinked, thinking of my first friend on the island who'd disappeared last week without a trace. Where was he going with this?

"Yes."

"Well, that's because you *are* different," Tristan said

slowly, firmly. "You're not like the other visitors on Juniper Landing."

My chest constricted. "Different how?"

Tristan gazed down at my fingers for a long moment before looking me in the eye. There was no one else in the room right then. No one else who mattered. "You're a Juniper Landing Lifer. Like me."

"Like all of us," Joaquin put in.

"What?" I breathed. "What does that even mean?"

"It means you won't be moving on," he said quietly. "You're staying here. With us."

My fingers slipped out of Tristan's grip, and I pressed the heels of my hands against my eyes. I had just started to adjust to the fact that I was going to some ethereal place called the Light. That I would never see home again. Would never graduate from high school or go to college or med school or do anything that I had spent half my life planning to do. And now . . . now I was stuck here? Forever?

"Why?" I demanded, dropping my hands. "What makes me so special?"

"You died an unnatural death," Joaquin told me, his voice suddenly gentle. "At least, that's the first requirement you have to meet to become a Lifer. And in the last moment of your life, you achieved the second."

The room swam before my eyes, a wash of browns and

yellows and greens. "The second? What's the second?"

"You have to prove your selflessness. Either in the other world or once you're here," Tristan told me. "You used your last seconds of life to rid the earth of a sadistic killer. Even as you took your last breaths, you managed to make the world a better place."

One last image came spiraling back to me. A slow-motion reel of me, yanking the knife out of my stomach, turning it on the man who'd murdered my family and so many others, the look of shock on Nell's face as the blade arced toward his chest. A strangled sort of cackle escaped my throat.

"My selfless act was killing Steven Nell?" I said, aghast. "That wasn't selfless; that was revenge."

Tristan's brow knit. "Maybe on some level, but—"

"This has to be a joke," I said, looking around at the rest of them. Waiting—hoping—for one of them to crack. To start laughing and shout "gotcha!" But no one moved. "You're kidding, right? Tell me you're kidding."

"I wouldn't joke about something like this, Rory," Tristan said. "I wouldn't do that to you."

The room blurred in and out around me. The coffee cups scattered on the bar, the plaster cast of a jumping dolphin suspended over one of the couches, all the faces staring back at me—curious, pitying, concerned. I pressed one hand against my forehead and forced myself to focus on Tristan.

Only Tristan. His perfect lips, his strong jaw, his kind eyes. Right now he was the only thing that made sense.

I took a breath.

"So what you're telling me is, this is it," I said, the air catching in my throat, making my eyes sting. "This is where I'm going to stay."

"Yes," Tristan replied, his eyes shining. "This is your new home. Forever."

FOREVER

So now she knows she's here—forever. It's such a pretty word, *forever*. A promise, really. Found on so many Valentine's Day and anniversary cards, signed in thousands of yearbooks, uttered in daily prayers. Forever is the greatest promise there is. Who doesn't want to know that the thing they love, the thing they count on, the thing they believe in will never end? Who doesn't hope for immortality, for the chance to live on . . . forever?

Well, I've tasted forever, and here's what I know: It never, *ever* ends. Every day on this island is an eternity. The sun rises, the clueless invade, the fog rolls in, the clueless depart.

It's the same, day in and day out. The same faces, the same places, the same smells and sounds and sensations. It's like a never-ending loop of the most boring movie ever made, and I'm forced to live it over and over and over again. There is no end. There will never *be* an end.

I know I'm supposed to feel pride in my work, understand and embrace that I've been blessed with a higher calling, a purpose—that I've been given a gift. And I tried to believe that in the beginning. I did. I so wanted to believe it. But it's been so long now. So very, very long. And what do I have to show for it? Nothing. What will I ever have to show for it? Nothing. Because here, in this in-between, there is nothing to hope for, nothing to strive for, no going forward, no going back.

Or so they think. What no one on this boring rock knows is that I'm already working to change my fate. I will get out of here.

No matter what it takes.

THE DRIVE

The sun outside was piercing. I held my hand up against it and tripped down the first few white marble steps, grabbing onto the handrail just in time to stop myself from sprawling across the sidewalk.

"Rory, stop!" Tristan shouted behind me.

"Just let me go, Tristan."

On a grassy stretch of the park, near the burbling swan fountain, a young woman worked her way through a series of yoga poses on a purple mat. An elderly couple strolled by with steaming coffees, whispering to each other and smiling. A middle-aged man jogged toward us, clutching a surfboard under his arm, headed for the beach. I stared at him until he dipped down the hill and out of sight.

Dead. All these people were dead.

Two black crows swooped in, cawing as they grazed perilously close to my ears—so close I felt the soft tip of one wing graze my skin. They swung up and across the street, coming to rest on the wings of the swan at the center of the fountain. The two of them sat there, puffing their chests and glaring at me.

"Not until you hear what I have to say," Tristan said. He caught up with me and looked down at his feet. "Listen, I really am sorry about having Fisher grab you on the beach. I just—"

"No. I get it. It's fine." I paused and took in a sharp breath. "I mean, it's not *fine*, but I get why you did it. You were trying to help me . . . my family." My eyes welled up all over again as I thought of my dad and Darcy, how blissfully ignorant they were right then. "God. This sucks."

"I know. I'm sorry." Tristan shoved his hands into his hair, briefly lacing his fingers together behind his head, his biceps flexing beneath the sleeves of his black T-shirt. "You should know that they won't remember anything that happened last night, either—that Nell was here, that Darcy was kidnapped, that a search party was formed."

I balked. "Why not?"

"No visitor who encountered Nell while he was here will remember him, just like all the other visitors who have been moved on," Tristan explained. "Your sister and dad included."

I shook my head slowly. "This is insane. This whole place is insane."

"I know it seems that way," Tristan said, dropping his arms at his sides. "But listen, you can get through this. Look at what you've been through already. You were stalked by a serial killer and you survived."

I laughed bitterly as one tear spilled over. "No, actually, I didn't."

"No, I mean, your soul survived," he explained, grasping my arms gently. "And it's beautiful and strong and true. Look at you, Rory. Look what you did last night. You saved your sister. You faced your murderer and won. And now, thanks to you, he's in the Shadowlands. You did that."

When I looked into his eyes, I could tell that he meant what he said. That he thought I was beautiful, strong, and true. That he even admired me, and what I'd done. Gradually, my breathing began to slow, and I felt something new sparking up inside me. It felt a bit like pride, a bit like hope. It was small, but it was there.

Tristan turned me gently to look up at his house, the

sprawling blue colonial mansion hovering high on the bluff overlooking the ocean to the south, and the town to the north and east.

"You see the weather vane up there?" he asked, lifting his chin.

It was a gleaming gold embellishment atop the tallest turret—another proud swan. The arrow was pointing south, and it was still as stone, even though there was a good breeze coming in off the water.

"Have you ever noticed it never points east or west?" he asked, lifting one eyebrow.

"Yes," I told him, feeling a little rush of realization. "It never actually moves with the wind."

"Exactly." His smile made me blush with an odd sense of accomplishment. "If the person goes to the Light, the weather vane points north. If the person goes to the Shadowlands, it points south. That's why it's pointing south now," he added, watching me carefully. "For Steven Nell."

"Why am I not surprised?" I said quietly.

Tristan smiled, and so did I. A small, tentative smile. "Come with me," he said, tilting his head. "There's something I want to show you."

I glanced over my shoulder toward the ocean, toward home. A huge part of me wanted to go back, to be with my

family, even if I couldn't tell them anything. But Darcy and
my dad—both late sleepers—were probably still in bed, and
I had a zillion questions only Tristan could answer. This
was his home, his reality, his existence.

We crossed the park and headed down a side street
toward the water. The marina was a wide horseshoe shape
lined by slatted docks that opened into a large parking lot.
A dozen sailboats—some wooden, some fiberglass—were
moored in the sapphire-blue water, while a few motorboats
were tied in individual slips. One, I noted wryly, was named
Eternity.

Out on the choppy bay, I could see the ferry moving
slowly toward the dock. I hadn't laid eyes on the boat since
the day my dad, my sister, Darcy, and I had arrived on the
island, and I realized now that I'd never really looked at it.
The enclosed areas had dozens of windows, all of which
gleamed as if this run was the boat's maiden voyage.

Tristan walked to a weathered wooden guardrail overlooking the dock and the parking lot just below us. We
waited in silence as the ferry slid into its berth. There were
a few shouts from the dockworkers as they tied the boat off,
and then the walkway was lowered. Before long, the first
passenger stepped off the boat. He was a short, wiry man
with thinning hair and a wide nose. He looked confused
but not unhappy. Behind him was a chubby girl about my

age, wearing a yellow sundress, her dark hair cut short so that it curled in a pixie-ish fashion around her ears. She was followed by a middle-aged couple holding hands, his ebony skin a stark contrast to her freckled pink complexion.

"So these people . . . they're all . . ."

"They're our new arrivals," Tristan confirmed, glancing at me. "Fresh souls."

My grip on the guardrail tightened, remembering my first few moments on the island. How Tristan had watched me so closely as my dad drove past him and his friends outside the general store. I'd felt our connection even then—this sense that somehow we knew each other, that we belonged together.

"I've gotten pretty good, over time, predicting who's destined for the Shadowlands and who's moving on to the Light," Tristan said, leaning his forearms into the top of the fence.

"How long have you been here?" I asked.

Tristan stared across at the gangway, turning so that all I could see was the back of his ear. "A long time."

I bit my lip, feeling as though I'd accidentally crossed a line.

"Check it out," he said, his tone light. He stood up straight and pushed his hands into the back pockets of his shorts. "Good. Good. Very good," he said, nodding as each passenger appeared on the gangway. "Bad but thinks he's good. Good. Bad." Then, all of a sudden, his expression darkened. "Okay . . . bad. Really, really bad."

His gaze was on a boy who looked to be a few years older than I was, with shaggy dark hair, a silver stud earring, and ripped jeans. He carried a stuffed green rucksack and wore a blank expression as he looked around at the peppy dockworkers and the carved wooden sign welcoming him to Juniper Landing. But he had a baby face, and his shoulders were hunched in a way that made me feel more like he was a victim than anything sinister.

"He looks normal to me," I said. "Just . . . sad."

"You'll get the hang of it, the longer you're here," he said, looking me up and down. "You're meant for this place, Rory Miller."

My heart skipped a beat at hearing Tristan say my real name.

"There's something I have to ask you," I said, steeling myself.

"Anything," he replied.

"What about my dad and my sister?" My voice caught. "They died unnatural deaths, too."

A shadow crossed Tristan's face, and I held my breath.

Please don't take them from me. Not now. Not after everything. Please, please, please.

"They did," he said. "The jury's still out on them. They might stay or they might—"

"Don't," I said, my gut suddenly wrenching in pain. I had thought I was ready to hear this, but I wasn't. "Just don't."

"But there *is* a chance they'll stay," he assured me. "We just have to wait and see."

"Okay," I said with a nod, trying to hold the tears back. "Okay."

"Rory, it's not all bad news. Being here, being a Lifer . . . it's a good thing," Tristan said, placing his hand on my back. "You'll get to usher souls to their final destinations. You'll be playing a huge role in their journey from life to afterlife. It's an amazing thing. You'll have a purpose now. A mission."

I took in a sharp breath and looked out over the water. "I had a mission," I said, trying not to feel suddenly sorry for myself—for the hopeful planner I'd been. The girl who had no idea she would never achieve all the goals she'd always dreamed of achieving. I was going to med school. I was going to cure cancer. I was going to make sure that no one else ever had to suffer the way my family did when we lost my mom. "And now all of that . . . it's just gone."

At the edge of the marina, I noticed a figure move in the shade of an elm tree. She flinched when I spotted her, then emerged from her position, half tucked behind the trunk of the tree, and walked off quickly, her head bowed. It was Mohawk Girl. Now I was certain she had a crush on Tristan. She looked up once, her eyes glittering black, before turning her back on me and heading for the bay.

"You don't get it," Tristan said, oblivious to the girl. "That's what makes you all the more perfect as a Lifer. You want to help people. You have the drive. You wanted your life to have meaning. Now it can."

A smile twitched at my lips. "You mean my afterlife will have meaning."

He laughed. "Exactly."

I gazed past Tristan toward town, studying the worn wooden shingles of the buildings on the square; the windsocks fluttering in the breeze; the joggers and the bikers and the morning strollers; the shopkeepers sweeping their walks, propping their doors open, greeting the first customers of the day.

If I had to live someplace forever, this certainly wasn't the worst place to end up. Even so, I felt the frightening pull of the unknown in the pit of my stomach. The sharp heaviness of the truth threatening to crush me if I chose to let it, if I chose to wallow. It had happened to me once before, after my mother died. It had sucked me into the darkest period of my life, a period I refused to revisit. Even now.

"I can't tell you how difficult it's been for me, keeping all this from you," Tristan said quietly, his voice thick. "You mean a lot to me—you know that, right? I can't wait to share all of this with you."

My heart swelled. This was Tristan's life. His world. And he wanted me to be a part of it. He wanted to share it with *me*.

"So tell me about this whole ushering thing," I said, squaring my shoulders. "How soon can I start?"

Tristan grinned. "Tonight. Meet me at the Thirsty Swan at nine."

"Okay, then." I smiled back. "It's a date."

MY FIRST

"I still can't believe *you* asked *me* to go out," Darcy said, hand to her chest as we walked down the hill toward the docks that night. My friend Aaron strolled along next to her, his dark hair spiked up and gelled in the front. He wore a blue-and-white-striped rugby shirt that made his tan look even deeper. "I mean, this is unprecedented."

"You've mentioned," I said wryly.

Up ahead, the calm water of the bay glittered in the light of a low-hanging moon. A buoy bell clanged, and I heard the faint sound of a boat motor chugging way out in the darkness.

"It's just, you're my antisocial sister. It's been one of the constants in my life ever since you hit puberty," Darcy said, pushing her fingers into her dark mane and fanning it out over her shoulders. "I'm sorry if it's taking my brain a couple of minutes to wrap itself around the concept."

"Try a couple of hours," I muttered under my breath, crossing my arms.

She'd practically fallen over when I'd gone down to the beach and suggested that we round up Aaron and hit the Thirsty Swan after dinner. Not that I could blame her. She was right. I'd always hated parties. It was practically my motto. But Tristan had told me to meet him tonight at the bar where he worked so he could start walking me through this whole Lifer thing, and while I knew we'd have to do that alone, the very thought of leaving my sister behind stopped me cold. After everything Tristan had told me, I didn't want to let her out of my sight. I would have even brought my dad along if he wasn't so busy working on the latest draft of his long-ignored novel—and if it was socially acceptable to invite your dad to a bar. There was a real possibility I might not have that much more time to spend with them *or* Aaron—my one true friend on this island. That soon they might be moving on . . . forever.

Our feet had just hit the rickety boardwalk, and I reached out to grab the nearest pylon, the wind knocked right out of me.

"What's wrong?" Aaron asked.

This was why I couldn't allow myself to brood, to wallow, even to ponder too much. Because if I did, there might be no coming back. I had to believe that they would all become Lifers somehow. Aaron's life had ended unnaturally, too, after all. Something I had realized after way too much pondering earlier. He'd told me all about it on the first night that we met, although neither of us had realized it at the time. There had been a fire at his uncle's house in Boston. A fire he'd supposedly escaped unscathed. But now that I knew where we really were, how we'd all gotten here, I suspected that wasn't exactly true.

"Nothing," I said with a tight smile, trying not to dwell on whether he'd suffered, whether he'd been scared, whether the rest of his uncle's family had survived. "I'm fine."

Aaron reached his arm around my back. "I don't know about this wallflower reputation of yours," he joked, holding me close to his side as we caught up with my sister. "I've only known Rory for a week, and I've seen her at not one but *two* parties," he said to Darcy.

When I turned to shoot him a grateful smile, I noticed a tall, solid man strolling along one of the paths in the town square. He wore a standard-issue blue uniform, polished black shoes, and what looked suspiciously like a gun in a holster on his hip. I recognized him instantly. It was

Officer Dorn, the man who'd laughed me out of the precinct when I'd reported Olive missing last week. He paused for a second to talk to a man reading the *Daily Register*, Juniper Landing's newspaper, under a streetlamp. When the two of them shook hands I could have sworn I saw a flash of white.

"Rory?" Aaron prompted.

I snapped back to the conversation. "Sorry, what?"

Aaron nudged me good-naturedly. "I said, isn't Darcy way too good for Joaquin?"

"Oh, yes, of course," I said, glancing back at the park. Both the man with the paper and Dorn had vanished.

"God, I hope he's not working," Darcy said as we approached the life-size carving of a wooden swan outside the door of the bar. The sounds of drunken laughter, clinking glasses, and loud rock music made the screened-in windows that lined three of the dive's four walls tremble.

"Why not?" Aaron asked. "You look totally hot and you're going to flirt with other guys. I hope he *is* working so he can eat his own heart out."

Darcy grinned. "I knew I liked you." She smoothed the front of her glittery top and quickly ran her tongue over her teeth to clear away any residual lip gloss. "Okay," she said with a nod. "Let's do this."

Then she lifted her chin and strode through the door, held open by a pockmarked gray rock at our feet. I expected

Aaron to follow her first, but he stopped to pull out his cell phone, holding it up toward the sky. My stomach turned. He wasn't going to be finding a signal anytime soon. Or ever.

"Still trying to call your dad?" I asked, shoving my hands under my arms.

"Just hoping I'll catch that fifteen-second window when a satellite happens to fly over this godforsaken rock." He sighed and pocketed the phone, then slung his arm around my shoulders. "Shall we?"

I swallowed hard, my guilt hot inside my chest.

"We shall," I said with a tight smile.

The Thirsty Swan glowed with the brightness of a non-stop party and was packed from wall to wall. I tried to get a glimpse of the counter to see if Tristan was working, but the crowd at the bar was three people deep. The girl with the pixie haircut from that morning's ferry was sitting at the end of the bar, sipping a soda and staring at Joaquin, who was slinging drinks like a pro, that big Cheshire grin of his charming everyone in the room. Darcy strode right past him without so much as a glance and took the empty stool between Fisher and some new guy with curly blond hair, an upturned collar on his polo shirt, and a pair of flip-flops with whales embroidered on the straps. The two of them were working together on a pretty serious shot-glass pyramid, and Fisher's tongue stuck out as he concentrated on placing the next piece. Aaron was right behind Darcy and instantly started chatting up the prep.

"Rory!" Joaquin shouted, shooting beer into a mug and spraying froth over his hand. "How's it hanging?"

The pixie girl turned to look at me, and her face fell. I hoped she wasn't thinking I was some kind of competition for Joaquin's heart. As far as I was concerned, she could have him. If she wanted the trouble.

"Can I get a Coke?"

"Don't you ever get tired of being sober?" he asked me, tilting his head as he reached under the bar for a glass.

"It's my only state of being, so . . . no. Is Tristan here?" I asked, fiddling nervously with the zipper on my jacket. Just the anticipation of seeing him was making me fidgety.

"Nope," Joaquin replied.

I waited for him to elaborate, but he didn't. "But he told me to meet him here."

Joaquin gave a short laugh and tossed a glass up end over end, catching it casually. "Sorry, but I'm not Tristan's keeper."

I rolled my eyes.

"Look, if Tristan said he's gonna be here, he'll be here. He's our resident Boy Scout," Joaquin assured me. "This is Jennifer, by the way," he added, nodding at the pixie girl. "She just got here today. Jennifer, Rory; Rory, Jennifer."

"Hi!" Jennifer's smile was somehow both eager and wary at once. She had a cute little birthmark above her lip, and as she held her straw between her fingers, I noticed her bubble-gum nail polish was chipped. "How do you and Joaquin know each other?"

"Oh, we're old friends," Joaquin said, sliding the soda glass across the counter toward me.

At the far end of the bar, Darcy laughed. She laid her hand on Fisher's arm and he smiled down at her, clearly enjoying her attention. To my surprise, Joaquin's smile died. He plucked another mug from under the bar, filled it, and slammed it down on the counter.

"Sister's moving on, I see," he said.

"What's the matter?" I asked as a round of laughter rose up from a nearby table. "Jealous?"

He leaned both hands into the bar. "Not in the least." But I could tell by the twitch at the corner of his right eye that he was lying. "What's there to be jealous of?"

"I don't know. Why don't you tell me?"

We faced off, each waiting for the other to blink.

"Um, I'm gonna go check out the jukebox," Jennifer said, sliding off her stool.

I took a seat and rested my elbows on the bar, my head in my hands.

"So. You've had an interesting couple of days," Joaquin

said, his voice going quiet and uncharacteristically gentle. "You okay?"

"Do I *look* okay?"

He chuckled. "You look like you're gonna be fine. It takes a little while to adjust, but there is an upside to being stuck here forever."

"You mean the sense of fulfillment you get from ushering souls to their ultimate destinations?" I said.

Joaquin's smile froze. "God! You sound like a Tristan Parrish disciple. No, woman!" He filled another mug with beer and slid it down the bar. "I was *going* to say that you get to hang out with me."

I barked a laugh. "You're such a jerk."

"I've been called worse," Joaquin said lightly. "But honestly, there are definite perks to being a Lifer. Other than what Tristan the Serious tells you."

I raised one eyebrow. "Like what?"

Joaquin leaned into the counter to get closer to my ear and lowered his voice. "We can't get sick, we can't *die*," he said, his eyes sparkling. "And we also get to stay young and hot forever." He stood up straight and threw his arms wide as I rolled my eyes. "In Juniper Landing, there's nothing to be afraid of."

"Yeah. Except the concept of eternity," I muttered.

He waved a dismissive hand at me. "Eh. You get used to that."

Shaking my head, I looked over my shoulder at Jennifer. "So, I'm not really sure how all this works," I whispered. "Do you know how she died?"

"Brain tumor," Joaquin said matter-of-factly.

My stomach clenched. "Oh my god."

He popped open a bottle of beer and took a swig. "Yeah, it was pretty quick, though. Only a month between diagnosis and *pffft*." He made a deflating sound with his lips, like letting the air out of a balloon.

"Wow. How very respectful of you," I said sarcastically.

"What? She doesn't know she's dead," he said quietly. "All she remembers is that she was diagnosed. As far as she's concerned, she's on vacation, and she'll be outta here in a day, anyway. Kid spent half her life volunteering with underprivileged children and the other half being polite. It's just too bad she won't be here longer so she could get a chance to sow an oat or two." His eyes flicked over her like he was considering the possibility of helping her out with that particular situation. I shot him a withering look and turned my back on him.

"Hey! I'm just doing my job."

"Whatever," I said. "So how do you—"

But when I glanced over my shoulder, Joaquin was already gone. He'd moved down the bar to tend to the clamoring throng, leaving me with my unanswered questions. Like how, exactly, he knew all these things about Jennifer. Whether he was going to be the one to usher her. How these new souls were assigned to Lifers in the first place. *Were* they assigned? Or was I supposed to just start chatting someone up and see if they were ready to move on?

I took a deep breath and sighed, wishing Tristan would show up already.

"I know, sucks in here, right?"

Startled, I looked over and found myself staring into the dark brown eyes of one of the new arrivals—the guy in the ripped jeans who'd seemed so lost when he'd stepped off the ferry today. He had a tiny scar through his eyebrow and didn't seem to know what to do with his hands; he touched the back of his neck, crossed his arms, then hooked his thumbs into the front pockets of his jeans.

"Totally," I said.

"You live here?" he asked, standing next to me and gazing down at the drinks menu.

I hesitated for a split second. "Yep, uh . . . yeah. I'm Rory. Rory Thayer."

"Brian Wohl," he said, lifting a hand. "Just got here from North Carolina."

"It's nice to meet you."

"You, too." He looked up at Joaquin, who had reappeared in front of us. "Can I get a beer? Whatever's on tap."

"You got it." Joaquin quickly filled a mug for him.

I wondered whether he had the same gut feeling about Brian that Tristan had had this morning, but he just went right along tipping bottles over glasses, digging ice out of the freezer, and chatting with the customers. Brian sipped his beer while the room around us buzzed and hummed and laughed and clinked.

"So, Rory. That's a nice name," Brian said eventually, leaning one elbow on the bar. I felt awkward, sitting while he was standing, but there were no seats to be had.

"I'll tell my dad you think so," I joked. He raised his eyebrows at me in question. "He picked it."

"Oh." Brian took a swig of beer, then sucked his teeth. "I don't know who picked my name. I never thought about it."

"One or both of your parents, I'd guess," I said.

"The thing is, I can't really imagine them doing it," Brian replied. He ran one finger around the rim of his mug on the bar, his eyes downcast. "I can't imagine them caring long enough to think about it."

"Oh." Now I was the one who didn't know what to do with my hands. I tucked them under my thighs and cleared my throat. "That sounds rough."

"Sorry," he said, his neck turning blotchy. "That'll kill your conversation, right?" He let out a sharp sort of laugh as the blotchiness spread to his cheeks.

"No, no. It's fine."

I had the sinking feeling that I was very out of my element and glanced down the bar toward my sister, as if she could somehow telepathically tell me what to do. But I couldn't even see her from where I was sitting, the crowd around her was so thick. Brian sighed and shook his head, like he was annoyed at himself. At least we were in this sinking boat together.

"So . . . uh . . . what brings you here?" I asked, then immediately regretted it. He had no idea what had brought him here. He didn't even know what *here* really was.

"I had to get away from my family," he said, looking away.

"How come?" I asked.

His eyes flashed. "You always ask so many questions?"

My face burned. "Sorry. I just . . . forget it." And Darcy wondered why I hated parties.

"Not everyone has parents who like them," Brian said tersely.

"I know," I replied, my voice thick. "For a long time I didn't think my dad liked me. All he's done for the past four years is bitch at me and my sister, so—"

"I bet he never threw you out of your own house."

He tossed back the rest of his beer and dropped the heavy mug on the bar like a punctuation mark.

My heart broke for him. "That's . . . Brian, I'm so sorry."

Brian sat forward and rubbed his palms together. His fingers were dirty, the cracks in his knuckles dark with grime.

"Yep. Nothing was ever good enough for them. I graduated, got a job in a garage . . . but it still wasn't enough, so . . ." He shook his head and shrugged. "Anyway, it's okay, because now . . . I'm free."

He spread his arms wide and smiled. There was a gap between his front teeth that gave him a charming, boyish look.

"I guess there's always a bright side," I said, forcing a smile. He had no idea just how "free" he was.

He pressed his lips together, considering this. "Always a bright side," he said. "I like that."

A relieved smile crossed my face. Finally, I'd said something right. A pack of raucous guys in the corner erupted in a cacophonous round of jeers and shouts. Brian winced.

"This isn't really my scene. You want to get out of here for a bit? Go for a walk by the water?" he asked, grazing the center of my back with his hand.

As soon as he touched me, I felt a spark, like static electricity, only sharper—hotter. My back felt prickly even after he dropped his hand—like my skin was vibrating—and a flutter of anticipation sprung up inside my chest. Maybe this was it. Maybe I was about to usher my first soul. I glanced around for Tristan again, but he was still nowhere to be found.

Then I had a thought, an inkling, a suspicion. Maybe this was how they trained the new Lifers. Maybe this was why Tristan hadn't shown up. I was being thrown into the deep end of the pool on my first day so they could see how I'd react, how I'd handle it. There was a familiar rush inside my chest. The feeling of rising to a challenge. The anticipation of making Tristan proud.

"Sure," I said, sliding off my stool. "This isn't really my scene, either."

Brian smiled and grabbed his rucksack, which had been leaning against the wall. He lifted the strap over his shoulder as he stepped aside to let me walk out first. When I crossed in front of him, I had to bite back a grin.

This was it. My first ushering. My new life was about to begin.

SAVED

The calm bay water lapped at the sand lazily, thinning out and sloshing back at an even rhythm. Brian kicked at broken seashells, their pale fragments gleaming against the sand, and sighed. Gray clouds flitted across the bright moon, and each breeze seemed cooler than the last. I flipped up the collar on my thin jacket, ducking my chin down deep.

Someone whistled in the dark—a slow, mournful tune—and I shivered. My eyes darted to the black waves; I was half expecting Mr. Nell to rise up out of the bay and drag me under. But instead I saw something gleaming in the moonlight, a long black splotch with a silver streak. I took a tentative step forward and my stomach turned. It was a pile of fish. Dozens of black and silver fish, all washed up on the shore, eyes fogged over. Dead. The whistling grew louder. I froze.

"What's wrong?" Brian asked.

"Do you hear that?" I hissed, my heart pounding as I whirled around. "Do you—"

A shadowy figure appeared on the boardwalk, and I clutched Brian's arm. A moment later, the whistler strolled under one of the lights outside the Crab Shack, illuminating the face of one of the Lifers—the guy I'd never met who'd been loitering in the corner of the basement this morning with Mohawk Girl and another nameless female. Relief flooded my body. He stopped momentarily when he saw us, and his whistling ceased. He wore a black sweatshirt with the hood up over his reddish hair, and his pale skin seemed to glow in the darkness. His eyes, dark and fathomless, held mine for several long breaths. Finally, he kept on walking, his heavy black boots crunching on the sandy slats of the boardwalk.

Brian and I both watched until the guy stepped out of sight. Then Brian looked down at my hand, still gripping his arm. Embarrassed, I released him and tucked my hands into my pockets.

"Sorry," I said.

"No worries," Brian told me, walking a few paces up the beach, putting distance between us and the fish. "Actually, I wanted to say that *I'm* sorry."

"For what?" I asked, walking beside him.

"For spilling all over you about my parents." He dug a groove in the sand with the tip of his sneaker.

My heart thumped with sympathy. "Oh, it's fine," I said, then hesitated. "I'm . . . glad you came over to me."

"I'm glad I did, too," he said with a grin.

And then his fingers caught me around the waist. The words *What are you doing?* were still forming in my mind when he leaned down and kissed me. His lips were dry and tasted sour. I yanked my face away as quickly and politely as possible.

"Oh, Brian, I'm so sorry," I said, taking a slight step back. "I didn't mean to make you think I—"

"Think what?" he asked darkly. "That you wanted me?"

His hands gripped my waist tighter now, and he pulled me against him, pressing my pelvic bone against his. Then his mouth came down on mine again, his nose pressing mine flat so completely I could hardly breathe.

Panic coursed through my body. This wasn't happening. This could *not* be happening.

I lifted my hands and pressed them against his chest, but

his grip was like a vise. I couldn't force even an inch of space between us. With a screech, I managed to turn my head away from his, but then he swept my ankle with his foot and sent me sprawling on the sand. My cheekbone hit something hard—a rock or a large shell, and hundreds of tiny dots of light exploded across my vision.

"Don't be a tease, Rory," Brian spat, climbing on top of me. He pinned my thigh down with his knee and my shoulder with one hand. With his other he worked the zipper on my jacket, yanking it open with three quick jerks. "You knew what you were doing when you came out here with me. We both knew what you were doing."

"Get off me!" I cried, kicking my legs.

Brian laughed coldly. He dipped his head closer, and I saw the sharpness in his dark eyes. The determination. "That's not gonna happen," he said icily. "So you may as well just relax and enjoy yourself."

He mashed his lips against mine again, and suddenly my whole body was on fire. My brain exploded with images. Faces. Girls. A blond with terrified blue eyes, blood dripping from her nose and over her lips as she tried to writhe free. An Asian girl with dark, wet hair, a scrape across her forehead, whimpering as she curled into a ball. Another girl scratching and screaming and begging him to stop. A fourth who'd gone catatonic, staring off into space while he had his way. Each memory assailed me with such stark details that my stomach curled and lurched and burned as I recoiled in horror, but I also felt this odd satisfaction, this tingling pleasure. I opened my eyes and looked into Brian's, and just like that, I knew.

Those positive sensations were coming from him. He'd done this before and enjoyed every minute of it.

I tried to knock him off me with my knee, but it was like he had four legs and ten arms. I felt my jeans unzip, and I did the only thing I could think to do. I screamed at the top of my lungs.

Brian laughed. He was just gripping the waistband of my jeans when all of a sudden something crashed into him so hard he was flung backward into the sand. A bare foot flew by my face and I sat up on my hands, scrambling backward on the cracked shells like a startled crab. In the darkness, I saw Tristan rear up, his blond hair a brief flash in the night. He lifted his fist high over his shoulder and swung. The crack was sickening. Final.

I pulled in a broken breath, fumbling for the zipper on my jeans, but my hands were shaking so hard there was no catching it. Somehow, I pulled myself up to standing and forced myself to take air into my lungs. Tristan's sandals lay a few feet away, one on the sand, one on the steps, where he'd kicked them off, probably to gain more speed.

"Are you all right?" Tristan asked, approaching me slowly. I covered the V of my exposed underwear with one hand, clutching my opposite shoulder with the other. Brian lay crooked and still behind Tristan, blood dripping from his nose.

"I . . . I . . ." It was the only syllable I could get out without bursting into tears. Tristan glanced down, and the rush of heat to my face was so intense I almost passed out. He shrugged out of his sweatshirt and tied it backward around my waist, so that the bulk of it was covering my front.

"Rory," he said, hands on my shoulders. "Are you all right? Say something. Anything."

I couldn't believe how badly I had screwed this up. I couldn't believe he'd had to rescue me. All this talk about being part of his world, one of the Lifers, having this mission, and I'd already failed.

"I'm so sorry, Tristan," I said. "I can't believe I—"

"You have nothing to apologize for," he said fiercely, one hand moving to cup my face. His thumb traced an arc back and forth across my cheek, and my skin hummed. "This is my fault. I'm sorry I wasn't here."

"But you were," I said, looking up into his clear blue eyes. "You saved me."

And then I burst into tears, burying my face in his chest. Tristan held me tightly to him, his arms locked around me as my body quaked with each fresh sob. I was still crying when the first fingers of fog rolled toward us with a low hiss, curling over the lights on the buoys, consuming the boats in their slips and finally the shoreline itself. Seconds later, the fog swallowed us whole, leaving me and Tristan alone in its cool, white grip.

ONE OF US

"Who the hell do you people think you are?" Brian seethed, kicking his legs as Joaquin and Kevin yanked him out of the pickup. His heels dragged through the dirt alongside the road, leaving two shallow, jagged trails behind him. "I didn't do anything. She wanted it."

He lifted his chin in my direction, and I stepped sideways behind Tristan. We had followed Joaquin in Bea's Jeep, a bright yellow rusted-out vehicle that wasn't much more than a go-cart with the top down and the doors removed. Tristan and I had huddled in the back, and I'd pulled his sweatshirt on to guard against the face-numbing wind, while Krista had ridden up front, holding her hair in place with both hands as we bounced over every bump and pothole.

I could hardly look at Brian. I couldn't believe how wrong I'd been about him, how thoroughly fooled. I felt like an idiot, standing there with the others. Like the stupid new girl. I hadn't looked Tristan in the eye since he'd saved me.

"Dude, just take this and get the hell out of here," Joaquin said, releasing him and slapping a gold coin into his hand.

Brian looked at it. "What is this?" he asked, his speech slurred either from the drinking or the punch he'd taken.

"Just go, already," Kevin grunted, pushing him toward the bridge so hard he almost stumbled.

"Go where?" Brian asked, throwing his arms wide even as he backed toward the bridge. It was as if there were a magnet inside the swirling fog, pulling him toward the open mouth of the path. "You can't pin anything on me. I can stay here as long as I want."

He had reached the precipice, the seam between dirt road and paved entry, and he paused, eyeing me derisively. My heart rate quickened, half expecting a hand to reach out and grab him and pull him shouting into the abyss. But nothing happened. He simply stood there while the rest of us stared.

"All right. That's it." Joaquin bent both knees and grabbed Brian around the legs, lifting him over his shoulder in a firefighter's carry.

"What the hell, man?" Brian spat, pounding on Joaquin's back.

Without replying, Joaquin strode toward the bridge and disappeared into the fog, the mist undulating around them. Suddenly we heard a slam and a pathetic-sounding "oof."

I glanced furtively at the others. "What did he just—"

But then Joaquin sauntered free of the thick, swirling wall, clapping his hands together, a cocky smirk on his face. Behind him, the fog suddenly whipped into a spinning gray vortex, and there was an odd sucking sound. A cold blast of wind nearly knocked me off my feet, its chill creeping around my heart, freezing it solid. Then everything went still.

"Seriously?" Tristan asked Joaquin, gesturing back toward the bridge.

"What?" he said, raising his palms. "I was sick of listening to him."

"Me, too," Bea said, unwrapping a piece of gum and popping it into her mouth.

Kevin spat on the ground in roughly the vicinity of Brian's footprints.

Krista hid a smile behind her hand. She lifted her shoulders at my surprised, somewhat judging look. "What? At least they're good for comic relief."

"Is it always like that?" I asked quietly.

"No," Tristan said, placing his hand on my back. "When they're going to the Light, it's really quite . . . peaceful."

"And sometimes when they're going to the Shadowlands, too," Krista added, reaching back to pull the rubber band from her long blond ponytail and retie it, smoothing the ratty strands that had been tugged free during our off-roading. "Since they have no clue where they're going."

"And normally we can each handle these things alone," Bea said, turning back toward where the cars were parked, their headlights making twin beams on the windswept reeds. "These last two just didn't want to go quietly, so—"

"When that happens, we bring backup," Kevin explained darkly.

"So, what do we do now?" I asked the group.

Tristan looked down at my hands, and I realized for the first time that I was clutching his sweatshirt at my sides, my arms wrapped around my stomach like two taut bungee chords.

"Well, you've just officially attended your first ushering," Tristan said, looking somehow proud and nervous at the same time.

"So Steven Nell didn't count?" I asked.

He shook his head. "You didn't know then that you were one of us."

"Consider sending that jerk to the Shadowlands your

initiation," Bea said, stepping up behind me. Somehow, that one action felt reassuring, like by standing behind me, she was saying she would always have my back.

Krista walked around her brother, her hair now smooth, her flowered dress perfectly fitted at the waist, the skirt billowing slightly behind her. She reached for my hand and held it, cupping my fingers in her own. The same warmth radiated off her as came off her brother, except there was a sweeter, less intense quality to hers. Almost tentative. I felt a pulse of anticipation.

"And now that you're officially one of us," Krista said with an excited smile, "there's something you need to see."

THE COVE

The rocky slope was steep and uneven, each step an act of faith as we walked in a straight line—Joaquin, then Tristan, then me, with Krista, Bea, and Kevin trailing along behind. The sounds of the waves rolling onto shore and the brief flashes of whitecaps far out on the surface signaled that the ocean was somewhere up ahead.

"Where are we going?" I whispered, tiptoeing over a slick rock.

"Trust, little protégé, trust," Joaquin said, his grin glowing in the darkness as he looked back over his shoulder.

"Don't worry. We're almost there," Tristan told me.

Suddenly my left foot slipped, and I went weightless, my arms flailing as my heart vaulted into my mouth.

Before I could even scream, Tristan grasped both my arms and hoisted me back up. Dozens of pebbles tumbled down a sharp drop as we grabbed on to each other. His breath was hot on my face, and even in the darkness, I could see the intensity in his blue eyes as he checked me over.

"You're okay. You're fine," he assured me.

I gripped his arms even tighter as the others caught up with us. "If you say so."

He smiled, his eyes slowly traveling over my face. "I do. This is one of the perks of being dead. You can't die again."

"Awesome, no?" Kevin said with a toothy grin.

"Keep it moving, Slimy," Bea said, nudging him as she rolled her eyes.

"Did she just call him Slimy?" I asked Tristan as Krista slipped past us, too.

"Bea has nicknames for everyone," Tristan informed me. "You'll get one eventually, but be warned—most of them are not all that nice."

"What's yours?"

"Golden Boy," he replied somewhat sheepishly.

I smirked. "Ah."

"Are you two coming or what?" Joaquin complained.

Tristan slipped his hand down my arm and took my

hand, wrapping his fingers around mine. "Don't worry. I've got you."

My heart bombarded my ribs with each beat. "Okay."

Up ahead, Joaquin flicked on a flashlight. The beam bounced over the jagged gray rocks until, suddenly, he dropped out of sight. The others, I noticed with a start, were already gone. I heard a thump and a squishing sound, and then Tristan squeezed my hand again.

"You have to jump here."

He leaped down, his arm stretching out straight to keep his fingers twined in mine. I hesitated. All I could see was his face smiling up from a few feet below.

"I won't let you fall."

Someone laughed in the darkness, and a few more flashlights flickered to life. When I squinted, I saw Krista, Kevin, and Bea standing there, waiting. I swallowed my fear and jumped. Almost instantly, the soles of my sneakers hit soft, damp sand.

"Rory!" Lauren rushed out of the darkness, slid between Bea and Kevin, and threw her arms around me. "You did your first ushering! Congratulations!" I could smell the alcohol on her breath and felt her fighting for balance. I patted her back awkwardly until she released me. She staggered sideways toward Bea and giggled.

"How did it go?" she asked, looking around at the others.

"He was . . . reluctant to leave us," Joaquin said, kneading my shoulders from behind.

The others laughed.

"But Joaquin took care of that," Tristan said.

"I'll bet," Lauren said knowingly. Then she hiccuped and covered her mouth with one hand.

"So, Rory . . . welcome to the cove," Joaquin said, smiling as he tilted his flashlight toward his face. The effect was eerie, lighting his mouth and nose but casting his eyes in half shadow. "Check it out."

He trained the beam up ahead, and the others did the same. The tall rock wall we had just descended formed a perfect C around a wide swath of white sand. Waves curled into the shore, but in a more timid, tame way than they did out on the open beach. Dotting the sand along the sheer rock were several colorful camping tents, all but one of them dark. Someone was moving around in the second-to-last tent, which was lit from inside by a lantern.

"Hey, Fish!" Joaquin shouted. "Get your ass out here."

The arc of the tent door unzipped, and Fisher stuck his head out. I half expected Darcy to be right behind him, since I'd last seen her flirting with him, but when he unfolded his large form in the small doorway, he was alone. A few beach towels were tucked under his arm, and he wore a white fedora at a jaunty angle.

"Hey, all." Fisher slapped hands with Joaquin, then slid his free arm over Lauren's tiny shoulders. "How you feeling, lightweight?" he asked her. She giggled, then hiccuped, then giggled some more.

"Okay, what's your deal?" Joaquin asked Lauren.

"Her new charge likes to drink," Fisher said, grinning.

"A lot," Lauren said, widening her eyes as she swayed. "Like, a *lot* a lot."

Everyone laughed. "Someone's going to be sleeping late tomorrow," Bea chided.

"What's a charge?" I asked.

"That's what we call the people we're supposed to usher," Bea explained.

"Brian was supposed to be mine," Tristan told me.

"Oh." My cheeks warmed, and I looked down at my sneakers, pressing my toes farther into the sand.

"It's fine," Tristan said, sliding a hand across my shoulders. "Don't worry. I'm going to teach you everything you need to know."

"Yeah?" I said, a hopeful flutter inside my chest.

"I promise," he replied. "Why don't you come by tomorrow morning? I'll take you on a tour of the town. A *Lifer* tour."

I grinned. "I'm in."

His smile widened, and my heart responded with an extra

hard thump. The weight of his hand on my shoulder felt comforting and meaningful. Here we were, in front of all his friends, and he had no problem keeping his arm wrapped around me for all to see.

"So where are Nadia and those guys?" Joaquin asked.

As if in answer to his question, there was a loud shriek, followed by a splash, and three people emerged from the water. One of them was Mohawk Girl, the second was the whistler from the boardwalk, and the third was their girlfriend from the basement that morning. They made their way over through the wet sand, and Fisher tossed each of them a towel.

"Rory, I don't think you've officially met Nadia," Tristan said, gesturing to Mohawk Girl. Her white bikini was practically see-through and her nose ring sparkled in the beam of Joaquin's flashlight. She stared me down as if I were an atom bomb sitting in the center of her beach.

"Hi," I said.

She didn't reply. She simply rubbed her hair with the towel, then tied the towel around her waist, covering up the bottom of her skimpy suit.

"And this is Cori," Tristan said, introducing the other girl, who had dark curly hair and olive skin and was wearing a modest one-piece. She had more curves than her friend, and a much more welcoming expression.

"Hey, there!" she said, earning a scowl from Nadia.

"And this loser is Pete," Fisher said, throwing his arm over the shoulders of the tall, gangly guy, who was jerking his head up and down, trying to clear water out of his ear.

He nodded at me, then turned his attention back to Joaquin. "We doing this or what?"

"Why? Got somewhere you need to be?" Joaquin asked.

Pete shrugged.

"Come on." Tristan tugged me forward, walking along the rock wall as everyone else fell in step. I didn't see the opening of the cave until we were right on top of it. It was an uneven triangle cut out of the stone, very wide at the bottom but tapering drastically as it reached the top, like a Hershey's Kiss listing to one side.

"You ready?" Tristan asked.

"We're going in there?" I demanded.

"If you dare," Pete said coolly in my ear.

Tristan shot him a look, and together, he, Krista, and I stepped inside the cave. The air was about twenty degrees colder, and the opening narrowed so swiftly that it forced us into a single line for a few feet before it widened into a huge, round chamber. The second we stepped inside, my jaw dropped.

The walls surrounding me burst with color. They'd been graffitied so thoroughly that hardly any of the black rock was visible beneath the intricate lettering and design work.

I stepped toward the nearest wall and ran my hand over the first name I saw. It had been spray-painted in red and yellow, the letters square and bold.

RYAN DUNN (CORRIGAN) 1995.

JACINDA RAND (LORNING) 2004.

MISTY CALLAIT (RABAT) 1982.

KRISTA KINCAID (PARRISH) 2012.

I stared at Krista, and she nodded, lifting a shoulder almost like an apology. "That's me."

I turned in a quick circle now, names and numbers assaulting me—2010, 2001, 1965, 1984, 1921, 1876.

"Eighteen seventy-six?" I gasped, gaping at the tight cursive. My words bounced off the high ceiling and echoed back at me, filling the chamber with their screeching tone.

"Every Lifer who ever came to Juniper Landing has written his or her name on these walls," Tristan explained, stepping up next to me. "The year marks the date they accepted their calling and received their full powers. For you, today is that day."

I glanced around the room at all the faces, every one of them watching me closely.

"Are you ready to become a true Lifer?" Krista asked.

I swallowed hard.

"I know it's overwhelming," Tristan said softly. "And I

know you're worried about your family, but look around. We're your family, too, now, Rory. This is your new home."

My heart thumped painfully. Kevin rubbed his nose with the back of his index finger. Bea gazed at me unwaveringly. Krista beamed, like I was her new baby sister. Pete tapped his toe, glancing over his shoulder. Joaquin shot me a small smirk, Lauren teetering and hiccuping at his side. Fisher smiled at me, like we were sharing a private joke. Nadia and Cori stood arm in arm, an alliance of two, while Nadia scowled openly.

I tried to believe what Tristan was saying—that these people could be my family—but my heart closed in on itself. I hadn't shared Christmases and birthdays and Thanksgivings with them. They'd never seen me win a science fair or run a race. They hadn't been there when I contracted the chicken pox at age six or when I broke my arm on the tire swing at my grandma's or when they lowered my mother's casket into the ground.

I knew who my true family was. *But you still have them,* I reminded myself. *You still have Dad and Darcy. At least for now, and hopefully for always.*

"If it means anything," Tristan said finally, "I think you're ready."

"We all do," Joaquin added loudly.

I looked at Nadia, who stared past me at Tristan, smoldering. It was obvious she didn't want me here. We might have been "family," but it was pretty clear we were never going to be friends. But I wasn't about to let her and her blatant feelings for Tristan stop me from accepting my new mission—or from being with Tristan.

"I'm ready," I said, my gaze locked on Nadia. "I'm beyond ready."

Her eyes narrowed at me for a brief second before she looked away.

"Yay!" Krista cheered. She produced some kind of string and held it out to me. It was a woven leather bracelet. I reached out my left arm and let her tie it to my wrist. The leather was hard, its pungent, tangy scent emanating from my arm. When I moved, it slid halfway to my elbow, then back down again. It was nothing like Tristan's, which was so worn the color had faded to a light tan, and so fitted it never moved from his wrist.

Joaquin let out a whoop, and everyone started applauding. The sound filled the cave, and the crowd collapsed toward me, hugging me like I was the long-lost kid sister they never knew they had. Krista threw her arms around me so tightly I thought she'd never let go, and Fisher put his massive hand on my head to ruffle my hair. As I turned into Bea's arms, I saw Nadia hovering near the edge of the cave, and a chill went right through me. She shot me a sharp, slit-eyed scowl before turning her back on the rest of us and disappearing into the night.

FOREVER

She's feeling it now. What it's like to be accepted. What it's like to be part of a group. I'll bet she didn't have a lot of friends in the other world. She was too serious for that. Too focused. But here, things can be different. There will be no graduation, no Ivy League to strive for, no stellar career out there waiting to be achieved. Here, she can relax. She can have fun. She can take risks and be wild and maybe even fall in love.

She's starting to feel it.

I did, too, once upon a time. But I've been here long

enough to know that this fairy tale doesn't last. The euphoria ends. That's why I've written a new happily ever after, *off* this make-believe island. The world is changing, and my new adventure is about to start. . . .

TOGETHER

I woke up early the next morning, the bright sun shining through the window behind my bed, and blinked in confusion. I didn't even remember dozing off. I'd been so wired after partying at the cove with my new "family" that I'd felt like I would never fall asleep. But as I stretched my arms over my head, I was oddly energized, and when my stiff new leather bracelet slipped toward my elbow, I knew exactly why.

Tristan had invited me to spend the day with him, learning everything I needed to know to be a Lifer. A whole day alone with Tristan. I tossed the covers off and yanked on the first clothes I saw—a T-shirt from the desk chair and jeans from the floor—then tore down the stairs, smiling at the now familiar sound of my dad pounding away on his keyboard inside his room. I was just headed out the front door when I heard the floor creak behind me.

"Where're you going?" Darcy asked.

I hesitated for a split second before turning to face her. She was already showered and dressed, uncharacteristically early for her. I saw the hopeful curiosity written all over her face and knew she wanted to get out of the house, but I also knew she couldn't come with me. Not on this particular errand.

"Um . . . for a run?" I said, guilt oozing out of my pores.

She narrowed her eyes. "In jeans?"

I looked down. Damn. One of the very few times in my life I was not sporting running shorts or sweats and she had to call me on it.

"A walk, I meant."

"I'll come with you," she said, grabbing her sunglasses off the front table next to the framed photograph of our family—me, my sister, my mom, my dad—the only one we still had of the four of us.

I bit my bottom lip. "Actually, I'm going to hang out with Tristan," I finally admitted, my face pulsating with heat.

Darcy's eyes widened; then she gave me a knowing smile. "I see. Have fun," she said meaningfully.

"Uh, thanks!" I said awkwardly. "We'll hang out later!"

Outside, the warmth enveloped me and I took a deep breath of the sweetly scented air as I sped up the hill toward town. On my way across the park, I saw Officer Dorn and his boss, Chief Grantz, standing close together, staring down at the paved sidewalk. A small white bird lay dead at their feet, half a dozen fat flies buzzing around it. I wrinkled my nose, and suddenly, both of the officers looked up at me, an accusatory gleam in their eyes. But for what? A dead bird?

Just then, Nadia rode across the street on a dirt bike and skidded to a stop right next to them. They shared a few words, and her eyes snapped up to glare at me, too. I shivered in the warm sunlight, then quickly turned my back on them and started walking again. As I started up the hill to the bluff, it took every ounce of self-control within me to keep from looking back. After what felt like an eternity, I knocked on Tristan's front door.

Krista answered, wearing her blue-and-white gingham general store uniform. "Hi, Rory!"

I smiled, Krista's ever-upbeat attitude instantly squelching what was left of my uneasiness.

"Hey!" I said. "Going to work?"

"Yeah. I was just heading out," she said, slipping past me onto the porch. "Listen, I wanted to ask you . . . I'm having this big party on Friday night, and I was wondering if you'd want to be on the planning committee."

I blinked. "The planning committee?"

She smiled and blushed, smoothing her bangs off her forehead with her fingertip. "Yeah. It's my one-year anniversary on the island," she explained, tilting her head and biting her bottom lip. "It's kind of a big deal, so the other girls are helping me plan it."

I fiddled with the end of my braid. Party planning was definitely not my thing. But she looked so hopeful.

"Sure," I said. "When do you need me?"

Krista squealed and grabbed me into a hug. "That's great! We're meeting here, Wednesday morning, at ten sharp."

"Okay. I'll be here."

"Cool. If you're looking for Tristan, he's up in his room. Just go upstairs. It's the second door on the left," she said as she jogged down the porch stairs.

"Thanks," I called after her.

She lifted a hand and hustled around the corner, out of sight.

I took a deep breath and walked inside, closing the door behind me. The foyer was huge and silent, lit dimly in the morning sun. The floors were a dark, polished wood, and matching wainscoting reached halfway up the walls. The decor was impeccable but impersonal: the nap of a deep red

Turkish rug was all swept in one direction, as if recently vacuumed. One perfect orchid in a gold vase sat atop a gleaming hall table. The walls were a warm, creamy white, bare of any photographs or portraits, aside from a landscape painting of Juniper Landing's town hall.

A tall, banistered staircase stood to my right, but before I could move, a floorboard creaked somewhere nearby. I saw a shadow under the edge of a door on the far side of the foyer. It hovered there, as if listening.

For a long moment, I just stood there, vacillating somewhere between an instinct to run and my yearning to see Tristan. Finally, the footsteps receded and a door slammed shut at the back of the house. Unfrozen, I took the stairs to the second floor two at a time, looking into each doorway until I saw Tristan. He was standing with his back to me at a drawing table, which was set up to face a bay window overlooking the ocean, and he was holding something in his hands. Suddenly he tossed the heavy item into the bottom drawer of a storage cabinet under the desk, locked the drawer, pocketed the key, then turned around before I could come up with a good excuse for my hovering there.

"Hey!" he said, his eyes lighting up at the sight of me.

My heart warmed and I instantly relaxed. "Hi."

He was wearing an aqua T-shirt that made his eyes stand out, even from across the room. There was something about seeing him there, in his own space, that made him seem vulnerable. He glanced around at the messy bedspread, the open trunk at the foot of the bed—filled with sneakers and flip-flops and what appeared to be a pair of fuzzy bear slippers—and the nautical-themed mirror with a crack in the right-hand corner.

"Um, welcome to my room," he said. Then he scratched the back of his neck, smiling sheepishly, and quickly whacked the trunk closed.

"Thanks," I said. "Krista let me in."

"So, are you ready for your tour?" he asked.

"That's why I'm here," I said, smiling.

"I'm glad you're still excited about all this," Tristan replied, picking at the carved edge of his bed's footboard. "Especially after last night. Sometimes when the first ushering doesn't go smoothly, new Lifers have a tendency to . . ."

"Freak out?" I supplied.

"To put it mildly," he replied with a chuckle. "I should've known you'd be different." He held my gaze for a long moment, so long I started to blush.

"So, where're we going?" I asked finally.

"Follow me," he said, heading for the door. He paused and looked back over his shoulder with a heart-stopping grin. "You're gonna love this."

ANYWHERE BUT HERE

"I knew it!" I shoved Tristan with both hands. "I *knew* some-one was watching me that day!"

Through the gleaming window I had a perfect view of the room across the street—the room Olive had occupied in the Freesia Lane boarding house last week when she was here. I'd gone looking for her there when she stood me up for breakfast, and I could have sworn someone was spying on me from this very room.

"Yeah, that was Lauren," Tristan said, holding the blue brocade curtain back. "She told me later that she was sure you'd spotted her over here. She had such a panic attack about it that Krista let her reorganize her closet to calm her down."

"That's calming?" I raised an eyebrow at Tristan.

He threw up his hands. "It is for Lauren."

"I saw the blinds move, but I didn't see who was behind them." It was weird, staring out that window, imagining my own curious face peering in from the other side.

"With practice, you get really good at not being seen," Tristan told me. His words hung in the air for a long moment, and I had a feeling he was thinking the same thing I was. He hadn't done such a great job of not being seen by me.

Tristan cleared his throat. "So, what do you think of the behind-the-scenes tour so far?"

I chewed on my bottom lip and glanced around the room. The wood floors were old and creaky, and the fraying lawn furniture haphazardly placed around the room left something to be desired. It had been like this in every "lookout" Tristan had taken me to—the library attic, which afforded a perfect 360-degree view of the town from its windowed rotunda, the widow's walk above the surf shop overlooking the ferry dock. Even the upstairs apartment at the Crab Shack had offered nothing more than a vinyl couch and a cracked cooler. Whatever Lifer life was like, it wasn't glam.

"Don't you guys ever want to, you know, get comfortable?" I asked.

Tristan laughed and leaned against the window, the sun illuminating his handsome face and highlighting the lines of his chest. I blushed and glanced away, focusing on the sidewalk outside. Fisher and Kevin walked by, in the midst of an intense conversation, and Fisher checked over his shoulder three times in the space of five seconds. Then they disappeared from view. I stepped closer to the window next to Tristan, to see if anyone was following them, but the street was empty.

"We're never in one place for very long, I guess," Tristan said. "But if you want to make any changes anywhere, feel free. You're one of us now."

He gave me this look that sent a warm glow through my chest, like he was glad, relieved, even, to finally be able to say that.

"Noted," I said, my heart rate skipping all over the place. "So, what's next?"

Tristan hesitated. He shifted almost imperceptibly from one foot to the other. "Well, there *is* one more place you should see."

It was clear that whatever it was, he didn't exactly want to show it to me. Intrigued, I followed him down the stairs and out into the bright sunlight. It didn't take long for me to figure out where he was taking me, and my pulse started to thrum as we stopped outside the gray house across the street from my own. Tristan had told me that his grandmother lived out there and that she liked to watch the world go by. That was how he'd explained away the moving curtains, my constant feeling of being watched, and the fact that he always seemed to be hanging out there. I glanced over my shoulder at Darcy's window, hoping she wasn't looking out. The house stared back at me, its two upper windows and double front door forming an accusatory face.

"You okay?" Tristan asked.

"Yep," I replied curtly.

"All right, then."

We strode up the steps and Tristan shoved the door. It let out a loud, painful squeal as it swung open. It wasn't until I stepped inside the cool, shadowy, empty house that I realized I'd actually imagined what it might be like inside. In my mind's eye I'd seen antique chairs set up around an ancient card table. I'd imagined lace doilies placed over the backs of upholstered sofas, a faded chintz rug, a fireplace decorated with knickknacks and framed portraits of grandchildren. Instead, what greeted me was a whole lot of nothing. The walls were gray and bare, the fireplace boarded up, and the only furniture on the first floor was a plain white desk, set up right in the center of the living room.

"Let's go up," Tristan said quietly.

I held on to the worn banister as I followed him up the stairs to the room that faced Darcy's. Here we found three white wicker chairs with faded and stained cushions, all of them facing the windows. I pushed a curtain aside and looked out. Darcy lay back on her four-poster bed, holding a magazine at arm's length up over her face. The view was so perfect I could see her blink.

"Wow," I said. "This is just—"

"Creepy?" Tristan supplied.

"Yeah," I said, turning away from the window.

"Maybe we should—"

Instead of finishing his sentence, he undid the faded tieback on the first curtain, and the fabric fell across the window, blocking the view of my house. Then he did the same with the other two windows, tossing the tiebacks onto the floor and casting us in relative darkness.

"I'm sorry," Tristan said finally. "It's just . . . it's what we do."

I tried to think back to all the times I'd been on the front porch or in Darcy's room. Tried to remember what he and his friends might have seen.

"What's the point?" I asked finally.

He seemed startled. "What do you mean?"

"I *mean* what's the point?" I asked, extending my hand toward the covered windows. "What's the point of all the watching?"

"Oh." He chuckled, as if relieved. He gently rested his

hands on the back of one of the wicker chairs. "We have to keep an eye on the visitors. We have to interact with them, because we're integral in sending them where they need to go."

A cold gush of fear crashed over me. "Wait a minute. You said you don't decide where people end up."

"We don't," Tristan replied.

"So what does that mean?" I asked. "How are you integral?"

He chewed on his bottom lip and looked up at the plaster ceiling, crisscrossed with cracks. "It's a little hard to explain, but basically, everything we see, everything we hear . . . it all goes into the ultimate decision."

"Do you have to write a report or something?" I asked, resting my hands on the chair across from his.

"No. Nothing like that," Tristan said with a short laugh. "The information we gather, it just goes where it needs to be."

"So what you're saying is, you're telepathic," I said.

He shrugged, tilting his head to one side. "Kind of. We all are."

"And you send telepathic messages to who? God?" I asked, almost laughing at the absurdity of the concept. Fortunately, though, I managed to hold my tongue. I didn't want to offend him.

"I don't actually know," Tristan said. "I've tried never to ask that question."

"How could you never ask that question?" I blurted out, my grip tightening on the back of the chair. "That's the single most important question there is! Why are we here? Why are we doing all this? If I'm going to be someone's eyes and ears, I'd kind of like to know who that someone is."

"I don't ask that question, Rory, because I'll never get an answer," Tristan said, his voice reaching a point very close to anger, a point I'd never seen him approach before.

I looked down at the floor, my face burning. "Oh."

Clearly this was a topic of some frustration to him as well. Only he'd been dealing with it for a very long time. I turned away from him and stepped over to the window. With one finger, I moved the curtain an inch to the side, looking out at my house, our house, the last house my sister, my father, and I would ever live in together, and my chest felt full. My eyes prickled and I gulped in a breath.

"Are you okay?"

I felt the warmth of Tristan's body as he stepped up behind me, the tickle of his breath on my neck. Instantly, my heart began to pound.

"Yeah," I said quietly. "I'm fine."

"I'm sorry," he whispered, sending a shiver down my spine. "I didn't mean to snap."

I turned my head ever so slightly to the side. My breathing

was shallow, my pulse skipping with him so near. "It's okay."

"I try not to question everything, because I know that what we're doing here matters," he said, his voice low.

I turned to face him, so fast that my braid brushed his bicep and our knees touched. I pressed myself back into the window, flattening the curtain behind me, but he didn't even flinch.

"How?" I asked hopefully, looking into his eyes. "How do you know?"

His eyes roamed my face, flicking from my lips to my cheeks to my eyes to my hair. "We're maintaining the balance of the universe," he said. "There's nothing that matters more."

His eyelashes fluttered and he stared down at my mouth. My lips tingled and my fingers itched to reach out and grab his hand, his waist, his arm. I recalled the feeling of his thumb tracing my cheek last night, the way he'd held me close at the cove, how he'd looked into my eyes yesterday when he told me how strong I was. How beautiful. How true.

In a rush of bravery, I stood on my toes and pressed my lips against his. For a split second, everything was perfect. His soft lips, the heady scent of sea and salt in the room, the sound of the waves crashing outside the open window. But then Tristan abruptly pulled away. He flattened the back of his hand against his lips, his eyes wide. It wasn't until that moment that I realized he hadn't kissed me back.

"I'm . . . I'm sorry," I stammered, flustered. "I didn't—"

"No, I'm sorry," he said, finally dropping his hand, an unreadable expression on his face. "I didn't mean to give you the wrong impression, Rory. I never meant to—"

This wasn't happening. This was *not* happening. I slid along the window, moving away from him, mortified. The things he'd said . . . all the touching, the stares, the obvious tension between us . . . how could I have misread him so completely?

But clearly that was exactly what I'd done. Of course I had. I'd only ever kissed one guy before and he had most definitely kissed me first. Besides, Tristan was perfect. He was the Golden Boy. The guy everyone looked up to, the guy every other guy wanted to be, and probably the guy every girl wanted to be with. I bet he'd kissed hundreds of girls over the endless years of his existence. Maybe even thousands. I was just the latest pathetic, recently deceased loser to throw herself at him. And now I was going to have to live with this humiliation—this skin-searing humiliation—forever.

As he stared at me, I realized he was wishing he could be anywhere but here. I knew the feeling.

"Forget it," I said quickly. "This never happened, okay? Let's just pretend it never happened."

I turned my back on him before he could see me break down for the second time in two days and stumbled toward the door, leaving Tristan and whatever was left of my pride behind.

DEATH SENTENCE

I tripped onto the sidewalk in front of my house, blinking back tears, and a few yellow leaves floated down from the magnolia tree in our yard before being caught up on the ocean breeze. As I shoved open the gate, I could feel him watching me from the gray house. Always, always watching me.

A wave of despair threatened to overtake me as I pictured the darkness of a forever without him.

Focus, Rory. Focus.

"Hey, beautiful."

I flinched at the familiar voice. Joaquin. Fantastic. Just

what I needed. He sidled up behind me and walked right through the gate as if invited.

"I'm not in the mood right now, Joaquin," I said, speed-walking toward the porch.

"Not in the mood for what? I just came by to—" Joaquin suddenly stopped and slapped at his neck. "Ow!"

"What?" I said, whirling on him.

His hand trembled as he gazed at his palm. Curled up in the center was a small, very dead, hornet.

"Are you okay?" I asked dutifully.

Joaquin didn't answer. He cupped the back of his neck for a second with his other hand and glanced around, as if waiting for the punch line. But there was no one but him, me, and the birds chirping in the boughs of the magnolia tree shading the walkway. When he looked down at the hornet again, his trembling grew violent.

"What? Is it bad?" I asked, alarmed now. "Are you allergic?"

"No," Joaquin said. "I just—"

He shook his head, and instead of flicking the tiny corpse to the ground, he shoved it into his pocket.

Joaquin shifted his weight and squinted out of one eye. "Where were we?"

"I think I was about to go inside and slam the door in your face," I said, stomping up the porch steps, which creaked and sagged beneath my feet.

"Okay, but just wait for one second," he implored, coming after me.

I threw up my hands. "Why?"

Behind him, the curtains on the upstairs window across the street fluttered closed. My throat closed, and I crossed my arms tightly over my chest.

Joaquin took a step closer. "Look, I just wanted to check in and see how you're doing today. Sometimes the second day is even harder than the first."

"How do you *think* I'm doing?" I asked, glancing behind me at the door. I just wanted to get inside before Tristan came out. There was no way I could handle seeing him again just then.

Joaquin touched his sting and winced. "At the moment I'd say . . . livid?"

"Do you have any idea how hard this is?" I ranted, yanking a geranium bloom from the nearest window box. "I spent all yesterday listening to my sister talk about finding her next hookup, and all I could think was *You're dead and you have no idea.* She's never going to graduate from high school or get that tattoo she's always wanted or save up for that damned leather jacket she's been talking about since last Christmas. She's never going to do *anything*, and I know it and I can't tell her. Do you have any clue how awful this feels?"

"Wait a minute. Darcy wants to hook up with someone else?" Joaquin asked, screwing up his face in consternation. "Is it Fisher?"

My jaw dropped. "Are you kidding me? That's all you took from what I just said?"

"All right, all right, calm down." Joaquin reached for me. "You've crushed the poor flower."

I looked down at the pink petals strewn all over my feet and released the head of the geranium from my sweaty grasp. Then I saw his fingers on my skin and yanked my arm back, angling myself away from him.

"Don't even try that Lifer mind trick on me. I'm not letting *you* control me."

"I wouldn't think of it." Joaquin crossed his arms over his chest and smiled in an amused way.

"What?" I said, tossing the flower to the ground. "Why are you looking at me like that?"

"I like this attitude," he said. "I thought you were a Goody Two-shoes, but I'm digging this whole defiant thing you've got going right now."

Defiant? He thought I was being defiant? More like I was turning into an emotional basket case. Little did he know my current manic state stemmed from a broken heart, nothing more. I glanced back at the gray house, but it was quiet.

"Me, I full-on lost it for at least a week," Joaquin said, leaning back against the porch railing. "When I first got here, they placed me with Ursula in that pink gingerbread house over on Sunset."

"Wait." I shook my head. "Placed you? And who's Ursula?"

"Oh, you know Ursula. The waitress at the general store? The one with the white hair? She's supposed to be my grandmother. We live together."

I thought of the cheerful woman I'd seen behind the counter last week. "*Supposed* to be your grandmother?" I echoed.

Joaquin shrugged. "Yeah. All of us who died when we were young were placed with adults when we got here so our living situations would look normal to visitors," he explained. "Like Tristan and Krista living with the mayor . . ."

"Huh?" I shook my head as I tried to keep up.

Joaquin sighed and sat back on the railing now, settling in. "The mayor isn't their real mother. Krista and Tristan aren't even related. You know that, right? She only got here last year, and he's been here forever."

I blinked. Krista and Tristan looked so much alike they were practically twins. How could they not be related? The sun suddenly felt much hotter than it had a moment ago.

"Anyway," Joaquin continued, "when I first got here, I

spent way too much time at Ursula's huddled under a flowered bedspread that smelled like mothballs and gardenias,
wailing like a baby. To this day, if I even walk past a gardenia
bush, I dry-heave."

"Can I ask you something?" I said, my heart fluttering
nervously as I traced a groove in the side of the porch swing
with my fingertip.

He looked me in the eye, crossing his arms over his
stomach. "You want to know how I died."

His gaze was unflinching. For the first time, I noticed
the gold and green flecks peppering the deep brown in his
eyes. I held my breath. "Is that a bad thing to ask?"

"No. Everyone asks eventually." He leaned back. "I
committed suicide. After I killed my mother and sister."

I froze. "You . . . what?"

Joaquin nodded, his jaw set. "It was 1916. I was kind of
a drunken asshole, and my dad had just gotten one of those
newfangled automobiles," he said sarcastically.

"Wait a minute, 1916?" I blurted out. "You've been
here for—"

"Yeah, I know. I look good for my age," he teased. "So
anyway, me and my friends went out joyriding on far too
much whiskey, and on the way home I was driving, if you
could even call it that, and there was an overturned grocery
cart in the road, and I didn't see it till the last second. And

when I swerved . . . I swerved right into my family. They were coming back from evening services, and I . . . killed them. I mean, not my dad. He wasn't there, but . . ."

He looked away and briefly touched the side of his hand to his nose.

"Anyway, my father stopped talking to me after that, and I stopped doing pretty much anything," Joaquin went on, his tone matter-of-fact. He leaned back and toyed with his leather bracelet, moving it up and down on his arm, though it only moved about an inch. "I couldn't sleep without seeing their faces, without hearing my little sister scream. . . . So one night I went up to the attic with a length of rope and—"

He made a little hanging motion with his hand and stuck out his tongue. I grimaced and looked away, disgusted.

"Don't do that," I said.

"Don't do what?" he asked.

"Make a joke of it. It's not funny."

"I know it's not funny," he said fiercely. "Believe me, I know. I thought by hanging myself I was escaping it, but instead, I landed myself here, and here I've been, for almost a hundred years, and every day I still see their faces. I can still hear her scream."

I looked down at the floorboards beneath my feet, my bottom lip trembling. He'd just confirmed my worst nightmare. Being here forever meant never forgetting. It meant never escaping. It meant I was going to feel this stupid, this humiliated, this small, for all eternity.

I could feel a black hole start to open up within me. This was not good. This was very not good.

The door of the gray house creaked open, and Tristan stepped out. He ducked his head, being careful not to look in my direction, not to even acknowledge me, then turned and hurried off down the street.

My eyes welled with tears. "I have to go," I told Joaquin, standing up and shoving open the door.

"Rory, wait," Joaquin said, scrambling to his feet.

But I just slammed the door behind me and sank to the floor.

Yesterday, forever had felt like a possibility, like a promise. But now I knew it was the exact opposite. Forever was its own death sentence.

CRACKS

All afternoon I've watched her sit on her porch, sighing out her heartbreak. One day and she's already figured it out: Forever isn't all it's cracked up to be.

I'd take her with me if I could, but she's actually what I pretend to be: good. She would never agree to my plan.

But I see it happening already, the cracks in the perfect facade. The sting is just the beginning. And I'll do what I've always done: smile, nod, and fool them all.

No one will ever suspect a thing.

THE JESSICA RULE

The Jeep pitched and dived as it climbed the rocky hill toward nowhere. All I could see in front of me were the sky and stars, and I clung to the roll bar, just hoping that Bea was as adept behind the wheel as she seemed to think she was. Next to me on the bench backseat, Krista smiled with her head tipped back, as if enjoying the sensation of her hair being nearly ripped from her scalp. To her right, Fisher stared straight ahead, his mirrored sunglasses on to guard against the wind. Joaquin and Bea occasionally spoke to each other in the front seat, but with all the whooshing air in my ears, and the frantic tripping of my heart, I couldn't make out what they were saying.

I had no idea where we were going. All I knew was it had taken Joaquin half an hour to wheedle me into the car, swearing left and right that whatever we were about to do was going to make me feel better about everything. It wasn't until he mentioned that Tristan wouldn't be there—he was working the closing shift at the Thirsty Swan—that I'd finally agreed to come.

"Just look at the stars!" Krista said, splaying out her arms.

"Yeah. They're . . . great," I replied flatly.

Up ahead, the ground seemed to just end, like we were coming to some sort of a drop-off.

"Um, Bea!" I shouted, leaning forward. "Maybe you should stop."

"Don't worry. It's fine," she called back, glancing over her shoulder at me.

"But you're heading for a cliff!" I yelled, watching the edge of the world rushing toward me at an alarming speed.

"Don't worry about it!" Fisher said with a smile.

My heart was in my throat. What was so cool about this? Were they going to drive me off a cliff just to prove I couldn't die?

"I *am* worried about it!" I cried, frustrated by their calm. "I'm sorry if I'm not used to being a Lifer yet, but I just got here and I don't want to—"

Bea suddenly applied the brake, and we skidded forward.

I closed my eyes as the Jeep turned sideways, the back wheels swinging toward the precipice. I heard the dirt and rocks spray out over the edge and clenched my fists, waiting to feel the ground drop out from underneath me. Dreading the weightlessness. And then, we stopped.

"We're here!"

"Everybody out!"

The Jeep bobbed as the others climbed out and jumped down onto the rocks. As my breathing began to slow, I could hear the waves crashing somewhere down below. Ever so slowly, I opened one eye, then the other. The stars winked overhead. I was still alive. Relatively speaking.

"What is the matter with you people?" I screeched, standing up on the seat. Instantly, the world swooped beneath me. The tire under my feet was aligned perfectly with the edge of the cliff and the water was miles below me. One wrong move and I would tip over the edge. Slowly, I sat down again, breathing in through my nose and out through my mouth. To my right, Bea and Fisher were stripping off their outer layers and walking to the far edge of the cliff, laughing and chatting along the way. Kevin parked his sleek black car nearby, and he, Lauren, and Cori clambered out, all of them shedding clothes along the way. There was no sign of Tristan. Or Nadia, for that matter.

Joaquin and Krista stood on the other side of the Jeep.

"Sorry. Bea's our resident speed freak," Krista said, tying her hair into a ponytail.

Joaquin stepped closer. "I'll help you down."

I slid across the bench and stood up shakily. Joaquin reached out and clasped my waist with his hands. I jumped down, assuming he'd back up, but he didn't, and we grazed hips. I looked up into his brown eyes. He was still holding on to me.

"Well," he said. "Maybe you're not such a goody-goody."

I blushed and stepped back. "What're we doing here?"

"Come see!" Krista said excitedly.

The others were all gathered at the very edge of the cliff. I walked toward them on quivering knees, clinging to the front of my sweatshirt with both hands. The fierce wind whipped my hair against my face. In the distance I could see the bridge, the fog swirling lazily around its legs. I stood behind the others on my toes and looked down.

All I saw was water. Water and foam and spray and rocks.

"It's a cliff," I said flatly.

"Yep." Shirtless, Fisher stepped backward toward the edge, tossing his sunglasses onto a pile of clothes. "And it's perfect for this."

My eyes widened. "Don't!"

But it was too late. Fisher had stepped off the edge. He let out a loud, merry shout as he fell. It seemed like five minutes passed before he finally hit the water. He was so far below us I didn't even hear the sound of the splash, but I saw the white water spray up around him.

For a long moment, no one said a word. I was sure I was never going to see Fisher again. No one, dead or alive, could survive a drop like that. But then, suddenly, the water broke and his head emerged. He let out a whoop and the crowd cheered. My shoulders slumped in relief as Fisher swam toward some low rocks and scrambled up onto them.

"That was awesome!" Joaquin shouted.

Fisher cupped his hands around his mouth, and a moment later I heard the faintest call. "Who's next?"

Joaquin, Lauren, Bea, Kevin, Cori, and Krista all turned to look at me.

"Oh no," I said, backing up. "No way. I'll just wait for you guys in the Jeep."

"Come on, Rory. It's an amazing feeling," Bea said imploringly.

"Here, look. I'll do it. It's fine," Cori told me.

Then she turned and jumped, disappearing from view in a snap. The rest of them cheered, hooted, and hollered. This time I didn't look, but I heard her shout up to us when she emerged.

"The water's perfect!"

Crazy. They were all crazy. Every last one of them. I

turned and walked away as fast as I could, my pulse thrumming in my ears. Krista, Bea, and Lauren came after me, but I threw my hands up at them, my sneakers crunching across the pebbles and sand.

"You guys do whatever you want to do," I said. "But just FYI, peer pressure is pretty lost on me."

"We're not trying to peer-pressure you," Bea said, screwing up her face as if I'd offended her. "If you don't want to do it, don't do it."

"Why are *you* even doing it?" I demanded, feeling annoyed and embarrassed that they were all so blasé about something that scared the breath out of me. "That has to be a twenty-story drop!"

Bea shrugged. "Because we can. There's a lot you can do when you realize you can't die."

My gaze darted past her to the edge. So that was what this was about. Illustrating Joaquin's point. I was going to "live" forever. Which meant nothing could hurt me. Not in a permanent way.

But still. That didn't mean I was ready to jump off a cliff.

"Hey, if you don't want to jump, don't worry," Krista said, reaching for my hand with both of hers. Her skin was warm and soft. "We'll sit this one out with you."

"We will?" Bea asked, disappointed.

"Don't let me stop you," I said.

"No. We want to hang out with you, right?" Krista said to the others as she tugged me toward a grouping of large rocks. "Let's sit."

Bea sighed, looking longingly over at the cliff. "Fine."

"I'm in," Lauren said with a shrug.

Krista and I settled down on a wide, flat, gray rock and Bea and Lauren perched around us. Bea sat with her knees together, her feet apart, and pushed her hair behind her shoulders, her jaw clenched. Lauren fiddled with the gold seashell she wore on a chain around her neck. I glanced over my shoulder at the waves far below, feeling awkward. Being the center of attention was not my thing.

"So," Krista began, biting her lip. "Are you okay?"

I froze. Had Tristan said something to her? "Yeah. Why?"

"Just Joaquin kept going on about how we had to cheer you up, and when Tristan came into the general store this morning after your tour, he wouldn't even look me in the eye," Krista explained. "Did something happen between you two?"

"Me and Tristan?" I squeaked. "No. Of course not. We're not, I mean, he's not—"

"Oh god. You like him, don't you?" Krista squealed.

"Ugh. Not another one," Bea said bluntly.

"What do you mean, another one?" I asked.

Lauren leaned back on her hands. "Just don't let Nadia find out."

"I knew it!" I exclaimed. "She likes him, doesn't she?"

Silence. The three of them exchanged knowing looks, and a new and awful thought occurred to me, one that would explain everything that had happened this morning and also make it ten times more embarrassing.

"Wait a minute. Are Tristan and Nadia, like, together?"

"Uh, no," Krista said with a scoff. "Please."

"Not that she doesn't *want* to," Lauren sang, pushing her legs out straight.

"Lauren!" Bea kicked Lauren's shin with her toe.

"What?" Lauren was wide-eyed. "I'm just saying! Rory should know. If you have a thing for Tristan, it's better to know. Trust me."

I blinked. Did Lauren have a thing for Tristan, too?

"What do you mean? Wait, is that why she's always lurking around and glaring at me?"

"She's been *lurking*?" Krista blurted out.

Bea sighed loudly and raised her eyes to the stars. "I don't know about the lurking, but Lauren's talking about the Jessica Rule."

"What's the Jessica Rule?" I asked.

Someone let out a loud whoop, and when we looked over, Kevin had disappeared from sight. We waited a couple of minutes until we heard him whoop again, his voice echoing up from the depths.

"Are you losers doing this or what?" Joaquin shouted to us.

"Keep your pants on!" Bea shouted back.

He laughed, then pulled off his shirt before diving over the edge.

"What's the Jessica Rule?" I repeated.

"Basically, the deal is this," Lauren began, tucking her glossy dark hair behind her ears. "Jessica was this Lifer who got here way before the three of us did, and apparently Tristan fell for her. Like, big-time fell. We're talking running barefoot through the fields, swearing undying devotion under the stars, epic kind of romance."

I squirmed, my toes curling inside my sneakers. "And?"

Lauren's eyes sparkled with mischief in a way that made me think of my sister and her friends back home. They got that exact same look on their face when they had good dirt. She leaned toward me conspiratorially.

"And *then* she—"

"Broke up with him," Bea interrupted curtly. Lauren whipped around to glare at her. "She broke up with him, broke his heart, and he vowed to never get into a relationship with another Lifer. Which is what Nadia found out when she tried to get together with him upon her arrival. What was it? Thirty years ago now?"

"Why not?" I asked. "I mean, why not ever get into another relationship? People break up all the time."

Krista took a breath. "Because she—"

Suddenly I was blinded by a flash of light. We all turned around at the sound of a gunned engine. A black sports car with a huge firebird painted on its hood came flying up the hill out of nowhere and skidded to a stop, spraying dirt and pebbles all over the place. Pete clambered out from behind the wheel and jogged over to the jumping point, leaving the engine running and the radio and lights on. He peeled a white tank top off over his head.

"Woo-hoo!" he shouted. And then he flipped off the edge.

Yep. Crazy people. I was living among a bunch of crazy people. I was just turning back to the conversation when the passenger-side door opened, and Nadia stepped out. She looked right at me with a cocky expression, slammed the door, and sauntered over. Her Mohawk was spikier this evening, and she wore thick black eyeliner that made her dark eyes look huge.

"What're you girls doing?" she said teasingly, pushing her hands into the pockets of her black vinyl jacket. "Getting a knitting circle going?"

They were the first words I'd actually heard her speak. Bea, Lauren, and Krista all turned to look at me.

"What?" Nadia said, looking down her nose at me.

I pushed myself up to my feet, my insides shivering and sliding. Nadia eyed me with interest.

"Do you have a problem with me?" I demanded. Bea, Lauren, and Krista all stood up around us, forming a circle.

She lifted a shoulder. "I have a few, actually," she spat, looking me up and down like I was dirt.

"What?" I asked, turning my palms out. "If this is about Tristan—"

"Tristan?" she barked indignantly. "Are you kidding me? This is not about Tristan. It's about the fact that I don't trust you."

My jaw dropped. "What did I ever do to you?"

Bea and Lauren exchanged an alarmed glance, as if they knew what was coming and didn't like it.

"Like you don't know," Nadia said, jutting her chin.

My fingers curled in frustration. "Enlighten me."

"Okay, fine," Nadia said. "Ever since you got here, something's off. All this strange stuff has been happening."

My eyes narrowed. "What strange stuff?"

"That's not her fault," Lauren said to Nadia, not defensively, but as if my innocence were obvious.

"How do you know?" Nadia demanded. "No one knows for sure."

"What strange stuff?" I repeated, looking around at the others.

"Stop acting like you don't know!" Nadia shouted, getting right in my face.

"Nadia, that's enough!" Bea shouted, grabbing her arm.

"Lay off, *Beatrice*." Nadia whirled on her. "You don't tell me what I can and can't say."

"If Tristan were here, he would say the same thing," Bea said, stepping toward her menacingly. She was a good foot taller than Nadia, with a lot more muscle. "So, shut. The hell. Up."

Nadia's pale face grew red. "Fine. But I know I'm right," she said, glaring at me. "And I'm going to prove it."

Then she turned around and took off, storming across the dirt and rocks toward Pete's car. No one spoke. Nadia got behind the wheel and peeled out.

"What was she talking about?" I asked when the growl of the engine faded to a dull hum. "What weird stuff has been happening since I got here?"

Krista opened her mouth to speak, but Bea shook her head, silencing her.

"Lauren?" I said.

"I can't. It's not my place," she told me, pulling her hands up under the cuffs of her sweatshirt.

Frustration burbled inside my chest, threatening to boil over. "Then whose place is it?"

No one said a word.

"Whose place is it?" I shouted. "Is it Tristan's?"

Still no answer. Lauren looked over her shoulder as if there were someone there who could help them out of this awkward mess.

"Fine. I'm outta here," I spat, striding away. "So glad I can trust my new family."

"Rory! Come on! It's at least two miles back to town!" Krista cried after me.

"Good thing I'm a runner!" I called back.

I kept walking, charging straight into the dark, my feet twisting and slipping over the uneven terrain. Trees rose up on both sides of the road, and a stiff wind sent a shower of curled brown leaves over my head and shoulders. I pulled my sweatshirt tighter and clenched my teeth.

I trudged around a bend in the road and froze when I saw a pair of headlights gleaming up ahead, illuminating a wild stretch of weeds. The car was sleek and silver, idling in the silence. The brake lights were on, and the window started to slide down as I arrived. Something moved off to my right, and I ducked down behind a wild berry bush, peering over the uneven branches. Officer Dorn slid down an embankment—an embankment from which he could have seen everything going on at the cliff—and walked over to the car, his black patent-leather shoes gleaming in the moonlight.

He leaned in toward the car window to talk to the driver, but I couldn't hear anything over the sound of the blood whooshing in my ears. The conversation went on for a few minutes before the window slid up again and the car slowly rolled away. Dorn stood up straight, sighed, and checked his watch before moving off in the opposite direction.

When I stood up on solid ground once more, my knees were shaking.

Dorn seemed to be everywhere lately. I thought of the accusatory look he and Grantz had given me in the park along with Nadia, and that odd feeling I'd had at Tristan's this morning, like someone was listening—watching. And was it just a coincidence that Pete had happened by on the bay last night, or had he been following me, too?

A cold wind blew all around me, and I shivered from head to toe. I raced up to the road and headed south as fast as I could. I wanted answers, and as far as I could tell, there was only one place on this island I could get them.

OBLIVION

Tristan was alone behind the bar at the Thirsty Swan, methodically moving a white rag in circles over the dark wood surface. I hesitated outside the screen door, all the dashed hope and hot humiliation from that morning rushing back, and I started rethinking this whole idea. But it wasn't as if I could avoid him forever.

Holding my breath, I pulled open the screen door and let it bang shut behind me. It was the first time I'd ever seen the place so still and silent, the only sound the even ticking of the fan at the center of the ceiling as it pushed the salty air around the room.

"Sorry, we're closed," Tristan said, looking up. When he saw me standing there, he paused, and a pained look passed quickly through his eyes. "Rory," he said, dropping the rag. I found myself staring at his hands. "What's up?"

Focus, Rory. Focus.

"Who's Jessica?" I asked.

Tristan reached out and gripped the edge of the bar. His chest went concave, as if I'd just shot him through the heart. Wow. Lauren wasn't exaggerating when she'd used the word *epic*.

"How . . . who told you about Jessica?" he asked finally, his voice a whisper.

I strode over to the counter, trying for cool detachment. All the chairs had been turned upside down and placed atop the tables, their spindly legs reaching toward the ceiling. Beneath my feet, the floor shone. I glanced toward the kitchen doors, the light glowing through the cracks, and wondered if anyone else was there.

"Lauren, mostly," I told him matter-of-factly. "Right before Nadia showed up and accused me of being responsible for all this strange stuff that's been going on. Any idea what that's about?"

Tristan's eyes flashed. "She shouldn't have done that," he said. "I'll talk to her."

I slid onto a seat. "So what happened between you and Jessica?" I asked, folding my hands in front of me.

Tristan sighed, pressing both hands onto the surface of

the bar. Outside, a bell dinged mournfully as a boat made its way into the marina.

"Jessica broke my heart," he told me, his jaw working. "I thought she was . . . perfect. But she turned out to be the exact opposite." He took a deep breath and looked me over as if deciding whether or not he should say whatever was on the tip of his tongue. "She was the first Lifer to ever go bad."

I felt as if the bar stool had just tipped beneath me. "What do you mean, go bad?"

Tristan turned his profile to me. He pinched his bottom lip between his thumb and forefinger, considering, then walked out from behind the bar, taking the stool next to mine. He turned toward me, and the outside of his thigh pressed against the inside of mine. My heart flip-flopped, heat radiating up my leg, through my chest, and all the way into my scalp. Then it flip-flopped again when he didn't move away.

"Do you remember yesterday when we told you what would happen if you told your father and sister what was really going on here?" he asked, looking into my eyes.

"How could I forget?" I said, my pulse thrumming quickly in my wrists, my ears, my chest.

"Well, Jessica decided that it was . . . immoral of us to keep that secret," Tristan told me. "She thought that the visitors deserved to know the truth. So she went from house to house . . . telling them."

"What?" I breathed.

Tristan nodded, staring past me with a far-off look. "What happened next was not pretty. It was devastating, actually." Suddenly his eyes welled and without thinking, I reached out and placed my hand over his. He froze for a second, his muscles tensing, then clutched me back. I held my breath, staring down at our fingers, feeling the warmth of his skin pressed against mine.

"What happened?" I asked.

"You have to understand this was a long time ago," Tristan said, touching his leather bracelet. "The people who were here at that time . . . they'd died during the first World War—they'd seen their brothers and sons go off and never come back. Some had gone with little or no food for weeks on end, watched their children suffering. The population of Juniper Landing was generally . . ."

"Pissed off?" I supplied, even as I absorbed this new information—that Tristan had been here at least as long as Joaquin had.

He looked at me and snorted. "Yeah. Pissed off." He blew out a breath. "So pissed off they formed a mob."

I gulped. "A mob?"

Tristan nodded sadly. "Mobs were big back then."

"What did you do?" I asked.

"There was nothing much we could do," he replied.

"We tried to reason with them, but once angry people get together and are out for blood, they're not satisfied until they get it. Fighting broke out and a lot of people were hurt, but eventually we got it under control." He pressed his lips together, chagrined. "We Lifers knew the island a lot better. We had what Dorn would call a tactical advantage."

My nerves sizzled at the mention of Dorn, and I thought once more of him whispering to the person in the silver car. "Was he here?"

Tristan shook his head. "Not yet. He's a lot newer. Showed up during the first Gulf War."

"Oh." I said, doing quick calculations in my mind. How long had Tristan been here that twenty years felt "new"?

"Anyway, we had to round up everyone Jessica had told and take them to the bridge," Tristan continued, his blue eyes dark with pain. "That was the worst part, sending all those people to the Shadowlands."

A twisting ache filled my chest. "But it wasn't their fault Jessica told them."

"Yes, but that's the rule," Tristan said emphatically. "It's there to scare Lifers out of telling people the truth and robbing them of their chance to resolve their issues, but Jessica clearly didn't care about that, and once it was done, there was nothing we could do to change it. I couldn't have sent them off to the Light at that point any more than I could have saved Jessica. It's the coins that make the decision, and the coins knew. They were all damned to the Shadowlands."

He released my hand and pressed his palms into his jeans, breathing in and out. He shook his head and glanced up at the ceiling with this look in his eyes, like he couldn't believe any of this had actually happened, even though it had been almost a hundred years ago.

"But that's so . . . wrong," I said. "Is there any way to change the rules?"

He looked at me and scoffed sadly. "I wish."

We sat in silence for a moment, listening to the fan tick, tick, tick overhead.

"What happened to Jessica?" I asked.

"Jessica," he said, then looked me in the eye. "Jessica was sent to Oblivion."

My hand went to my wrist, clutching my leather bracelet. "But you said there were only two destinations."

"There are. For the visitors," he said quietly. "Oblivion is a very specific, very awful region of the Shadowlands. It's reserved for Lifers who break the rules."

"So . . . wait a minute," I said, getting off the stool, my feet hitting the floor with a thud. "If I had left you at the ferry landing yesterday and told my family what was going on, not only would they have gone to the Shadowlands, but I would've gone to Oblivion? You didn't feel the need to share that little factoid with me?"

"I didn't have to," Tristan told me. "I knew you wouldn't tell them. You love them too much to do that to them."

"Is this why you . . . I mean—" I paused, trying to summon the guts to say what I wanted to say, what I needed to know. "Is this why you backed away from me this morning?" I fumbled out. "Because you think I'll go bad? Because you don't trust me?"

Tristan shook his head and stepped down from his bar stool. "No," he said. "I don't think you're going to go bad. I just . . . what Jessica did . . . it killed me. It killed me that I didn't see it coming. If I hadn't been so blindly in love with her, I could have stopped it from happening and saved all those people," he said. "Forget about trusting someone else. For a long time I didn't trust myself. And I realized somewhere along the line that I was going to have to live with that pain and uncertainty *forever.*"

I breathed in and out slowly. For a long moment we just looked at each other, and all I wanted to do was sink into him. To hold him. To wrap my arms around him and tell him that I was different, that I would never hurt him, that I wasn't Jessica.

But he didn't move, and neither did I.

"This is what's best, Rory," Tristan said finally, formally. I looked into his eyes and saw hardness that cracked my heart in two. "It's what's best for both of us."

WRONG

So now she knows. Not everything in this magical place is exactly what it seems. Whatever people say about trust and family, there are always secrets. Always half-truths. There's always more to learn. But now she knows the most important fact, that however idealistic we all make it sound, things can go wrong here. They can go very, very wrong. The question is, will she even realize that it's already happening? Will she be able to stop it before it's too late?

Not if I can help it.

THE MAYOR

The next morning, I stood in our kitchen, surrounded by cracked eggs and white powder. After several attempts, the pancake batter I'd made finally started to hold its roundish shape in the hissing pan. I placed another heavy skillet on the next burner and grabbed the matches. Today was going to be a normal day. Just me and my family, eating pancakes and bacon and sipping fresh coffee. No Lifers, no usherings, no insane accusations. Just a normal day. I struck the match, but nothing happened. I tried again. Nothing. I was just going for a third try when I saw something move outside the kitchen window. I was so distracted that the flame traveled down the match and burned my fingers.

"Ow!" The match dropped to the linoleum floor, and I stamped it out under my sneaker. "Great," I said to myself, sucking on my fingertips. "Burn yourself over a stupid bird."

But even as I said it, I saw another flash. Someone darting by the back window, right outside on our deck. Someone wearing a black sweatshirt. My heart hit the floor. Whoever it was had been watching me. Placing the matches silently on the counter, I tiptoed toward the door. The lurker had either sprinted down the steps to the beach or was standing in the blind spot between two windows, not three feet away.

I held my breath and slowly, shakily, reached for the doorknob.

"What're you doing?"

My hand flew to my heart. Darcy stood in the doorway between the kitchen and the front hall, eyeing me as if I were conducting chemistry experiments on the kitchen table.

"Making pancakes?" I said dumbly, trying to recover from my moment of panic.

"Oh, yeah? How's that working out for you?" she asked, padding over to the stove in her bare feet. She took a peek at the pan and wrinkled her nose at the gelatinous glop bubbling in the center of an oil slick.

"Not very well," I replied, my shoulders drooping.

She picked up the pan and threw the whole mess into the sink. I opened the door quickly and glanced outside. Nothing but the marigolds rustling in the ocean breeze.

"It's in the genes, I guess," she said. "Remember when mom tried to make penguin-shaped pancakes?"

"Of course." I smiled sadly as I closed the door. I would never forget that day. I was eight, and my mother had almost burned down the house with an oil fire, leaving a huge black stain on the kitchen ceiling, but instead of freaking out, she'd opened all the windows, dumped the pan and the remaining batter in the garbage, and found a coupon for IHOP.

"I think we polished off three dozen stacks that morning," Darcy said as she opened a bottle of water.

"I miss IHOP," I said with a nostalgic smile, wiping my hands on a kitchen towel. "The grease, the butter . . . the regret."

Darcy laughed just as a crow landed on our windowsill, cawing at us.

"That should be our first meal when we get home," she suggested, rinsing out the pan. "Rooty Tooty Fresh 'N' Fruity."

We locked eyes. "Extra on the fruity," we said together.

And we both laughed. It was my mom's line. Actually, it was my grandfather's line, but my mom had claimed it as her own.

Darcy reached for the pancake mix as tears filled my eyes.

Don't cry. Do not *cry over IHOP,* I told myself, clutching the dish towel. *There's no way to explain that.*

As I watched Darcy move around the kitchen, her graceful movements so much like my mom's, I wondered what kind of selfless acts Darcy and my dad would need to do to make them Lifers—and how I could help them accomplish those feats. I'd already said good-bye to my mother; I didn't want to have to say good-bye to them, too. Not if there was anything I could do about it.

"How about we start over?" Darcy said, pulling some eggs out of the fridge.

"We?" I asked, happily surprised.

She shrugged. "I've baked for a lot of bake sales. I must've learned something. Where's your measuring cup?" Darcy asked, taking a clean bowl out of the cabinet.

I reached past her for the ceramic coffee cup I'd been using, and she grabbed my arm, staring down at my leather bracelet. My cheeks burned and I snatched my arm back.

"Where did you get that?" she demanded.

"Nowhere," I said automatically. She gave me a "nice try" sort of look, and I sighed, busted. "Krista gave it to me."

"She just gave you one. Just like that," she said skeptically.

I shrugged one shoulder. Obviously Darcy had noticed,

117

just like I had early on, that Tristan, Joaquin, and their entire crowd all wore these bracelets.

"So . . . what? Are you part of their little clique now?" she asked, opening a drawer so violently all the utensils inside came sliding to the front.

"No! Of course not. She just thought I'd like it," I improvised. "It doesn't mean anything."

"Uh-huh." She took out a set of plastic measuring cups and slammed the drawer. "Whatever you say."

I swallowed hard, knowing how jealous Darcy must have felt. She was supposed to be the popular, cool girl, not me. If there was one thing she hated, it was being left out. Of anything.

"Darcy, I—"

At that moment, my dad came barreling down the stairs. I was about to ask him if he wanted pancakes when he entered the kitchen, and the question died on my tongue.

His face was flushed, his eyes wild, his normally neatly combed hair sticking out behind his ears. It was a look I knew well. For a long time, my father's temper had been beyond short, his ability to be patient nil. Whenever the cable guy was an hour late or they forgot his fries at the drive-through window or he had to wait at the doctor's for more than fifteen minutes, this was the look he got on his face—like that of a deranged madman.

"Girls," he said, half in, half out of the kitchen, "I just came in to tell you I'm driving over to the mainland."

"What?" I blurted out, gripping the counter as my legs gave way beneath me.

"Can I come with you?" Darcy asked at the same time.

"Why?" I demanded.

"Because we've been here for over a week and no one has contacted us," my father explained, shaking his fist angrily. "Not the FBI, not the U.S. Marshals. And I can't dial out from this damned island. I don't know about you, but I'd like to know what's going on back home and whether or not Steven Nell is still on the loose."

Sweat beaded on the back of my neck. Steven Nell wasn't still on the loose. He was dead, just like we were, except, according to Tristan, I'd sent him to the Shadowlands. We were completely safe right now. If you considered being dead a state of well-being.

"Dad, I'm sure everything is fine," I said, trying to keep the desperation out of my voice.

"No, it's not! This is not okay!"

I looked at my father, his eyes alight with hopeful concern. He was just trying to protect us. Just trying to get us home. I loved my dad in that moment. More than I had in a long time. But I could not let him leave this island.

"Dad, let's just wait a few days. Maybe by then—"

But he didn't listen. He closed the door so hard it shook the windowpanes. I had only made it halfway through the living room when he leaped into the car and gunned it out of the driveway.

"Dammit," I said under my breath, reaching back to untie my apron.

"Where're *you* going?" Darcy demanded, throwing a hand up as I ran out the door.

"I'll be right back."

"But what about the pancakes?" she shouted after me.

"I'm sorry!" I called back.

Out on the street, I chased after the car. My father took the left toward town at top speed and disappeared up the hill. I ran after him as hard as I could.

What am I doing? I thought desperately, trying to control my breathing. *There's no way I'm going to catch him.*

But I knew I had to try. His afterlife might depend on it.

When I emerged at the top of the hill, I saw my father's car across the park, turning toward the ferry docks. I took a moment, relieved. At least he wasn't going to the bridge.

The wind whipped, and from the corner of my eye I saw an odd flash coming from the rotunda windows of the library. My heart thumped. The flash came again. Then again. It was as if someone was sending Morse code, flashing the sunlight back out at the world with a mirror. I squinted but could make out nothing, and suddenly, the blinds fell.

My dad turned the corner, and I tore myself away from the window. Taking a deep breath, I sprinted across the park, then up the hill to the bluff. In the distance, bobbing over whitecaps, was the ferry. It was still a few minutes out, but once it was docked, my father was going to attempt to board it. I did the only thing I could think to do—I ran up to Tristan's front door and collapsed against it, pounding on the wooden panels as hard as I could with both hands.

Tristan threw open the door. He looked angry until he saw me. Then his face softened.

"Rory, what—"

"What happens to someone if they try to leave the island?" I demanded, grabbing his arm.

He turned pale. "What?"

"My father . . . he's on his way . . . to the ferry," I said between gasps. "He wants to go back to the mainland to find out what's going on with Steven Nell."

I managed to get the bulk of it out in one breath, then leaned against the wall. The world was starting to go prickly, and I had to bend over to keep from passing out.

"Are you okay?" he asked me, steadying my shoulder in his strong grip.

"Yes! But my father—"

"I'm on it," he said, turning toward the door on the far side of the foyer. I took a staggering step to go with him, but he placed his hand on my shoulder again. "You should wait out here. The mayor can be sort of . . ." He paused as I looked up at him through my sweaty bangs. "Just wait here," he said with an apologetic, grim smile.

"Okay. Just hurry. Please," I told him. Then I fell onto an antique bench against one of the front windows, leaning my head back against the cool pane. When I closed my eyes, all I could see was the determination in my father's face. If Tristan didn't automatically have an answer for this, then it was not good. I heard a door open and jumped up.

A tall woman in a cream-colored suit and matching heels strode out of the office, her long, tapered fingers clasped in front of her. Her makeup looked professionally applied, and there wasn't a single stray hair slipping out from her blond chignon. Diamond earrings dangled from her earlobes, and she wore a strand of pearls around her imperious neck. When she smiled at me, I ran my tongue over my own slightly crooked front teeth.

"Rory Miller," she said in a welcoming tone, her hand stretching out in front of her. "It is a distinct pleasure to finally meet you."

"Um, you, too," I said, shaking her cool, dry hand with my hot, clammy one. I glanced past her at Tristan. He raised his shoulders, as confused as I was. He'd made it seem like she'd be annoyed by my intrusion, but instead I was a "distinct pleasure"?

"Tell me . . . what is your father up to?" she asked, lifting her hand to her chin and tilting her head like a politician listening to a laid-off worker.

"He's trying to get off the island," I told her. "I didn't know what to do. What'll happen to him if he—"

"Interesting, interesting," she said, narrowing her clear blue eyes. "Well, I don't want you to worry about that for one more minute," she said, clasping her hands together again. "*I* will take care of it."

She smiled down at me, then at Tristan, like she was some kind of magician and we were two rapt kindergartners.

"Okay, but what—"

Tristan shot me a look that said to stop, so I did, and the mayor turned and strode back into her office. The door closed with a click, and two seconds later I could hear her talking in a low voice. Tristan stepped over to me, watching the door the entire time, as if expecting it to open again.

"What's she going to do?" I whispered.

"Don't worry," he replied. "If the mayor says she's going to take care of something, it gets taken care of."

"But what happens to people when they try to leave the island?" I asked, my heart racing.

Tristan's face was a blank. "I'm not sure anyone has ever tried before."

A door down the hallway behind Tristan suddenly closed. My heart skipped a beat.

"What?" Tristan asked, noticing my change in demeanor. "What's wrong?"

I walked past him and pushed the door open. In front of me was a wide, modern kitchen with every amenity from a microwave to a stainless-steel oven to a double refrigerator—the complete opposite of our quaint nineteen-fifties throwback. But the important detail was, it was empty. Not a soul was there, and not a dish was out of place.

"What is it?" Tristan asked again, coming up behind me and pushing the door even wider.

"Nothing," I said. "I could have sworn someone was back here. I saw the door move."

Tristan glanced around but saw the same thing I did. An empty kitchen.

"The house is drafty sometimes," he said. "I'm sure it was just the wind."

"Oh," I replied. "I guess."

But as I turned to go, I heard footsteps overhead, followed by a soft, keening giggle. And just like that I knew: Someone *had* been watching me. Because on this island, someone always was.

BRAINWASHED

My father never came home. I spent the entire day on the front porch pretending to read on my iPad, but I was really watching the road. Aside from a few bicyclists, a skateboarder, and one happy strolling couple, I saw no one all day. By the time the sun had started to dip behind the gray house across the street, I had about a dozen theories as to what the mayor had meant when she'd said, "I will take care of it," and none of them were good.

I looked up at the ceiling of the porch, leaning my head against the hard edge of the back of the swing. From the corner of my eye, I saw that one of the potted marigolds on the porch railing had withered and drooped, its formerly bright yellow bloom gone brown. I sat up fast. I could have sworn that a few hours ago, that flower had been alive and well, its stem curving toward the sun.

"Hey, Rory!"

I was so startled I almost jumped.

Aaron strolled toward me, a large take-out bag swinging by his side. I sat up as he opened the front gate, placing my feet on the porch floor.

"Hey," I said, trying to smile.

"I brought you guys dinner, enough for four."

Aaron lifted the bag, which was imprinted with the Crab Shack logo, and smiled back. He was wearing a red polo shirt with the collar turned up, just like the guy he'd chatted up at the bar the other night.

My heart sank at the reminder of my father. "Thanks. That's great. But my dad's not home, so it'll only be three."

"More for me, then," he said happily, reaching for the front door and holding it open for me. Amazing how the source of such anguish for me was a happy surprise for him.

"Darcy!" I shouted as the door swung closed. "Aaron's here."

I heard her bed squeak, then her door slam, and she appeared at the top of the stairs. Her hair was all done up and curled around her face, like she was getting ready for prom.

"Hey, there!" Aaron said brightly. "What's with the do?"

"Like it?" she asked, turning her head from side to side before tromping down the stairs. "I call it the Sheer Boredom."

Aaron laughed. "Very creatively named."

"What'd you bring?" Darcy asked, squiring him into the kitchen. "It smells yum."

Just as Darcy opened the bag, the front door opened and my dad stepped into the house, flicking on the porch light.

"Dad!" I shouted. He barely had time to open his arms before I ran into them. "You're back!"

"I am," he said, dropping his keys on the table next to the framed photo of my family. "What's with the hero's welcome?"

I hesitated. He wasn't acting like someone who'd gone on a fruitless mission to right his daughters' lives. In fact, he looked happy and relaxed. Beaming, even.

"Um . . . where've you been?" I asked.

He was already looking past me toward the kitchen, where Darcy and Aaron were unpacking the food on the Formica table.

"You'll never believe it," he said. "I was at the mayor's house, and she's going to help me get my book published!"

"Really?" Darcy squeaked, taking a bite of fried shrimp as she sat down at the table. "How?"

"Apparently, she used to be in publishing, and she knows all these agents and editors," my father said, strolling into the kitchen and eyeing the array of fish, fries, and sauces Aaron had laid out. "How're you, Aaron?" he asked, slapping him on the back.

"Doing well, sir. Help yourself," Aaron replied.

"Daddy, that's great," Darcy said as my father went to the cabinet for plates. "Are you done with it?"

"Almost," he replied happily. "She said she'll read it as soon as it's finished."

I walked slowly to the kitchen threshold, watching as the three of them settled in for their meals. They looked like some kind of brightly lit sitcom. The single dad, his pretty daughter, and her sweet little friend. For a brief moment I wondered if that was why this house was decorated like something out of the fifties. Were they—whoever *they* were—trying to paint the perfect American family backdrop before people moved on?

"That's where you've been all day? With the mayor?" I asked.

My father frowned, thinking, as he loaded his plate with fried clams. "No. I went for a walk, had lunch at the general store, then bumped into her at the library."

Untrue. Completely untrue. He'd stormed out of here on a mission and driven to the ferry. There was no way he'd spent the day wandering around. Someone or something had screwed with his memory—screwed with his mind. I looked at Darcy, waiting for her to ask about the mainland, but she didn't. She simply pushed herself up from the table and went to get everyone drinks.

They'd messed with her mind, too.

"Are you gonna have some?" Aaron asked, glancing at me over his shoulder. "If you are, you'd better start or I'm gonna eat it all."

I just stared at him. They were all brainwashed. Every one of them. If Darcy disappeared tonight, then tomorrow, Aaron wouldn't remember her. And if Aaron disappeared, too, my father wouldn't remember either of them. How did they do it? How did they erase everyone's memories and replace them with new ones?

"Rory?" my father said.

And even worse, if this was happening all around me, how did I know it wasn't happening to me, too? Everything that had occurred since I got here could be a lie.

"Actually, I'm not really feeling that well," I said, taking a step backward. "I think I'm just going to go to bed."

I raced up the stairs two at a time, ignoring my father's call to come back. What did it matter? There was every possibility he wouldn't remember any of this in the morning.

THE COIN

I saw it the second I awoke the next morning. Sitting dead center in the middle of my polished brown nightstand was a single gold coin. I reached for it, my fingers trembling, and laid it flat in the center of my palm. How had the coin gotten there? I felt like I had on every Christmas morning from the day my logic-loving, four-year-old brain had realized the improbability of Santa Claus. Every year for four years I'd tried to stay up to see how it all really happened, how those gifts appeared under the tree, but every year I dozed off and woke up with a start, amazed at the wonder of it all, but secretly angry at myself for failing, yet again, to see the truth with my own eyes.

Leaning back against my pillows, I flipped the coin over and over between my fingers, trying to keep the hovering sadness at bay, knowing I was just avoiding what the coin really meant.

Today was the day. I was going to do my first real ushering, all on my own. But instead of feeling full of purpose and light, my chest was impossibly heavy. I was going to begin my mission without Tristan.

I tromped downstairs and into the kitchen, focused on the coffee machine, but a blur of blue outside on the beach stopped me cold. It was Tristan. He was sitting on the beach behind our house, staring out at the water.

Suddenly, I could have sworn I felt the coin burning a hole in the front pocket of my jeans. I forgot all about the coffee and headed outside. Tristan didn't turn as I approached. He had his legs pulled up, his forearms resting across his knees as he played with a bit of broken reed between his hands. The wind whistled in my ears as, out on the ocean, a rainbow-striped sail bobbed over the waves. I dropped down next to Tristan and pulled out the coin. He glanced at it.

"Today's the day," he said.

"Do you know who it is?" I asked.

He shook his head and pushed his legs out in front of him, poking the reed into the sand at his side, making a long, straight mark like a tally. "Not yet. But you will, soon enough."

I swallowed hard, staring out at the water, my jaw set. "What're you doing here?"

"I wanted to check in about yesterday—"

"Yeah. About that—" I interjected.

Tristan hesitated for a beat. "What's up?"

"What the hell happened to my dad?" I demanded. "When he came home, it was like his memory was wiped."

"What did you expect to happen?" he asked neutrally.

For some reason, that blasé tone got right under my skin. This was my father's mind we were talking about. His memory. His emotions. He might be just another dead guy to Tristan and the mayor and the rest of Juniper Landing—just another visitor to keep in the dark—but he was my father. The only parent I had left.

"I don't know," I snapped, shoving myself up to my feet. "I thought you guys would pretend the ferry broke down or the mayor would . . . just convince him she'd find out what was going on with Nell."

Tristan got up as well, still holding the small reed. The wind blew his hair back from his face, and I couldn't help noticing how sharp his cheekbones suddenly seemed.

"What would be the point of that?" he asked calmly. "He'd only start asking more questions tomorrow."

Like memory wiping was an obvious and not at all insidious solution. I groaned and started to walk back toward my house. Tristan, of course, followed.

"Rory, look, I'm sorry if you find the whole thing disturbing, but that's just how it works around here," he said. "Would you rather your father be up there right now in a panic, planning his next attempt to leave?"

I looked at the windows of my dad's bedroom. He'd been up late working on his novel with renewed enthusiasm, now that the mayor had him convinced she could get it published. He was probably at his desk right now, editing and rearranging, muttering lines of dialogue out loud to himself.

"Of course not," I said. "But that doesn't make it right." I stared past him at the sailboat, wishing I could be on it, sailing off to . . . well, anywhere but here. "How does it work, exactly?" I asked. "Does the mayor have special powers or something? Did she sneak in here at some point and wipe Darcy's brain, too?"

"No. It's not like she has to touch a person or something," he said, his blue eyes serious. "Most of the time, the memory fix just happens on its own. Like when a visitor leaves and no one remembers them the next day. It's automatic. Your dad was a special case. She had to place new memories in his mind, and once she did that, Darcy's memories were changed to match his."

KATE BRIAN

I shuddered in the wind and hugged myself tightly. "How does she do that? Place new memories?"

Tristan ran his fingers through his blond hair. "It's kind of wild, actually. She just sits with the person, looks them in the eye, and tells them a story," he explained. "When she's done, whatever's she's told them, they believe it actually happened that way."

"So she hypnotizes people," I said.

"In a way. But she doesn't do it often," Tristan said. "Only in extreme situations."

I nodded, trying to swallow the lump in my throat. "Why can I still remember what happened?"

Tristan turned to face me fully. "Because you're a Lifer," he said, like it was obvious. "Our minds can't be altered."

"How do I know that?" I demanded. "How do I know that anything that's happened to me is real?"

"Because," he said, reaching out and placing his hand on my forearm, "I'm telling you. I swear to you, Rory. You're safe here."

I stared down at his hand, an accusation in my eyes. He quickly released me.

"Can you do that, too?" I asked, watching his hand as he pushed it into his pocket. "Implant new memories? Can I?"

Tristan sighed. He walked over to the bottom step leading up to our deck and sat down, sliding toward the railing to give me enough room to join him. "No. Only the mayor can do that."

"So she does have special powers," I said, sitting next to him but making sure no part of my leg touched any part of his.

"A few." He used the reed to draw a series of vertical lines in the sand on the step. "She was sent here after the Jessica thing happened," he said, keeping his eyes on his work. "She can tell if a Lifer with bad intentions arrives here, and if they do, she can send them straight to Oblivion."

My throat tightened. Somehow the wind suddenly felt colder than it had a moment ago. "Well, that's terrifying."

"What?" he asked.

"One person having that kind of power," I told him, wondering how he couldn't see it. "Has that ever happened? Has she ever sent anyone there?"

Tristan nodded. "Twice. Both men. I never even found out their names. She just . . . dealt with them."

"So they didn't even get to plead their case?" I asked. "They didn't have a chance to redeem themselves?"

Tristan looked me in the eye and shook his head. "We can't let it happen again, what happened with Jessica. We can't take that chance."

It seemed so extreme. But then, I hadn't been here when Jessica had sent their world teetering toward the brink. I couldn't imagine what it must have been like, the visitors rising up against the Lifers. All the fear and anger and paranoia. The wind hit me with such force at that moment that I shivered.

"Are you cold?"

Tristan moved to put an arm around me, and I automatically flinched. "Don't do that."

He blinked. "What? I was just—"

I stood up, trembling from head to toe as goose bumps popped up all over my skin. "You can't tell me you can't be with me and then keep doing things like that. It's not fair, Tristan," I said, my voice cracking.

He stood up and faced me, so close that our bare toes touched. My chest radiated heat with each pained thump of my heart. I crossed my arms over my stomach, holding on to myself for dear life.

Focus, Rory. Focus.

"Rory—"

"No," I said. "Please, Tristan. Just . . . don't."

He took a tiny step backward, and it was all the incentive I needed. I raced up the steps and across the deck, slamming the kitchen door behind me. Only when I was safely inside did I look back. And Tristan still stood alone in the sand at the bottom of the steps.

Watching.

MY NEXT

Running. Running was good. Running cleared my head. It upped my endorphins. It made me feel positive, like everything was going to be all right. Until I came around a turn into the center of town and saw the mayor's big, imperious mansion staring down at me, and a pulse of fear stopped me cold.

How could one person be allowed to wield so much power? If she could send people to Oblivion without even consulting with anyone else, what was to stop her from banishing every person who disagreed with her? Every person who looked at her wrong? Every person who wore a pair of ripped jeans or stepped on a flower or littered?

I jogged over to the general store and paused under the shade of its blue-and-white-striped awning. Bracing my hands against my knees, I gazed up at the turrets, the wraparound porch, the paned windows, and wondered what she was doing in there right now. Was she wiping someone else's memory? Deciding the fate of some poor Lifer?

Chill, Rory, I told myself, standing up straight again. *Tristan said it was only in extreme situations. There's nothing to worry about.*

The wind shifted, and I automatically looked at the weather vane. The fog had come and gone about an hour earlier, when my dad and I had been out on the back deck barbecuing burgers for lunch, and the vane was now pointing south. I wondered which unlucky soul had been ushered to the Shadowlands—and was thankful I had not been the one to do it.

Another stiff breeze yanked a rotten peach from a nearby tree, and it rolled to a stop at my feet. A fat black worm poked its head out of a slimy brown bruise in the peach's flesh. I grimaced and kicked the peach as hard as I could into the brush at the end of the sidewalk.

Taking a deep breath, I reached back for my ankle to stretch my quads. On the far side of the park, I saw the man whom Dorn had shaken hands with the other night jog up the steps of the library and duck inside. I lowered my foot and reached my arms back to open my chest. Kevin came around the side of the library, glanced quickly over his shoulder, and went in. He was soon followed by Dorn. Then Bea. I dropped my arms, curiosity tingling at the base of my skull. Sure enough, two seconds later, the door of the police station opened and Fisher and Joaquin appeared, toting two heavy bags each. They turned right and headed straight for the library.

I narrowed my eyes, my heart pounding furiously. What were they up to? I reached back to stretch my other quad and lost my balance.

"Gotcha!"

Aaron stepped up onto the sidewalk from the street and grabbed my arm. The second we touched, I had a flash. Aaron on a plank floor, crawling for the window, his fingernails digging into the wood while flames and smoke engulfed him. He reached for the windowsill, red and blue lights throbbing outside, knowing that if he could just get to his knees, if he could just signal someone . . . He tried to breathe, but his throat was closed, his lungs turned inside out. Someone outside was screaming his name. He collapsed on the floor and shut his eyes, sputtering, choking, gone.

"Hey! Are you okay?"

I blinked, my eyes bleary, until Aaron's handsome face came into focus. His smiling, innocent, sweetly clueless face. I sucked in a breath and coughed, doubling over.

"Rory?" he asked, patting my back and sounding alarmed. "Rory? Talk to me. What just happened?"

I shook my head at the bricks beneath our feet, trying not to sob out loud. I heaved in a loud breath and stood up straight, reaching for his shoulder to steady myself, but then recoiled in fear of another flash and grabbed one of the columns supporting the awning instead. My leather bracelet slipped from my sweaty wrist toward my elbow.

"I don't know," I gasped. "I just . . . got dizzy."

"Are you okay? Maybe we should go inside for some water," Aaron suggested. "Or ice cream. It's on me."

I stared at him, trying not to let the horror and sadness shine through. "Sure," I said, mostly just to make him stop being so solicitous, so I could think and regroup. "I just need to stretch some more. I'll meet you inside."

"You sure you're okay?" Aaron asked again, his brown eyes concerned. He reached out to squeeze my shoulder and I flinched, holding my breath, but this time, nothing happened. I stayed right where I was, in this world, with the breeze blowing fresh air all around us, the low hum of conversation emanating from inside the restaurant.

"I'm fine," I said. "I swear."

"Okay. I'll get a table." He strolled inside to the sound of jingling bells and was finally, mercifully gone. I walked to the corner, out of sight of the windows, and covered my mouth with one hand.

Poor Aaron. He'd been so alone. So scared. So desperate. Someone as amazing as he was shouldn't have had to die that way. No one should ever have to die that way.

Suddenly a hand came down on my shoulder, and I jumped, whirling around. It was Krista, wearing her waitress uniform, a pencil tucked behind one ear.

"You okay? I saw you through the window and I thought you were going to pass out."

"Yeah, I almost did." I checked to make sure we were alone. The couple I'd seen get off the ferry yesterday skated by holding hands, and Yoga Girl was back in the park, executing a perfect handstand. "Just now when Aaron touched me, I got the most vivid flash of the way he died."

"Oh, yeah. That," Krista said, with a sigh. "That sucked when I first got here. I mean, it always sucks, but the first few times were awful."

"What the hell was it?" I asked.

Two crows swooped over and perched on the back of one of the outdoor chairs. A third joined them, forcing them to bounce sideways and adjust their talons on the wrought iron bar.

"That's what happens when you touch the next person you're going to usher," Krista told me, twisting her long blond ponytail around her finger. "Since their death is something they can't tell you about themselves, it gets 'revealed to you,'" she added, throwing in some air quotes. "It lets you better understand them so you can help them through whatever they need to get through."

I barely heard a thing after the words *next person you're going to usher.*

"Wait a minute," I said to Krista, waving my hands in front of me. "Wait a minute, wait a minute. Are you telling me that my next charge is . . . Aaron?"

Krista bit her bottom lip. "Looks that way," she said. "I'm really sorry."

The door behind her opened, and Joaquin's "grandmother," Ursula, stuck her head out. "Krista, hon? You got orders up."

"I gotta go," Krista said apologetically. Then she paused as she held the door. "You'll be okay. I mean . . . right?"

"Sure," I said, nodding absently. "I'll be fine."

She squeezed my hand once before turning in a swirl of gingham and lace and heading back inside. Ursula, however, stayed.

"Can I get ya anything, hon?" she asked sympathetically, her leather bracelet clinging to her thick wrist.

I tried to smile. "No, thanks. I'm good," I lied.

As soon as she was gone, I sank to the sidewalk, sitting with my back against the wall of the building as the crows cawed and screeched. My insides were hollow, numb.

Aaron was leaving. Before I knew it, he'd be out of my life for good. And I was going to be the one to make him go.

CONFESSION

"Do you think Darcy will come out and join us?" Aaron asked me that night, folding both arms behind his head.

We were both on lounge chairs on the back deck, staring up at the stars. My pulse pitter-patted nervously. In the pocket of my jeans, Aaron's coin pressed heavily against my thigh.

We'd spent all day together, and as much as I wanted to focus on enjoying the time I had left with him, the same thoughts kept hovering in the back of my mind: *When? When was it going to happen? How would I know it was time?* I felt constantly on edge, like at any second a bomb was about to go off.

"Probably not. She has a date with Fisher," I said.

Aaron lifted his head, intrigued. "Really?"

I sighed. "Second one in two days."

"You don't approve?" Aaron joked, narrowing his eyes.

"It's not that," I said, only half lying, picking at my fingernails. Overhead, a cloud of gnats hovered around the outdoor light. "It's just . . . I miss her, I guess. I'd rather she spend time with me."

"Aw! That's so sweet!" Aaron said, nudging me with one hand. "So tell her!"

I scoffed. "Yeah, right."

Aaron pushed himself up on one arm and rolled to face me. "No. I'm serious. You should. Just be honest about how you feel. That's what I'd do if I could talk to my dad."

His eyelids fluttered down for a second, and I could sense his whole body tightening at the thought of his father.

"What happened with you two?" I asked gently, somehow speaking past the lump in my throat. "You never said."

"I know," Aaron responded. When he opened his eyes again, they were full of tears. "It's because I'm embarrassed. He was just trying to look out for me, and I—"

Out of nowhere, Aaron started to sob, a silent, racking kind of sobbing. He rolled over onto his back again and placed his hand over his eyes. I sat up and placed my feet on the ground, twisting my leather bracelet around my finger.

"Oh . . . god. I'm so sorry, Aaron. I didn't mean to upset you." Suddenly I felt hot all over, and I was grateful for the cool ocean breeze on my back. "You don't have to talk about it if you don't want to."

"No, I do." He took a deep breath through his nose and sat up, pulling his knees up to his chest. "I do," he repeated in a calmer voice. "I was going out with this guy," he said with a sniffle. "Charles. My dad never approved of him. Said he was disrespectful and immature. I thought it was just that he didn't want me with any guy, so I ignored him. I liked Charlie *because* he seemed dangerous. I thought it was exciting that he drove a motorbike and lived in this tiny shack by the water. I thought it was *cool*." He said the last word with venom in it.

I inched forward on my seat, leaning toward him and placing my hand on his back. The second I did, all of his anguish, all of his sorrow and self-doubt and anger, rushed through me so fast the pain was almost too much to take.

And just like that, I knew. It was time. Aaron was getting ready to move on, and this was how I was supposed to help him. I was supposed to listen, to be here for him, to let him confess everything.

"So what happened?" I asked quietly.

"One night my family went out to dinner, and we came home early because my sister had taken ill. We found the door to our house was open," he said, giving me this knowing look, as if he expected me to see where this was going. "My father told everyone to wait outside, and he went in on his own. Two seconds later we hear shouting, and all of a sudden Charlie comes running out of the house and tears off down the street. We heard the motorbike getting away before my father even made it back down the stairs. Charlie had known we were going to be out all night and had used the opportunity to try to rob us."

My heart gave a horrible, sick thump. "Oh my gosh. Aaron, that's—"

"Awful. I know," Aaron said. He swung his legs over the side of the lounge chair and faced me, which forced me to pull my hand back. "But the worst part is, I defended him."

With that, Aaron buried his face in his hands and cried. I covered my mouth, unsure of what to say. All I knew was I didn't want to interrupt him. He needed to get this out of his system, and I was going to let him. After a few minutes, he wiped his nose with the back of his hand and sighed.

"I'm sorry."

"No, it's fine," I told him. "Go on."

"Well, I told my father that he deserved it. That he was such a closed-minded prig it was no wonder Charlie felt the need to punish him," Aaron said. "I accused him of shoving our wealth in Charlie's face all the time, of practically tempting him into doing it. Then I told him I was going to run away with Charlie and I wasn't coming back."

"Wow," I breathed, staring at Aaron's blotchy face. "What happened?"

His eyes took on a distant blankness, as if he wanted to hold himself apart from whatever he was going to say next. I reached out and took his hand, entwining my fingers with his. My fingers instantly began to throb with the strength of his regret.

"When I got to Charlie's, he was gone. The place was wiped out," Aaron said, looking down at our hands. "He just bailed. And when I tried to call him, his number had been changed. No explanation, no apology, not even a breakup e-mail. He just left." He breathed in shakily and let it out. "So I came to America to stay with my uncle and get away for a while. It was a chat with him that made me realize how wrong I was, actually. But then the fire happened, and I haven't had a chance to call my father since."

The fire. The fire that had taken Aaron's life. And because of that, he would never have a chance to call his father.

"I'm just so sorry, you know?" Aaron said, his lower lip trembling as he looked me in the eye, squeezing my hand so tightly it hurt. "I just want him to forgive me. I just want him to forgive me for being such an ass."

I let go of his hand, sat down next to him, and wrapped my arms around him. Aaron buried his face against my shoulder, holding one hand over his eyes as he cried. I felt all of his sadness and regret crash through me again, and this time it was so overwhelming that tears welled up behind my own eyes. I blinked them back, but it was no use. Before long, his striped shirt was dotted with tears.

"It's okay," I told him, my voice wet. "He forgives you. I know he does. He loves you. He knows everyone makes mistakes, and he forgives you."

"You think so?" he asked wearily.

"I know he does," I replied.

Slowly, Aaron's sorrow began to subside. The ache in my heart ebbed, replaced by a distinct, comforting, warmth. Aaron pulled away and looked me in the eye. He seemed a different person suddenly. Like he was calmer, gratified, maybe even happy. And I had made him feel that way. Confessing to me, hearing me say his father forgave him, had given him peace.

I let out a shaky breath and smiled. But it wasn't until Aaron smiled back in a relieved sort of way that I realized, suddenly, how naive I'd been. Being a Lifer wasn't about Tristan. This wasn't even about me. This was about Aaron. It was about helping him let go of all this awfulness and move on. It was about leading him through the biggest transition he'd ever make.

This was a true purpose.

Something tugged gently at my hair, and when I looked down, the fog had already engulfed Aaron's feet. It rolled in over the deck floor, colliding with the glass door and surrounding the planters. But this time, something was different. I could see a clear path through the fog, leading away from the chairs and toward the beach. There was a creak on the stairs, and I turned around. Tristan climbed up to meet us.

"Hey, man," he said.

"Hey," Aaron replied.

Tristan stepped toward me. I stared at the Tevas on his feet. "You ready?"

"Yeah," I said quietly. "I think we are."

Aaron's expression was confused, but not scared. I, however, was terrified. I was about to say good-bye to him, forever. I was about to send him into the beyond.

Tristan held a hand out to me, then quickly thought better of it and shoved it into his back pocket. "It's time."

SURPRISES

As we stood at the end of the bridge with the fog swirling around our ankles, Aaron looked from me to Tristan with innocent bemusement, kind of like a little kid standing outside on the playground on his first day of school, wondering if his parents really were going to leave him there alone.

"What are we doing here?" he asked.

Tristan looked down at my hand. I felt the cold weight of the coin cupped inside my palm. I cleared my throat, and my eyes welled up.

"We're here to say good-bye," I said.

KATE BRIAN

Tristan dipped his head and took a step back on the sandy, rocky road, giving us space.

Aaron looked at me quizzically. "Are you going somewhere?"

"No," I said sadly. "You are."

I handed him the coin, and he held it up between his thumb and forefinger, studying it. "Where am I going?"

"Someplace amazing," I told him, my heart aching like crazy. "Someplace where you'll be happy and . . . at peace."

That was how I imagined the Light would be. The way I hoped it would be.

Aaron smiled. "That sounds fairly awesome."

I grinned, struggling to hold back the tears, and put my hand on his back, turning him toward the bridge. "All you have to do is hold on to that and walk across the bridge," I told him. "You'll be there before you know it."

Aaron took one step, then looked back at me. "I wish you could come."

"Me, too." I reached out and hugged him as tightly as I could, trying to solidify the feeling of him, his clean scent, in my memory. "It's been so nice knowing you," I whispered.

"You, too," he told me. "Thanks for everything. I mean it, Rory. You've been a really good friend."

I looked over at Tristan. It was almost as if Aaron knew where he was going. Maybe some small part of him did.

152

"Good-bye," Aaron said to Tristan rather formally.

Tristan lifted a hand in a wave, and Aaron strode into the fog surrounding the bridge. The second he was gone, I dropped my face into my hands and cried, feeling guilty and selfish for it. Aaron was going to be fine. He was going to the Light. It was me I was crying for.

Suddenly I felt Tristan's warm hand slide up my back and clasp my shoulder. "Rory," he said, his voice full of anguish and grief and comfort and hope.

I turned toward him, knowing my face was covered in tears, knowing my nose was swollen and my eyes were red and my lips were dry and puffy. Knowing and not caring.

Tristan reached up and ran his thumb over my cheek, tilting my face so I had to look him in the eye.

"Rory," he said again.

"I'm sorry," I blubbered. "I just . . . I didn't want . . . I didn't want him to go."

"I know," he said, drying one cheek with the pad of his thumb. "I know."

He took in a sharp breath, and then before I could realize what was happening, he kissed me. He kissed me so hard that I staggered backward until he tightened his grip on me to hold me up. I slid my hands up his broad back and tangled my fingers up in the soft, thick hair at the nape of his neck. Tristan kissed me like a guy who'd never kissed anyone before. Like a person who was so starved to be kissed he'd never stop. Not that I ever wanted him to. It didn't even matter that my skin was smeared with tears. I'd never experienced a kiss so perfect. I'd never experienced *anything* so perfect.

When he finally pulled away, his hands gripped the back of my T-shirt and we were standing so close I couldn't tell whose legs were whose. We both gasped for breath, our exhalations mingling between us.

"I thought you said—"

"Forget what I said," he interjected. "I'm just sick of it."

"Sick of what?" I asked, my brow creasing.

"Sick of trying to keep away from you," Tristan said with a sigh. He held the back of my neck with one hand. "I've only been doing it for ten days, and it feels like an eternity."

He kissed me again, and I smiled beneath his lips. He'd been counting the days, struggling all along to keep from wanting me, and now he was breaking the rules for me— breaking *his* own rules. Everything felt lighter suddenly. It was as if some chokehold on my heart had loosened and now it could really breathe.

Tristan broke off the kiss and wrapped his arms around me. For a long time we just stood there, folded against each other. My eyelashes were still wet, my heart brimming.

I leaned back to look him in the eye again, but then

Tristan's expression suddenly darkened. I glanced over my shoulder to see what had caught his attention. Along the side of the road, a swath of the green reeds had dried out and turned brown, bending toward the road. Some of them were broken, sticking out at violent angles, like bony fingers reaching up from a grave.

"What is it?" I asked.

"Nothing," he said, forcing a smile. "It's nothing." He entwined his fingers with mine. "Let's walk back."

"What about your car?" I asked, glancing over at his Range Rover, parked near the foot of the bridge.

"I'll get it later," he told me. "Right now, I'm in the mood for a nice, long stroll. With you."

I grinned. "I like that plan."

Our hands swinging between us, we walked down the hill toward town. Tristan pointed out various landmarks to me—a tree he used to climb when he first arrived on the island, trying to see across the ocean; a steep hill he and Joaquin had once raced down on bikes before crashing into each other at the bottom; the spot in the park where he and Krista had picnicked when she'd first learned the truth about Juniper Landing and her role here. I sensed how much Tristan loved this place—not just his mission, but this island.

Downtown Juniper Landing was bustling, full of people

headed to the docks for dinner or strolling through the park with ice-cream cones. The trilling music of a flute wafted out through an open window somewhere as screen doors squeaked and people laughed. Everything seemed so peaceful, and the grass beneath our feet glimmered from the moisture left behind by the fog.

"And this is where I was standing the first time I saw you," Tristan said, pausing in front of the general store.

"You remember that?" I asked with a blush.

"I'll never forget it," he said, sounding nostalgic.

I laughed suddenly.

"What?" he asked, squeezing my hand.

"I still can't believe you kissed me," I said.

He took a deep breath and blushed. "I just finally decided . . ."

"What?" I asked, biting my bottom lip. "You decided what?"

He lifted one shoulder and looked me in the eye. "I decided that you're more important."

For a second I couldn't breathe, but in a good way. There was so much meaning in that one sentence, so much surrender and trust, it actually took my breath away.

I was just rising up on my toes to kiss him when his eyes flicked past me and he tensed. I turned to see that Nadia had just walked out of the general store and now stood rooted to the sidewalk, a stunned expression on her face. My mouth went dry as her eyes slowly trailed down to our hands, still clasped between us.

"Nadia," Tristan said.

Her dark eyes were like daggers. "Unbelievable," she said, stepping off the sidewalk. "So much for the rules, huh, Tristan?" she yelled, throwing her hands wide as she walked backward across the street.

She grabbed a dirt bike that had been tossed on the grass in the park and quickly pedaled away, heading down toward the beach. Tristan sighed.

"I'm guessing that's not good," I said quietly.

"No, probably not," he replied.

I was about to ask him about Nadia, about what exactly had happened between them and what she had meant the other night when she'd confronted me—when I glimpsed the weather vane from the corner of my eye.

Instantly, all the activity around me faded to black. All I could see was the golden swan, sitting up there fat and proud atop its arrow. The arrow that was pointing south.

My vision grayed. I grasped his arm, the dizziness hitting me so hard I thought I might go down. "Tristan," I gasped.

He turned to look, and his jaw went slack.

"It . . . it can't . . ." I stuttered. "It can't be. That doesn't mean . . . Aaron didn't go to the Shadowlands."

A line of concern formed between Tristan's eyes. He seemed to be weighing his response. Weighing it for far too long.

"Tristan!" I shouted. A couple who was sitting at a table nearby turned to gape.

"Come here." Tristan pulled me gently but firmly around the corner at the end of the block, away from the prying, curious eyes of the visitors. I pressed back against the shingled outer wall of the general store, my heart pounding desperately inside my chest.

"This isn't happening. It can't be happening," I told him.

"I'm sorry," he said firmly. "But it is."

"No!" I wailed. "He's a good person. You should have felt the regret and sorrow coming off of him tonight when he talked about his father. There's no way he could have ever done anything awful enough in his life to warrant being sent to the Shadowlands."

"I'm sorry, Rory, but this happens sometimes," Tristan said calmly, soothingly. He ran a hand over my hair, then rested it comfortingly on my shoulder. "We think we know these people, but—"

"But nothing!" I shouted, flinging his hand off me and pushing away from the wall. "We have to help him. We have to get him out of there. We have to—"

"No!" he spat.

I stopped short, surprised at being shouted at. Tristan looked away, but I wasn't sure whether he was ashamed at having barked in my face or taking a breath because he was so angry.

"We can't," he said more calmly.

"What do you mean, we can't? There's been a mistake. There must be something we can—"

"No one ever comes back from the Shadowlands," Tristan said ominously. "Or the Light. Once it's done, it's done."

My eyes brimmed. "But Aaron's—"

"Even if we could get him out of there, we wouldn't," Tristan interjected, his jaw clenched. "The coins are never wrong."

I pressed my hands into my forehead, unable to comprehend, unable to accept what he was saying. I had brought Aaron up there and told him he was going somewhere to be happy and at peace. I had sent him on his way with that trusting smile on his face. He'd told me I was a good friend. He'd *thanked* me for all I'd done. And I'd sent him straight to hell.

"No, Tristan. No!" I cried, backing away from him. "This can't be right. We have to do something. We have to!"

"There's nothing we *can* do, Rory," Tristan said grimly, looking past me at the weather vane. "If Aaron went to the Shadowlands, then that's where he was supposed to go."

IMAGINGS

It's happening. It's finally, finally happening. It had to be this way, of course. He had to go. A person in my position needs a few sacrificial lambs. And isn't it always more powerful when that lamb is special? When it's cared for? When it will be missed?

Rory thought he was headed to the Light, whatever that means. I imagine it's different for everyone, whatever a person's version of heaven would be. If what you loved in life more than anything was your family, you'd spend forever in some great, big resort, surrounded by them, having huge dinners every night filled with conversation and laughter. If all you cared about was sports, you'd spend eternity attending Super Bowl games and World Series finals and Olympic events, and whomever you're rooting for would always win.

When I picture the Shadowlands, however, there is nothing. Nothing but blackness. You'd feel alone and scared and sad and lost forever, always wondering why you've been abandoned, always searching for some speck of light you'll never find. In the Shadowlands, you'd be cold. Not just in-need-of-a-blanket cold, but truly and utterly, painful-to-the-bone cold. The kind of cold no one on earth has ever felt. The kind of cold that breeds despair and desperation.

Not that I'll ever know for sure. Because I have found a way out of Juniper Landing, out of my own personal hell. And now that it's started, it's just a matter of time before I am free.

THE BALANCE

Wrong. Everything was wrong. I had just started to believe in this place, started to believe what Tristan had said about us playing an important role, somehow helping maintain balance. I'd begun to believe in our purpose. But if Aaron could be relegated to the Shadowlands, then the balance was seriously off.

I plodded around the corner onto Magnolia Lane, then hid in the shadows cast by a huge peach tree, waiting to make sure the house was silent. I didn't want to talk to anyone, afraid that I might break down and say things I shouldn't, or start crying with no good explanation and never stop.

When I finally entered the house, I opened the door slowly, to keep it from creaking, then held the knob so the catch wouldn't click. When I let it go ever so carefully, the bolt silently slid into place. I was sure I was home free. Until I turned around and found Darcy standing at the bottom of the stairs with Fisher.

"Sneaking around?" she quipped.

"God! You scared me," I said, my eyes darting between the two of them. Her hair was disheveled, and his T-shirt was on inside out.

"Sorry," she said.

I started past them up the stairs, which forced Fisher to stumble down the last two steps to the floor.

"Rory, wait," Darcy said. "Are you all right?"

I paused, wishing I could tell her everything—wishing I could tell her *anything*—but I couldn't. I couldn't even whitewash it and tell her I was sad because Aaron had left the island, because she wouldn't remember that Aaron had ever existed. This was what our relationship was going to be like now. Me keeping secrets and trying to keep track of what she could and couldn't remember.

Unless she became a Lifer. *Please let her do something self-less and earn the damned bracelet she wants so badly so I won't have to deal with all this alone.*

I looked into Fisher's eyes, and he shot back a

questioning glance of concern. I saw his hand move to his bracelet, and he turned it around and around. He could tell something had spooked me, and he was worried about me. I would have loved to talk to him just then—to talk to any other Lifer and find out what they thought. But I couldn't exactly ask Fisher up to my room with Darcy standing right there.

"I just have a headache," I told her, staring at the floor. "I'm gonna go lie down."

She started to say something else, but her words were drowned out by my heavy footsteps as I raced up the stairs. By the time I got to the third floor, the tears had started to fall. I threw myself onto my bed, pressed my fists to my temples, and tried to breathe.

"It's okay," I told myself aloud. "It's okay. Everything's going to be okay."

But I was lying to myself, which just made the frustration burn hotter beneath my skin. Aaron was suffering. Right now, at this very moment, he was suffering in the Shadowlands. What if souls were tortured there? Or what if it was one, big, yawning nothing—a vast empty plane of loneliness? Was he in pain? Was he scared? Was he wondering why I did this to him?

Of course he was. He had to be blaming me, because I was the last person he had spoken to, the last person he had touched, the one who'd sent him off to eternal damnation with a tearful smile and a wave.

I rolled over onto my side, clutched my pillow to me, and cried. My stupid imagination went wild, conjuring images of fire and demons, Grim Reapers and cold graves, whispery taunting voices and empty eye sockets and yawning dead mouths—slime, muck, and tears. I pressed my eyes closed and tried not to see it, but I couldn't. As bad as my theories were, I would never know exactly what was happening to Aaron, and that was the worst part of all. The not knowing.

"No."

I sat up in bed, pulling the pillow onto my lap, and gritted my teeth together. There had to be a way to reverse this. It was a mistake, and it needed to be rectified. I was not going to let Aaron suffer forever, thinking I had sentenced him to a fate worse than death. I was going to make this right.

GUILT

I woke the next morning with tears streaming down my face, my nose clogged, and the sound of Aaron's screams—which had plagued my dreams all night long—echoing in my ears. Gasping for breath, I pressed my hand to my forehead. My heart skipped a beat, and I whipped around to look at my nightstand. No coin. Thank god. I couldn't handle ushering anyone else today.

A glance at the clock told me it was already past ten. It took me a good minute to remember it was Wednesday; I was supposed to be at Krista's house right now.

I whipped the covers off, changed quickly into a T-shirt

and sweats, and wove a new braid into my hair. Then I jammed my worn Princeton baseball cap over my dirty hair, and headed out.

I crept downstairs as quietly as possible. Behind his closed door, my dad tapped away at his keyboard. I tiptoed over to the open door of my sister's room. She was lying on her back on her bed, reading a magazine. I slipped past as silently as possible. I couldn't handle her questioning where I was going again; I had no idea what kind of excuse I could give this time.

Outside, the sun warmed my shoulders as I speed-walked across town, my eyes trained on the ground. If Nadia or Dorn or Pete was skulking about, watching me, I didn't want to know. I just wanted to get to Krista's as quickly as possible and find out if anyone had a clue about what had happened last night. As I climbed the path to the bluff, the big blue mansion seemed to loom threateningly overhead, and there was the weather vane, still pointing stubbornly, heartbreakingly south.

Somehow, knocking felt pointless. I gripped the cold gold doorknob with a trembling hand and pushed open the door. The first thing I heard were angry voices shouting behind the closed door of the mayor's office. I froze in my tracks.

"I'm telling you, they're all clean!" the mayor snapped, sounding frustrated.

"But that's just not possible," a male voice answered. "Have you checked the—"

"Yes! Of course I have! Do you take me for some kind of imbecile?"

"Hi, Rory!" Krista said loudly.

I jumped. Krista stood at the top of the stairs in a blue-and-white-striped sundress, her blond hair down around her shoulders. The moment she spoke, the shouting stopped. I stared at the office door, waiting for the mayor to come out, but nothing happened.

I wondered what she would do if I simply knocked on her door and told her what had happened with Aaron. Wouldn't she want to know if someone had been ushered to the wrong place? Wasn't that the sort of thing one was supposed to bring to the attention of those in charge?

"Come on up!" Krista said. "We're just working on some garlands and stuff."

I hesitated, staring at the mayor's door.

"Rory?" Krista said.

"Coming!" I replied reluctantly, following her up the creaky stairs. Krista's room was huge and pink, with dark wood accents and a stone fireplace on one wall. There were floral throw rugs everywhere, and Lauren sat on the edge of the biggest one, stringing beads onto thick white yarn. Krista sat down across from her and carefully pushed a needle and thread through the back of a small cloth flower. Bea was sacked out on the queen-size canopy bed, flipping through magazines. Strewn all over the hardwood floor were hundreds of the flowers, cases of colorful glass beads the size of Ping-Pong balls, and bags full of large white and pink feathers.

"You can help Lauren with the garland," Krista suggested as I hovered in the doorway.

"Garland. Sure."

"The pattern is pink-pink-yellow-pink-pink-white," Lauren instructed me, pointing at one of the boxes of beads as I sat down next to her. "Because we have more pink than any other color."

I glanced up at Bea, who laughed. "She's anal-retentive," she explained.

"All righty, then," I said. I pulled the box of beads toward me, grabbed a spool of the heavy-duty string, and got to work, wondering if I could broach the subject of Aaron's ushering.

"Where did all this come from?" Joaquin asked, suddenly appearing in the doorway.

"Would you believe it was all in the relic room?" Krista asked. There was a lightness about her this morning. The wispy, light fabric of her dress made her tan skin glow, and she hadn't stopped smiling since I arrived. She suddenly tossed her head as if something funny or pleasing had just occurred to her, but she didn't share.

I wished I were in her mood, wherever it had come from. "What's the relic room?" I asked.

"It's this big bedroom downstairs that Tristan converted into a storage closet," Bea said, idly flipping a page. "It's where we put all the visitors' stuff once they move on."

"And we kind of go shopping in there whenever we need anything," Lauren added.

I gulped, feeling suddenly hot around the collar of my T-shirt. I knew the room they were talking about. I'd stumbled in there accidentally the previous week and seen the guitar strap that had belonged to the musician from the park, hanging from a shelf. I wondered if all of Olive's and Aaron's stuff was down there now—her guitar and his windsurfing gear, her flowy sweaters and his preppy jeans—just waiting to be picked over and claimed.

"You're kidding," Joaquin said. "When did we have Barbie's circus come through here?"

Bea snorted. Joaquin glanced at my blank face. "At least someone around here thinks I'm funny."

"Pink-pink-white-pink-pink-yellow," Lauren muttered under her breath as she strung each bead.

Joaquin reached for a bag of feathers and tore it open. It exploded all over everything.

"Joaquin! I'm trying to concentrate!" Lauren chided him, dusting a pink feather off her leg. A white one fell directly on top of my head, the end hanging down to touch my nose. I blew it off, annoyed. I couldn't believe I was there doing this while Aaron was trapped in the Shadowlands.

"Sorry," Joaquin shot back. He looked Krista up and down as she pushed a needle and thread through the center of one of the flowers. "What're *you* doing?"

"Making flower leis!" she replied happily.

"And you?" he asked Bea.

"Resting my arms after carrying all that crap up here," she said, not looking up from her magazine. "And I just learned how to do the perfect cat-eye with gray shadow and black eyeliner," she added in a wry tone. I doubted she'd ever worn eye makeup in her life.

"So then I guess I should—"

"Have you guys ever sent a soul over the bridge and then found out they ended up in the wrong place?" I blurted.

Bea stopped page-flicking. Lauren stopped muttering. Joaquin stared.

"Are you kidding? Never," Krista said, her knee bouncing as she tied off the end of the thread on the lei she'd just finished. I wasn't sure whether to feel relieved at that answer or more confused. When no one else chimed in, she looked around at the group. "But then, I haven't been here that long. Why?"

Everyone else was still gazing at me, and I started to feel exactly how I didn't want to feel—stupid. Joaquin's attention was somehow more intense than the others', his brown eyes sharp, like my question hadn't just startled him, but scared him.

"Yeah, why?" Lauren asked.

"No reason," I said, lifting a shoulder. My fingers trembled as I reached for the next bead. "Just trying to learn the trade."

"It happens," Bea said finally, sitting up. "It sucks, but it happens."

"Usually it's someone you think is supposed to go to the Light who ends up in the Shadowlands," Lauren said. The tiny pink end of her tongue stuck out as she started to concentrate again. My stomach clenched.

"Really?" I said.

"Some people are just very good at hiding their true natures," Joaquin confirmed, gathering up the fallen feathers around him and shoving them back into what was left of the plastic bag. He did it more vehemently than necessary, and his fist suddenly tore another hole in the back of the bag, rendering it useless. He tossed the whole thing aside, making an even bigger mess. Lauren sighed, but Joaquin didn't seem to notice. "But the really bad ones are pretty obvious. I don't think I've ever seen someone I was convinced was bad end up in the Light. Only the other way around."

"Oh," I said. "That's . . . interesting."

So maybe Tristan was right. Maybe Aaron had me totally fooled. But I just couldn't wrap my brain around that.

Suddenly, Lauren's posture slumped. "Rory! It's pink-pink-yellow-pink-pink-white! Not white-white-yellow-pink-pink-white!"

I looked down at my garland and saw that I had, in fact, strung the last few beads incorrectly.

"That's okay. They don't all have to be perfect," Krista said, patting my knee.

"Yes, they do!" Lauren protested.

"No, they don't. It'll be eclectic!" Krista replied.

"Eclectic is for amateurs," Lauren muttered. She grabbed the garland out of my lap and yanked. "I'll start it over."

Krista and I exchanged a look, and I almost laughed. Almost.

"Ooooh-kay," Joaquin said, standing. "This whole decorating-committee thing is a little too intense for me, so I'm just gonna—"

"No! You just got here," Krista whined, getting up.

But Joaquin was already halfway out the door. The second his foot hit the hallway, he stopped, startled. "Oh. Hey, man."

"Hey," Tristan said.

Tristan stepped around the corner, his ears red. At the

sight of him, all the intense feelings surrounding our kiss came rushing back, prickling my skin, and making me blush, but they were quickly crowded out by the memory of him shouting at me. He'd obviously been hovering outside the door, and I wondered if he'd heard our conversation about the bridge.

"Are you gonna help?" Krista asked him hopefully. "Because if you want, you and Joaquin could go check on the tent and make sure all the pieces are there. I know it's a little girlie in here, so—"

"Actually I stopped by to remind you," Tristan said, pressing his palms together, "there's someplace you're supposed to be."

Krista's eyes widened, and she covered her mouth with one hand. "Crap! I'm supposed to be clearing out Aaron's stuff."

My skin tingled. Tristan glanced at me apologetically. It was clear he hadn't wanted that said out loud.

"Sorry." Krista dropped her lei on the pile of finished versions next to her bed. "I'll go now. Guess the party's over, people."

"*Yes!*" Bea cheered under her breath, flinging the magazine toward a pile on Krista's nightstand. It slid right off the top and fluttered to the floor, where it landed with a *thwap*. Bea made no move to pick it up. Lauren, meanwhile, had put my beads aside and started organizing Joaquin's feather mess.

"I'll do it," I volunteered.

"What?" Tristan said.

"Really?" Krista asked.

"Yeah, I want to." I wanted to find out if there was some clue as to why Aaron had ended up where he did. Maybe if I had proof that the coin had made the right decision, I would somehow start feeling better about all this. "I'm supposed to be learning how to do these things, right?"

"That'd be awesome, Rory," Krista said, looking down at her project. "I have so much to do. Including baking cupcakes. Actually, can you come help with those tomorrow? At two," she asked brightly, gazing at me with wide blue eyes.

"Sure, no problem," I answered distractedly as I stepped over the box of beads I'd been working on and navigated my way around the piles of flowers and feather bags. As I was heading out the door, Krista grabbed Bea.

"You can take her place at the beading station," she suggested happily.

Bea groaned. "You'll pay for this, Miller!"

"Sorry!" I called over my shoulder.

"I'll go with you," Tristan offered.

"You don't have to," I said tersely.

His face fell. "Do you even know where he was staying?"

I narrowed my eyes, thinking back. "He mentioned a room, but . . . no. He always came to my place." Was that some kind of clue? Had he been hiding something from me?

"I can take her," Joaquin offered.

We both tensed. For a second, I'd forgotten he was even there.

"That's okay. I got it," Tristan said, angling around my side as if to block Joaquin out.

We walked down the stairs together, conspicuously not touching. Near the bottom step, I glanced back up and caught Joaquin lingering at the top, watching us with a brooding expression.

Tristan held the front door open for me, and as we passed through, I saw that the door to the mayor's office was slightly ajar. A second later, it banged shut.

"Did you see that?" I whispered.

"See what?" he asked, closing the front door behind us.

My reply caught in my throat. The fog was creeping in slowly from all sides, rolling over the grass and crowding out the flower beds at the foot of the stairs. Just like that, the mayor was forgotten.

"Someone else is being ushered," I said flatly.

"Looks that way," Tristan said.

I bit my tongue to keep from saying what I wanted to: *I hope they end up in the right place.*

PERSPECTIVE

I stood in the doorway of Aaron's room, a small, square chamber at a one-storied bayside motel called, in a very dead-on way, the Bayside Motel. Tristan hovered a few feet behind me, keeping a respectful distance while the fog continued to thicken around us. I waited for some sort of epiphany to strike me—a deep thought to occur that would put everything in perspective—but all I could think was this: Aaron was a minimalist.

There wasn't a shred of clothing in sight. No soda cups or candy-bar wrappers or magazines. No razors or cookie crumbs or crumpled tissues. The only personal items were his canvas beach bag, which was slung over the back of a desk chair, and a hardcover copy of *Tales of the City*, which lay on his nightstand next to the motel's old-school telephone, its spine perfectly aligned with the edge of the table.

"So . . . what do I do?" I said quietly.

"Find his suitcase, pack everything inside, and—"

"And then we take it back to the relic room," I finished, turning to look over my shoulder.

Tristan cleared his throat. "Yes."

"So everyone can go through it and take what they want," I said bitterly.

"It's not like that," Tristan replied, shoving his hands in his pockets. "People don't just raid the place every time someone moves on. We just leave it there, and it may or may not eventually get used."

I nodded as the hissing fog swirled around us. "However you want to say it, it still doesn't seem right to me."

Tristan's blue eyes looked pained. He glanced down, dragging his toe across the wood-plank walkway that stretched the length of the building, serving as a sort of front porch. "Rory, about last night—"

My heart thumped. I wasn't ready to talk about this with him. Not yet. "I should get started."

I took a deep breath and stepped over the threshold. The gray carpet inside the motel had been worn paper-thin, just like in a real motel in the real world. I wondered why they couldn't fix up the place a little bit, considering it was the last stop before eternity. Would visitors really get that suspicious if the rooms in the motel happened to have new carpet?

"Do you want me to—?"

"No," I told Tristan. "I'm fine."

I looked in the small closet and found Aaron's newish tweed suitcase, which I placed on the bed. The opening of the zipper sounded like a bomb going off in all the fog-induced silence. When I opened the top drawer of the dresser, a chill went through me that was so fierce I had to stop and force myself to breathe. There was Aaron's rugby shirt, the one he'd worn to the Thirsty Swan with Darcy and me just a few days ago. His folded beach towel. His plain white T-shirts. I lifted them out and got a whiff of Aaron's cologne. The scent brought tears to my eyes.

Suddenly, all I could think about was getting this over with. I placed his things in the suitcase and moved on to the next drawer, trying to ignore the pang in my heart when I touched the wetsuit from our windsurfing lessons last week. When I found the sneakers he'd worn on the beach my first night on the island—the ones that had made me feel like less of a loser for having worn mine—I had to bite back a sob. I tossed them in the bag and closed it.

There were no drugs, no alcohol, not even a pack of cigarettes. I didn't uncover a journal filled with maniacal, violent drawings illuminating the inner workings of Aaron's mind. No serial killer–style magazine tear-outs with faces x-ed out in red. No lists of names of the people who'd wronged him and deserved revenge. No beheaded dolls or dead puppies or bags of hair. I did, however, find a folded picture of David Beckham in his underwear drawer.

Yep. This guy was a real threat to society.

I emptied Aaron's bathroom of its perfectly aligned bottles of shampoo, conditioner, gel, and body wash, checked under the bed, then opened the drawer on his bedside table. Something slid out from the back and knocked against the front stop of the drawer. My heart caught in my throat. It was his cell phone.

Glancing over my shoulder, I saw nothing but the open doorway; Tristan was giving me my space. Shakily, I turned the phone on, and it let out a loud, jaunty *bing* as it powered to life. There were, of course, no new messages, but when I scrolled to Aaron's outgoing calls, a tear slid down my face.

There were twenty-three calls to his father over the past three days with a few to his brother and sister mixed in. Next to each of them was the awful message: CALL FAILED.

I sat down on the bed, clutching the phone in both hands, silent tears pouring down my face. Aaron had been a good son who wanted to make up with his father. I knew it. I had *felt* it last night when I'd held him. He was sorry for what he'd done, and all he wanted in the world was to have his apology heard. There wasn't a bad bone in Aaron's body, and this room proved it. He was just a person, a good person who had befriended me and my sister, all while suffering with his guilt.

The light in the room shifted, and I looked up at the four-paned window. The fog was starting to roll out, revealing the empty parking lot, the manicured hedge across the street, a seagull-shaped windmill stuck in the center of the front lawn across the street.

Tristan stepped into the doorway, his expression pained. "Are you all right?"

"No," I replied bluntly. I turned the phone screen toward him. "Look at this. Just look. All he tried to do the entire time he was here was call his father so he could apologize. That was all that mattered to him. How can he deserve to be in the Shadowlands?"

Tristan blew out a sigh. He sat down next to me on the bed, the weak mattress buckling beneath our weight.

"I'm sorry, Rory," he said, putting his arm around me. "I'm sorry you have to go through this on top of everything else."

Anger flashed through me, so hot and sudden it made me

spring to my feet. "Stop it!" I demanded. "Just stop! I don't want you to tell me how sorry you are. I want you to fix it!"

"I can't," Tristan said, shaking his head. "I can't fix it."

"You're telling me that you guys sent all those poor people off to the Shadowlands over a hundred years ago and you haven't even tried, in all that time, to figure out a way to get them back?" I demanded.

An awful jolt of pain crossed Tristan's face. "How can you say that to me?" he demanded, rising from the bed. "I told you how awful it's been for me to live with that. You don't think I would have brought them back if I could have?"

"There must be a way, Tristan," I said. "There has to be."

"Rory, look, I know that you're a problem solver," he said, irritated. "That you're a questioner and a scientist, but I can tell you that this is one problem you'll never find an answer to."

"I can't believe you," I said, turning toward the door. "It's like you don't even care. Like you *want* him to rot in hell."

Tristan just stood there, glowering at me, his jaw working under his skin.

"How can you be so complacent?" I ranted.

"You know what, Rory?" Tristan said, his eyes on fire. "I think we both need to cool off a little. I'm going to head out." He slipped right past me out the door and into the bright sunlight.

"But what about Aaron's stuff?" I shouted at his retreating back.

"Leave it!" he yelled without looking back at me. "I'll get it later."

He got to the end of the sidewalk, turned the corner, and was gone. At that moment, the phone on the nightstand rang, its old-fashioned bell pealing so loudly I jumped. A moment later, it rang again. Slowly, I walked over to the table and picked up the receiver, my hand shaking as I brought it to my ear.

"Hello?"

Outside the window, four crows landed on the fence across the street, watching me with their glassy black eyes. On the other end of the line, there was the faint sound of slow, rhythmic breathing. My heart hammered against my rib cage.

"Hello?" I said again, clutching the phone.

Laughter echoed through the line. Quiet at first, but growing rapidly louder. I banged the phone down and bolted from the room, leaving the door wide open behind me.

AN ALLY

I ran for home as fast as I could, my pulse throbbing in my eyes, my ears, my fingertips. The chill ocean breeze did nothing to cool my overheated skin. Had that call been intended for me? Had it been placed by someone who knew Tristan and I were there, or was it just a random coincidence? A crow cawed overhead as I raced across the square, and I got this awful feeling in my gut. A feeling that on Juniper Landing, there were no coincidences. I tore through the park, turned the corner onto Freesia, and smacked right into someone.

"Where're you going in such a hurry?" Officer Dorn

asked, staring down his nose at me with piercing eyes.

I took a step back, shaking like a leaf. "Nowhere," I said automatically. His eyes narrowed. "Home."

He moved, infinitesimally, out of my way, and I took off again down the hill. When I got to the bottom, I checked back over my shoulder, and my heart thumped. Dorn hadn't moved; his suspicious glare was still fixed on me.

I clenched my jaw and kept moving.

"Rory!"

I collided with Joaquin's shoulder so hard he had to grab the trunk of the nearest peach tree to keep from going down. A startled bird flung itself from the tree's branches, raining dozens of shriveled brown and gray leaves onto our shoulders. It swooped across the street, disappearing behind the flowery hedge on the opposite side. Joaquin reached for my arm, but I wrested it away.

"I don't want to talk to you right now, Joaquin," I said, pushing past him. "I just want to be—"

"Stop!" he shouted. "I need to know why you were asking about people being ushered to the wrong place."

I froze in my tracks. The breeze lifted my hair from my neck and sent chills down my arms. Slowly, I turned. Joaquin was gasping for breath, like he'd just been sprinting. Sweat dotted his upper lip and hairline.

"Why?"

"Because I just ushered that girl—Jennifer? The one with the pixie cut?" he said. "And she went to the Shadowlands."

I blinked "Wait. How is that even possible?" I asked. "You were with us when the fog rolled in."

"I . . . *got the call* about two seconds after you left, so I went over to her room and got her," Joaquin explained. "I wasn't that surprised, because she was so simple. There was no unfinished business there, so it wasn't like she'd need my help to get ready to move on. I just picked her up and brought her to the bridge. But then, when I got back to town . . ."

"The weather vane was pointing south," I finished flatly.

"Yeah." Joaquin tipped his face toward the ground for a second, his hands on his hips. When he looked up again, his normally cocky gaze was searching, almost pleading. "What you said before at Krista's, about someone going to the wrong place . . . Why did you ask us that?"

"Oh, that was just—" I looked away. My knee-jerk reaction was to keep the peace, to not make any more waves than I already had.

"Rory, don't mess with me right now. Please," Joaquin said in an urgent voice that cut me to the core. "Jennifer didn't . . . she doesn't deserve what she's getting."

He was desperate. I could see it in his eyes.

"Aaron was sent to the Shadowlands last night," I told him. "And I know for a fact that he doesn't belong there."

Joaquin dropped my hand, his eyes going flat. "And let me guess, Tristan told you that's just the way it is. That you had to accept it and move on."

"He did," I said.

Joaquin pivoted and took a few steps away. His fingers curled into fists, then stretched. Finally, he took a deep breath and faced me.

"There's something you should know," he replied. "All this?" He looked down at the leaves that blanketed the sidewalk. "It shouldn't be happening."

I squinted, confused. "What? You mean the leaves changing? I know it's early, but—"

"No! You don't get it. This stuff never happens," he said, pacing the width of the sidewalk in front of me, the dry, dead leaves crunching beneath his feet. "Leaves don't turn, flowers don't die, birds don't drop out of the sky, fish don't pile up on beaches, and there are definitely, *definitely* no hornets."

I shook my head. "But the other day, you got stung right outside—"

"I know, Rory. And in almost a hundred years on this island, that was the first hornet I've ever seen," he said vehemently. "We have bees because we have flowers, but no hornets, no wasps, no other insects, nothing like that."

"That's insane. It's—"

Then, ever so slowly, realization began to dawn. Joaquin's weird reaction to the hornet sting. The marigolds withering in their pot on the porch—alive one minute, dead the next. The reeds near the bridge that had made Tristan go pale.

"And these things . . . when did they start happening?" I asked, Nadia's accusations ringing in my mind. "Was it when I got here?"

"I don't know," Joaquin replied. "No one really knows *exactly* when it started, but it's definitely been recent. They think that it might be because the balance of good and evil around here has been thrown off somehow. That maybe a Lifer has—"

"Gone bad," I breathed. My gut twisted as I thought of Jessica. "Joaquin, the other night Nadia accused me of being responsible for all this strange stuff that's been going on around here. Does that mean she thinks *I'm* the reason things are *dying*?" I demanded. "Does she think I'm pure evil or something?"

Joaquin just stared at me. I felt like I was going to throw up. What if Nadia took her suspicions to the mayor? What if the mayor believed her?

"She's going to get me sent to Oblivion," I said under my breath, my vision blurring.

"No," Joaquin said. "Rory, she's not. No one thinks she's right about you."

"Dorn does!" I insisted. "And maybe Grantz, too. What if she starts convincing other people? What if she convinces everyone?"

Joaquin reached for my shoulders and held on tight. "That's not going to happen," he said, looking me in the eye. "I won't let it. Tristan won't let it. Nadia is just grasping at straws. Now, take a deep breath."

I did, and blew it out slowly through pursed lips. I felt slightly better. But only slightly.

"Okay?" he asked me.

I nodded. "Okay."

"Good." He released me. "Look, I know you're not the cause of all this, but there's definitely something up. And now, on top of everything, good people are going to the Shadowlands. Whatever it is, it's not good."

I cleared my throat. "So what do we do?"

"There's only one person to talk to around here when something's wrong," Joaquin said, starting for town. "And whatever Saint Tristan thinks, something is clearly wrong."

"We're going to the mayor?" I asked tremulously.

Joaquin nodded, his fists now tightly clenched. "We're going to the mayor."

A GNAT'S BLINK

Joaquin walked right into Tristan's house without knocking. Somewhere nearby I heard voices whispering urgently, but they fell silent when I closed the door. Joaquin was already striding toward the mayor's office.

"Just go," I heard Tristan's voice hiss.

A female voice answered. "But, Tristan, you have to understand—"

"I don't want to hear it! Go!"

I was still trying to figure out who the girl's voice belonged to when Tristan and Krista appeared from around the corner in the living room.

"J.," Tristan said, his eyes smoldering. "We need to talk."

I hesitated in the center of the entryway. Krista fidgeted with her bracelet. A door near the back of the house banged shut.

"Not now, man," Joaquin replied. He walked right over to the mayor's office and rapped loudly on the door.

"What the hell are you doing?" Tristan demanded, following him.

"Reporting a problem to the mayor," Joaquin replied.

Tristan got between him and the door, pushing him backward. "You can't just storm in here like that."

"Get off of me!" Joaquin yelled, windmilling his arms to throw Tristan off.

"This is my house!" Tristan yelled.

Joaquin laughed in a sarcastic way. "Don't even start with that shit, Tristan."

"What shit?" Tristan countered, shoving Joaquin in the chest. "What do you mean?"

"You *know* what I mean." Joaquin shoved back.

Tristan's nostrils flared.

"Rory, do something," Krista pleaded, hugging her arms to her chest.

"Guys! Cut it out!" I shouted, trying to get between them. "We didn't come over here to fight."

"Well, then get him out of here," Tristan spat. "The mayor's gonna kill us. You know she hates it when we—"

The door behind him suddenly flew open, and the mayor stepped out. My heart seized up at the sight of her. She wore a crisp blue pantsuit, a light pink shirt, and a politician's smile. Her blond hair was pulled back so tightly from her face it made her skin appear stretched. She seemed taller somehow. Broader. More intimidating.

This woman could send me to Oblivion. She could send all of us there if she felt like it.

Tristan slid out of the way, taking position behind Joaquin like he was getting ready either to back him up or throw him out. The mayor started to close the door, but not before I saw that someone was sitting in the chair across from her desk, tucking two black Converse sneakers out of sight just before she banged it shut.

"Can I help you, Mr. Marquez?" the mayor asked, clasping her hands together in a patient way. When her eyes flicked to me, I felt a chill in my bones.

"Yeah. There's something going on around here, and I think you should know about it," Joaquin said, his chest heaving. "Something aside from the obvious."

Tristan shot me a betrayed sort of look, as if asking whether this was about what he thought it was about.

"All right, then," she asked. "What is it?"

"Nothing," Tristan said, trying to drag Joaquin away. "It's nothing."

A tiny crack snaked through my heart. He really didn't believe in me. In Aaron. He truly thought the coin was in the right. He was embarrassed that Joaquin and I were wasting his "mother's" time.

"It's not nothing," Joaquin said, staring the mayor in the eye with impressively unyielding determination. "I just sent a girl to the Shadowlands, someone who didn't belong there, and Rory did the same last night. The weather vane has been pointing south a lot more often than it ever has before. All these people can't belong in the Shadowlands."

The mayor glanced at me over Joaquin's shoulder, then tilted her chin toward the floor and chuckled. My palms went slick.

"Mr. Marquez, the coins are never wrong," she said simply.

My fingers curled like claws, red-hot adrenaline rushing through my veins.

"They were this time," I said, my pulse pounding in my ears.

"Excuse me, but you don't know anything about this," she replied condescendingly. "Correct me if I'm wrong, but you haven't even done a solo ushering yet, have you?"

She looked at Tristan. He shook his head, mute.

"But I do know that Aaron was a good soul," I protested, my voice quaking. "I *felt* it. Doesn't that mean anything?"

The mayor's blue eyes crackled with anger.

"It means you're still new here," she said sharply. "And you have no clue what you're doing."

"Now, wait a minute," Tristan said, squaring off next to Joaquin.

"Maybe the weather vane's wrong," Krista piped up suddenly, her voice reed thin. My heart swelled both with gratitude toward Krista and with hope. The weather vane being wrong would mean that Jennifer and Aaron had actually gone to the Light and the vane had simply indicated the opposite.

Another chuckle from the mayor. "Sweetie, the weather vane is never wrong."

"Well, it is now," I said, stepping toward her as calmly as I could. "Please, if we could just talk about this," I implored. "Something is wrong. I know what I felt. I know that Aaron was a good person. If you'd just—"

"Stop!" the mayor thundered. She stepped around Joaquin and Tristan like their wall of muscle was nothing more than a puddle on the floor and came to a stop right in front of me. Terror seized my gut, and I staggered back a step. "Do you even hear what you're saying? Weren't you some sort of scientific genius in your former life?"

I said nothing. At that moment it was hard enough to breathe.

"What do you think is more likely? That a system that has been in place without a single hitch since the dawn of time has suddenly gone haywire, or that you, someone who has existed in this realm for less than a gnat's blink, has made an error in judgment?" Her lips curled into something that resembled a smile but felt more like a threat. "What do you say, Ms. Miller? What's your hypothesis?"

My whole body shook under her scrutiny as she looked me slowly up and down. I clamped my teeth together and held my tongue.

"That's what I thought," she said smugly.

"Look, we all know something's off," Joaquin said calmly, patiently. "Flowers and animals dying, leaves changing, hornet stings . . . Did you know Kevin found a nest of worms in his yard this morning? And there are spiders and flies and—"

"I'm well aware of what's going on, Mr. Marquez," the mayor said. "I don't need you of all people coming in here to tell me."

"So you won't even listen to what we have to say?" Joaquin asked. "You won't even consider the possibility that people are being misplaced?"

She lifted her head and looked at Joaquin and Tristan. "I think you've wasted enough of my time. I'd like you to leave now," she said, striding back toward her office, back to whomever was waiting in that chair. She paused next to Tristan and looked down her nose at him. *"All* of you."

Next to me, Krista made a sound somewhere between a squeak and a squeal.

"Let's go," Tristan said to the rest of us. He walked over to the door and held it open. Krista was the first one through, fluttering like a startled butterfly. Joaquin hesitated for just a moment but eventually tromped out.

I was just passing by Tristan when the mayor's voice stopped me.

"Oh, and Ms. Miller?"

I stopped and looked at her. In the shadows cast by the curtained window next to her, her face looked like a skull.

"Don't come back without an appointment."

Then she walked into her office and slammed the door.

ALWAYS

Outside, Joaquin flung Tristan's arm off his and stormed to the edge of the bluff. In the distance, storm clouds gathered, lightning flashing deep within the dark gray cover. I took in a deep breath and tried to relax, but the mayor's last words to me still rang in my ears. In two short days, I'd gone from being a "distinct pleasure" to being someone who needed an appointment. Someone who got the door slammed in her face. Was it just because I was siding with Joaquin, or was it something more?

"What is the matter with you?" Tristan demanded, charging after Joaquin. A gust of wind blasted his hair back from his face as they neared the drop-off. "You know she hates it when we just barge in."

"Do you really think I give a shit?" Joaquin asked, whirling to face Tristan. "Something's going on around here, Tristan. Something bigger than the random shriveled magnolia or the centipede you found at the gazebo. Don't you feel it? Because I do. I can feel it in every inch of my body."

Tristan scoffed. "You're so melodramatic."

Krista and I hovered a safe distance away as the boys faced off. I could feel the mayor watching us through her office windows, but I refused to turn. Krista, however, kept glancing furtively back at the house. Along the front of the porch, the garden that had once been bursting with daisies was now a square of dry brown thatch.

"What if she never lets us back in?" she whispered, biting her bottom lip.

"I'm sure she will. It's your home," I replied.

"Yeah, but not really," Krista said. "It's not like she's really my mother. And I've never seen her that angry before."

Krista toyed with her bracelet, looking at the ground.

"We can't keep letting this happen!" Joaquin shouted, the veins in his neck bulging. "You know the weather vane has been pointing south a lot more often than usual. If people are being sent to the wrong place, then what's the point of all this? What's the point of our existence?"

Another cold wind whooshed in off the ocean, leaving me momentarily breathless. The clouds were moving in at a fast clip; they were an ominous shade of steel gray. Krista took a few steps back toward the porch and away from the drop-off.

"People aren't getting sent to the wrong place," Tristan replied stubbornly. "The system works, Joaquin. It's *always* worked."

"Always?" Joaquin asked, raising his eyebrows.

Something passed between them. Some unspoken communication. Tristan stood, stock-still and silent, as if weighing his response. I smoothed my braid. Was Joaquin talking about Jessica, or was there something else going on?

"You've been here longer than anyone, Tristan," Joaquin said, shifting his weight from one foot to the other. "You know that things aren't always what they seem. That the system can be circumvented."

"No," Tristan said firmly. "Not like this. Nothing like this has ever happened before. It can't happen, J. It's just . . . it's not possible."

They stared each other down, the wind blowing the sleeves of their shirts tight against their arms, until Joaquin finally chuckled and backed off.

"Screw this; I'm outta here," he said, storming past me.

Krista looked at the ground as he went by.

"So you're really not gonna help us?" I asked Tristan, my voice nearly drowned out by the swirling of the wind.

He turned his palms out, his eyes determined but still full of sorrow. "There's nothing to help with. This place isn't broken, Rory. It *can't* be broken."

I pressed my lips together, hesitating. "But . . . Jessica broke it, didn't she?"

An angry shadow crossed his face. "That was different," he said fiercely. "She willingly ignored a rule, but once she did that, the mechanics worked as they were supposed to. The people who had been compromised went to the Shadowlands, as they were supposed to. You're trying to say that the coins can be altered, that the final decision can be wrong. That can't be."

"But I know Aaron didn't belong in the Shadowlands. I know it." I looked down at my sneakers, gripping my fingertips until they hurt. It was nothing compared with the pain inside my chest. "What if we could bring them back?"

"We can't," Tristan said, pushing his sleeves down.

"But what if we could? What if there was a way to—"

"It wouldn't matter anyway," Krista interrupted. "If Tristan's so sure they are where they're supposed to be, then we *shouldn't* bring them back."

"Exactly," Tristan said, his face like stone.

"But they're not where they're supposed to be!" I wailed.

"We can't keep having the same conversation, Rory," Tristan said firmly. "Trust me. Nothing's broken, and no one is coming back."

Suddenly, my whole body felt hollow. There would be no getting through to him, no making him understand how awful, how wrong, how desperate I felt. Something or someone had sent Aaron to the Shadowlands when he belonged in the Light. And nothing Tristan said was going to change my mind about that. He was right about only one thing: we couldn't keep having this conversation.

"Rory," Tristan said, taking an imploring step forward.

I instinctively backed away. "I have to go," I said, my heart breaking along with my voice.

"But you don't understand—"

"I have to go."

I turned and jogged after Joaquin, the wind making me tear up. As I came around the corner of the house, my foot caught on a rock and I stumbled. From the corner of my eye, I saw a pair of dark eyes staring at me through the office window, and the second I did, the blinds snapped shut.

I shoved myself up to my feet and ran. "Joaquin!" I shouted.

He was crossing the patio out back, headed for the woods on the southwest corner of the island.

"Joaquin, stop!" I shouted again as the clouds moved in to block out the sun.

Joaquin finally paused near the tree line, but he didn't turn around. A rumble of thunder sounded nearby as I jogged to catch up with him, shoving my knotted hair away from my face. One huge drop of rain plopped onto my cheek.

I blew out a breath, choked with anger, confusion, and despair. "What are we going to do?" I asked, my hands on my hips.

"I don't know," he replied simply.

"Why won't he listen to us?" I asked.

Joaquin sighed. "You've gotta understand. . . . If Tristan admits that something is wrong, if he even starts to think about it, then he'll have to question everything. It's like we're asking him to give up on his whole belief system. Without this place . . . without the whole 'balance of good and evil' thing, he has nothing."

He'd have me, I thought as the rain started to come harder.

"Well, why didn't he tell me that?"

Joaquin looked me in the eye. "Maybe you should ask him."

I pushed my hair away from my face. It didn't escape me that even though Joaquin was pissed off, he was managing to see Tristan's side of things. "You guys are really good friends, huh?"

Joaquin smirked. "When we're not fighting, yeah. Tristan's like a brother."

Just like Darcy and me. The two of us could fight like crazy people, but in the end we'd always be there for each other. And I suddenly understood why Krista had been so eager to be my friend since I'd arrived in town. As the newest girls here, we had a lot in common. She was probably dying for a best friend, a sister figure. But I already had a sister. A sister I intended to keep with me forever, if I could only figure out how.

"We have to do something," I said. "With or without Tristan. We have to—"

"Look, you should get inside," Joaquin said, glancing toward town. "I have someplace I have to be right now. We'll figure this out in the morning."

As he started to move away from me, the sky opened up, rain flattening the grass all around us and soaking my clothes right through. The leaves on the trees turned upside down, and some of the smaller ones bowed toward the ground. I started to shiver.

"We can't wait until the morning," I protested, hugging myself against the sudden chill. "What if someone else gets taken tonight? What if they get sent to the wrong place?"

"That's not going to happen," Joaquin replied, shaking his head. Water dripped from his eyelashes and chin. "No one ever gets taken in a storm."

I laughed sarcastically. "Oh, and there's no chance *that* rule is going to be broken?"

Joaquin gave me a hard look. "I'm sorry, Rory, but there's something I have to take care of. You're just gonna have to trust me. I'll be at your place first thing in the morning."

Then he turned and slipped into the woods, disappearing between two huge trees. I just stood there, soaked and baffled, my teeth chattering, waiting for the punch line. He had something to take care of in the middle of the woods, right now, when two seconds ago he'd been about ready to throw down with Tristan?

Shaking from head to toe, I turned to look back at the mayor's house. I'd never seen it from this angle before, and for the first time, I noticed the large garage facing the driveway. The door was open, and sitting inside, safe from the rain and wind, was a sleek silver convertible. The very same car I'd seen idling near the cliff the other night.

The mayor had met with Dorn. Dorn, who was watching me just like Nadia was. A chill went down my spine, and as I turned to go, I saw Tristan standing on the porch under the cover of its wide roof, staring out at me.

You've been here longer than anyone, Joaquin had said. And Tristan hadn't argued. Was that really true? How long was "longer than anyone"? And was it even possible that one person had been sent to Juniper Landing alone, with no one there to guide him?

Slowly, I headed back toward town. Joaquin didn't want to deal with this tonight? Fine. As of that moment, I had my own mission to carry out.

1766

Navigating the descent to the cove that night in the pouring rain and pitch dark was terrifying. The wind was so fierce it drove the rain sideways, each droplet a sharp dart against my skin. Halfway down the rocky decline, my foot slipped on the rocks, and as my arms flung out to grasp at the nothingness, I was sure I was about to fall to my death. Then my back hit a jagged point and I remembered: I couldn't die. But I could feel excruciating pain.

I scrambled to my knees and checked the pocket of my rain jacket to make sure my flashlight hadn't tumbled out. Shakily, I pushed myself to my feet and took baby steps all the way to the bottom of the hill. When I could finally see the sand, I unclenched my jaw and jumped the last few feet. The ground squished beneath the soles of my sneakers, bubbling up around the rubber treads with the consistency of oatmeal.

I could just make out the shadowy humps of the tents in the distance. Not surprisingly, they were dark and still. I flicked on my flashlight and ran it along the rock wall to my left, inching forward until I finally found the opening of the cave. It looked smaller somehow, as I stood there in front of it alone. Threatening. For one brief moment I thought I saw something flicker deep inside, and I almost turned around and ran.

No one's here, I told myself, listening to the rain as it thwapped against the vinyl cover of my hood. *They'd have to be crazy to come out in this.*

Of course, I was crazy just for being here. And after seeing the Lifers storm-surfing last week and the cliff-diving the other night, I already knew that some of the others weren't exactly on the right side of sane. But this place was mine now, as much as it was theirs. If someone was inside, they were just going to have to deal.

I took a deep breath and slipped into the cave. The narrow opening was clogged with smoke, the heady, ashy kind that billows up after dousing a fire. As I came around the corner,

I covered my mouth with my sleeve and ran the flashlight's beam along the floor. Sure enough, the fire pit was smoldering. A few small embers still glowed bright orange in the darkness, and thick gray smoke snaked up from the center of the charred logs, disappearing near the high ceiling of the cave.

"Anyone here?" I called.

No response. Somewhere in the deepest depths of the cavern, water dripped at a steady rhythm.

This made no sense. If someone had been in here just before me, I would have bumped into them coming out, either on the beach or on the rocks. Unless there was a back entrance to the cave, or some other way out to the cove that they hadn't shown me.

Forget it, I told myself. *You came here for a reason.*

I tried to ignore my trembling hands as I aimed the flashlight beam at the wall to my right. I found Krista's name again, the bubbly flowery lettering proclaiming her arrival. A few feet away, Nadia had written her name in slanted, sophisticated script: NADIA LINKOVA (NASH) 1982. Right under hers, Cori had added her name: CORI HERTZ (MORRISON) 1982. No wonder they were so close. They'd shown up here around the same time. Another reason why Krista probably expected the two of us to become BFFs. I moved on, illuminating unfamiliar names like Corina Briggance (Horrance) from 1993 and Wallace Brooks (Garretson) from 1979. I paused when I found Kevin's name, huge and jagged, near the top of the wall, an intricate fire-breathing dragon painted above it, the tail curling around his year, which was 1965. Kevin had come here the year my father was born.

Slowly, I made my way along the wall, reading name after name after name. Toward the back of the cave the years got older and older. 1921, 1915, 1906, 1899. Some looked hastily painted, in thick white paint. Others seemed to be written in chalk, probably the only instrument they could find in those days. I couldn't imagine that some of the people I'd seen on the street had been here for almost two hundred years. How was that even possible? How was that survivable?

I squinted in the darkness, trying to make out the words that had faded with time, holding my breath as I waited for my light to find the name I was looking for. When it finally did, I was at the innermost point of the cave. And there, etched into the stone at eye-level, was Tristan's name.

TRISTAN SEVARDES (PARRISH) 1766.

I inhaled sharply. He'd been alive before the U.S. was even a country. Had, in fact, died before the Revolutionary War. He was over two hundred years old.

There was a noise, like a scraping, near the mouth of the

cave, and I dropped my flashlight. When I grabbed for it, it slipped through my fingers and hit my toe. Cursing under my breath, I picked it up again and shone the light near the opening. The fire still smoldered.

"Hello?" I said, my voice sounding weak and scared. My toe throbbed angrily. I cleared my throat, tried to sound more authoritative. "Who's there?"

No reply. I took two tentative steps forward.

"Come on, you guys. This isn't funny," I said.

I listened hard for the sound to come again, but it didn't. All I could hear was the deafening rasp of my own breathing, and the faint echo of the surf crashing outside.

I looked at Tristan's name again. 1766.

Suddenly, my whole body started to shake. The manic scribble on the walls closed in. I tried to take a breath, but my throat squeezed shut. I had to get out. I had to breathe. I pressed one hand against the cold wall and lurched for the exit. That was when a crackling sound stopped me cold.

"Hello?" I called again.

I took a tentative step forward. Another crackle. Something in the corner of my vision flashed. There was a piece of white paper stuck to the bottom of my sneaker.

Nice. *Way to be paranoid, Rory.* I reached down and plucked the page from my sole, then kept moving.

Outside, the rain had reduced to a light drizzle. I took a deep breath of the cool night air and tipped my face toward the sky, letting the rain soothe my face. After a while, the rhythm of my breath returned to normal. I leaned back against the rock wall and trained my light on the paper. It was a small, rectangular sheet torn from a standard notepad, the kind reporters scrawled on in old movies. Someone had drawn a line down the center and made hash marks on either side, each set of four slashed through with a long mark—the old method of counting by fives. In one column there were thirteen slashes. In the other, only nine.

Someone was keeping score, but of what?

"What've you got there?"

I was so startled by the voice, I staggered backward and tripped, slamming my head into the sharp rock wall. Suddenly three flashlights flicked on, and Nadia, Pete, and Cori appeared as if from nowhere, dark hoods pulled over their hair. Before I had time to move, Pete stepped forward and snatched the page from my fingers.

"Wait!" I yelled.

Nadia shone her light on the paper. Her black eyes widened. "Holy crap. Is that what I think it is?" She turned the light on my face, effectively blinding me. I threw up my arms and squinted, but all I could see were a dozen purple dots and three looming shadows. "Are you actually keeping a log of all the people you damn to hell?"

"What? No! I just found that in the cave!" I protested. "It got stuck to my sneaker. Look, you can see the tread marks."

I lunged forward to grab it back, but Pete pulled it up and out of my reach.

"Nice try," he said with a sneer. "You think I'm gonna let you destroy the evidence?"

The three of them stared me down. Even Cori's normally friendly face had gone taut and tense. I glanced back at the solid wall behind me. There was nowhere to go. Nowhere to run.

"We know it's you," Nadia sneered. "It all started when you got here."

"It's the only explanation," Cori said coldly, crossing her arms over her chest as Pete stared down his nose at me.

"It's not," I told them, trying to keep my voice from quavering. The skies opened up again, heavy raindrops pelting down on me. "I swear to you. It's not me."

"Yeah? Well, we'll see what the mayor has to say about that," Nadia spat, grasping my wrist, pinching the skin between her thumb and fingers.

Suddenly someone jumped down from the slope and

squatted right next to me. I dropped my flashlight. Cori screamed, but Nadia's grip only tightened.

"Get off her," Joaquin growled, pushing his black hood off his face. Nadia instantly dropped my hand and backed up three feet, stepping right into the beam of my fallen flashlight. I stopped breathing.

Black Converse. Nadia had been in the mayor's office this afternoon. My worst fear was confirmed; the girl who thought I was responsible for everything wrong on the island officially had the mayor's ear. Maybe that was why the mayor's attitude toward me had shifted so abruptly.

I was screwed. I was so very, very screwed.

"She's guilty, Joaquin," Pete said, shoving the tally into his pocket. "You and Tristan have to stop protecting her."

"Dude, she just got here," Joaquin pointed out. "Do you really think she could be responsible for everything that's been going on?"

"It's *because* she just got here that we know she's responsible," Nadia shot back, shooting me a slit-eyed look. "It can't be one of us."

"I say we take this to the mayor right now," Pete said, advancing on me.

Joaquin moved sideways to stand squarely between us. "Back off her, Pete. I'm not kidding."

Nadia laughed, shaking her head at the ground.

Thunder rumbled in the distance. "You're so predictable, J. Do we really have to remind you what happened the last time you and Tristan got into a pissing match over a girl?" Her gaze flicked to me. "Anyone tell *her* about it yet?"

My heart squeezed. Lightning flashed, and I caught a glimpse of Joaquin's profile. His jaw was working hard, and his hands clenched at his sides.

"This is nothing like that," Joaquin said through his teeth. "And you weren't even here yet, *Nadia*." He spat her name like a curse word. "Don't talk about things you don't understand."

"Well, I do understand one thing," Nadia said, stepping forward and tipping her head back to square off with Joaquin. "You might not want to get too close with her. You never know where you might end up."

Lightning flashed again, a deafening thunderclap hot on its heels. I was so startled I reached for Joaquin's hand. He froze. Nadia's eyes darted to our fingers, and for a split second I was sure he'd pull away. But instead, he lifted his chin and curled his fingers through mine. His skin was warm and rough.

"I'm not worried," Joaquin said clearly.

"Yeah, well. You should be," Pete said, lifting his chin. "Come on. We've got something to show the mayor."

The three of them turned and strode away. I sucked in a few broken breaths, the rain battering my face, trying to ignore the searing sting of tears behind my eyes. Joaquin just stood there, half a foot in front of me, still holding my hand. When he finally turned, he stared down at our clasped fingers before looking up at me. His dark eyes penetrated my fear.

"What did he mean, they've got something to show the mayor?" he asked.

"I found something," I said. "In the cave. Some kind of tally. I have no idea what it even is, but they think it's mine and they think it means something." My stomach clenched. If the mayor suspected me, I was as good as dead.

Joaquin stared at the ground, fixated on the few mushy, wet inches of sand between the toes of our shoes. I started to shiver, and the longer he was silent, the more violent the shaking became. Did he think I was guilty, too? He was the only person who believed in me, who wanted to help save Aaron. I couldn't handle this, any of this, if Joaquin wasn't on my side.

"Here." He released my hand and unzipped his heavy jacket, flinging it over my shoulders in one, smooth motion. The inside had been warmed by his body, and its comforting, musky-tart scent enveloped me. My shivering instantly stopped.

"Come on," he said as I pushed my arms into the sleeves. "We should get you home."

"But what about—?"

"Don't worry," Joaquin told me, looking darkly in the direction the others had gone. "I'll take care of them."

TALLY

Nine down, eleven to go. And pinning it all on perfect, saintly Rory? Gravy.

DUE NORTH

I didn't sleep all night. I just sat up listening. Waiting for Dorn to come banging on my door. Waiting for an angry mob of Lifers to drag me off to the mayor's for my sentencing.

But nothing had happened. All night long I'd stared at the ceiling, clutching my pillow, and nothing. So by the time Joaquin held open the door of the general store for me on Thursday morning, I was like a wired zombie. My eyes were at half-mast and I dragged my feet, but I was still hyperaware of every curious gaze, every movement around me. I was awaiting the ambush.

The door chimes tingled over our heads. Outside, the sun was shining again, and the shop was bustling with people, sipping their coffee at the counter, leafing through old magazines, and chatting about the storm.

"Did you see all the flotsam washed up on the beach?"

"A huge tree came down on Hermit Crab Lane."

"They're having a big I-Survived-the-Storm Party at the Thirsty Swan tonight."

Joaquin sighed. "Guess I'm getting called in to work later."

All the tables were taken, and it looked like we weren't going to find a seat. Then I spotted Krista and Fisher in the booth farthest from the door. I was surprised Fisher was up so early, considering I'd heard him sneak Darcy back into the house after 3 a.m. As he lifted a hand to flag us down, Krista turned around in her seat like an excited kindergartner.

"What're they doing here?" I asked Joaquin, stifling a yawn.

"They wanted to come," he replied.

"Hi, Rory!" Krista patted the blue vinyl seat next to her, and I slid into it, while Joaquin squeezed in next to Fisher, the two of them taking up the entire bench. There was a half-full glass of orange smoothie in front of Fisher, but Krista had only water.

"What's up?" Fisher asked, his light green eyes almost startling so close up.

"No one else has been ushered since yesterday morning," Joaquin reported.

"And I got to sleep in my bed last night," Krista assured me, touching my leg, as if her and Tristan's getting back into their house had been weighing on me all night long.

"Um, good," I said. I reached for the saltshaker, just to have something to do with my trembling hands. "That's good."

"Fisher brought someone over two days ago, and they ended up in the Shadowlands, too," Joaquin explained.

"No way Alec should've gone there," Fisher said, taking a long pull on his straw. "No way. Dude was a priest."

"Really?" I asked, passing the glass saltshaker back and forth on the table's surface.

Fisher squirmed and cleared his throat. "No, I mean, not literally, but in his life he sure as hell acted like one."

Krista giggled, and everyone stared at her. "Sorry."

"What'll you kids have?" Ursula asked, appearing at the end of our table. She looked at Joaquin as if the rest of us weren't even there.

"Good morning, Ursula," Joaquin said with a smile. "You're looking rather fetching today."

Ursula sniffed. "Don't even try it. You left the seat up again this morning."

Fisher chuckled and shook his head.

"Did I? I'm sorry. I swear I'll make it up to you," Joaquin teased.

"Yeah, yeah. I've heard it all before." She sniffed again. This time her gaze flicked around the table. "So what'll you have?"

"Um, coffee?" Krista said.

"Coffee's fine," I added. Ursula glared down at the still-moving saltshaker, and I stopped, blushing. "Sorry."

She cleared her throat and looked at Joaquin.

"I'll have the Spanish omelet with extra peppers, a side of fries, and a short stack of pancakes," Joaquin said. "Oh, and chocolate milk."

"It's your intestines." She shoved her pen behind her ear and started to turn. "And don't forget to pick up some tea bags on your way home."

"What's your obsession with tea lately?" Joaquin asked. "I've never seen you drink tea before this week."

Ursula scowled. "Just get the tea."

"Slave driver," Joaquin said with a grin. For a split second, I thought she was going to smile, but then she was gone.

"She's in a mood," Fisher commented.

"Right? She's been like that for a few days," Joaquin replied, rubbing his palms on his thighs. "Like instant personality shift."

"I noticed it, too," Krista said. "Yesterday when we were working together, she kept zoning out."

"Do you think something's wrong?" I asked, glancing over at the counter, where Ursula was pouring coffee for a couple of guys. The yoga woman from the park was sitting on the stool at the very end, glaring at me. I turned around again, my heart in my throat.

"What could possibly be wrong? She lives with me," Joaquin said, lifting his chest.

I stared him down, trying to ignore the feeling of the yoga woman's eyes boring into the back of my skull.

"Can we get back to the reason we're here?" I asked. "So no one got ushered yesterday. What about today? I didn't have a coin this morning. Did any of you?"

"Nope," Joaquin said.

"I did," Krista said, raising her hand slightly.

"Me, too." Fisher placed his coin on the table. Joaquin picked it up and studied it.

"Do you think they could be tampered with somehow?" I asked, thinking of Nadia's theory—that I was purposely ushering people to hell. If someone wanted to do that, wouldn't they have to somehow "fix" the coins?

"It looks normal to me," Joaquin said, placing it in front of me and Krista, sun-side up, so we could see it. "They're all the same. When the person who's moving on touches their coin, it basically turns depending on whether the person is good or evil. Until that moment, the coin is nothing but a hunk of gold."

The door chimes tinkled, and I looked over my shoulder. Yoga Woman had just exited the building. I sighed with relief.

"Okay, so maybe I was right," Krista said as Ursula delivered our coffees. She pushed the coin back across the table to Fisher and waited for the waitress to walk away before continuing. "Maybe it's the weather vane that's gone all freaky."

"I guess it could be," Joaquin said.

"Why not? Maybe it got bent in one of the storms," Fisher suggested, pushing the coin into his back pocket and reaching for his smoothie. "There've been a lot of them lately. Maybe it just keeps pointing south because it's off-kilter."

"We should keep an eye on it," I said, hope springing up inside my chest again. "If it never points north, we'll know something's up. I mean, it's not like every single person coming through here right now is inherently evil." I paused and looked around at them. "Right?"

"Right," Joaquin said.

"No way," Fisher put in.

I spun the saltshaker between my thumb and forefinger, hesitant to make my next suggestion. "What if we stop ushering souls?"

For a second, Krista, Joaquin, and Fisher just sat there, looking at one another.

"We can't do that," Krista said finally. "If we do, then the fog will roll in and never roll out again."

"Plus, it'd get pretty crowded around here," Fisher added, sipping at his smoothie.

"What's a little overcrowding compared with sending a bunch of good people to the Shadowlands for all eternity?" I said harshly.

Ursula placed two plates heaping with food in front of Joaquin. Steam rose from the omelet plate as if the eggs had just been removed from the pan, and the smell of the fried onions and spicy peppers filled my nostrils, making my empty stomach growl. As Ursula turned away from the table, she let out a huge sneeze.

The shop fell silent. Krista tensed up next to me. I looked over at Joaquin. His face had gone ashen.

"Bless you," one of the visitors called out.

Joaquin got up and put his hands on Ursula's shoulders. "Are you . . . what are you—?"

Then Ursula burst into tears and fled the restaurant.

Some of the diners exchanged baffled looks. Krista and Fisher stared at each other as if they'd just seen a news report of a terrorist attack.

"What just happened?" I asked, flattening my palms against the edge of the table.

"Ursula sneezed," Krista whispered, looking up at Joaquin warily.

"So?" I asked as the conversations around us started up again.

Joaquin turned and pressed his hands into the side of my bench, leaning all his body weight into it. "So Lifers don't get sick, remember?" he said through his teeth. "We can get hurt by, like, falling off a bike and scraping our knees—"

"Has to look authentic for the visitors," Fisher interjected.

"But we don't cough, we don't sneeze, we don't even hiccup," Joaquin finished.

"Maybe it was just a random itch," I suggested.

Fisher shook his head. "Doesn't happen."

I shakily folded my napkin in my lap. Another facet of Juniper Landing life gone awry. Another hitch in the system that was supposedly hitch-free.

"Do you think that she's really . . . sick?" I asked quietly, looking up at Joaquin. "I mean, do you think that's why she wanted the tea?"

Realization swept over Joaquin's face. "That's why she's been so weird. She didn't want to tell me."

"Poor woman's probably terrified," Fisher put in.

Joaquin laced his hands behind his head, his elbows out like wings, and took a deep breath. "I'm going after her."

Fisher looked toward the door, and his face dropped. He rose slowly from his seat. "You guys, the fog."

I turned around in my seat, pushing myself up on my knees. Sure enough, the fog had slipped into town lightning fast, blotting out the park and the library and all the buildings on the other side. The room grew hushed as everyone stopped to watch.

Joaquin walked toward the door. The rest of us followed. Some visitors eyed us curiously as Joaquin shoved open the door, making the bells ring, and stepped out into the mist. Krista, Fisher, and I joined him one by one, huddled close together under the general store's striped awning. The fog was so thick it instantly wet my skin and hair and clogged my lungs.

"What do we do?" Krista asked.

"We wait," Joaquin replied.

He stepped to the edge of the sidewalk and looked to the left, in roughly the direction of Tristan's house. My breathing was shallow as I silently recited the entire periodic table. Then I counted to one hundred, then counted again. And again. Fisher tapped his fists against one of the pillars holding up the awning while Krista paced behind us. After what seemed like an eternity, the gray cloud all around us began to thin.

"This is it," Joaquin said, staring at the retreating wisps of fog. "If the weather vane turns south, there's definitely something wrong with it. There can't have been four evil souls in a row. There's no way."

"If it turns south I'll climb up there myself and fix it," Fisher said grimly.

The last fingers of fog pulled across the park, leaving behind their wet trails and a clear blue sky. Atop Tristan's house, the weather vane turned slowly. And turned. And turned. The wind was blowing in from the east, whipping the flags on the flagpoles all along Main Street toward the west, but the weather vane paid it no mind. It took one last turn, and stopped, pointing due north.

"Okay, so that's good," Krista said.

"No, it's not," Joaquin snapped. "If the problem isn't the weather vane, if it's not telling us people are going south when they're not, then that means Jennifer and Aaron and Grant all ended up in the Shadowlands when they shouldn't have."

Krista turned pink around her ears. "Oh."

"What the hell is going on around here, J.?" Fisher asked, squaring his broad shoulders. He looked like he was ready to beat the crap out of someone and was just waiting for an opponent to show himself.

"That's it," Joaquin said. "I'm calling a meeting. Tell everyone we're getting together at the Swan at midnight. I want to know if this has happened to anyone else and how many times. If we get enough people together, the mayor will *have* to listen to us. In the meantime, I'm gonna go check on Ursula."

"Good luck, man," Fisher said, clasping Joaquin's hand. "I'll hit the beach. Pete and them are probably down there."

"No," Joaquin said, glancing over at me. "Don't bother with them."

"Why not?" Fisher asked, drawing his head back.

"They're not . . . They don't want to hear it," Joaquin said. "But get Bea, Lauren, and Kevin."

Fisher screwed up his face in confusion, and he knocked his fists together. "Um . . . okay," he said dubiously, as Joaquin jogged away. He looked over at me and Krista, as if waiting for an explanation. I just lifted my shoulders. "All right, then. Kevin's probably sleeping one off at the cove, so I'll go there."

"I'll find Lauren and Bea. Wanna come with me?" Krista offered.

"What about Tristan?" I asked.

"I'll tell him when I get home," she said with a shrug. "Unless you want to go do it."

I glanced over my shoulder at the huge blue mansion

on the bluff, where Tristan, who didn't believe in me, lived under the same roof with the woman who could send me straight to Oblivion. My throat was suddenly dry.

"Actually, I think I'll go home and check on my family," I said.

"Okay, well, then, I'll see you later?" Krista asked hopefully.

I blinked, confusion written all over my face.

"We're baking cupcakes?" she reminded me, knitting and unknitting her fingers. "For the party? Two o'clock."

"Right. Right. Sorry," I said. "I'll be there."

"I'll walk with you," Fisher offered, putting his large hand on the small of my back. "I'm going that way anyway."

"Okay."

We left Krista, turning north up Main Street and headed for Freesia Lane. We'd only taken two steps when I saw something out of the corner of my eye—something that stopped my blood cold. Darcy.

She was standing near the fountain at the center of the park in her favorite sundress, glaring at me. Me and Fisher. The boy she was falling for had just put his arm around me.

"Darcy!" I called. But she just turned on her heel and disappeared over the crest of the hill.

PILLS

Darcy wasn't home. I'd gone back to the house, ready to explain, but she wasn't there. And my dad was tapping away at his laptop, as always. Even with the sun shining brightly through the windows, the place felt desolate, and I spent the entire morning on edge, waiting to hear the door open downstairs. Anticipating the confrontation. But Darcy had never returned. Which meant she was seriously pissed.

She still wasn't home when I left for Krista's. As I cut across the park, I twisted my hands together in front of me, trying to ignore my mounting fear of going to the mayor's house. Instead, I focused on Tristan and what I was going to say to him to get him to believe me about the usherings.

I understand why you're scared, but I can't accept this, I thought. *Aaron doesn't belong in the Shadowlands.*

I shook my head, laughing tersely at myself as I passed the fountain. I'd only said the exact same thing a million times yesterday. Why would his response be any different? Maybe . . .

I understand why you're scared, but there clearly is something wrong around here, I thought. *Don't you want to help us figure out what it is?*

I bit my lip. That might work better, keeping Aaron out of it.

I was just squaring my shoulders and starting to psych myself up for this whole walking-into-the-lion's-den thing when I saw them. Pete and Cori, straddling their dirt bikes not ten feet away, glaring at me.

My steps automatically slowed as frustration burbled up inside me. *What?* I wanted to yell. *What's your problem with me?*

But then Officer Dorn and Chief Grantz strolled over to join them. And then Yoga Woman from the park. And the grocer. And two other people I didn't recognize. I stopped in my tracks, adrenaline and fear surging through me. All that was missing was Nadia and her piercing black eyes.

Dorn leaned toward Grantz's ear, and they both fixed

their angry gazes on me. The others seemed to shift as one, as if primed for an attack.

Tristan's voice echoed in my mind: *Once angry people get together and are out for blood, they're not satisfied until they get it.*

I ducked my head and kept walking, faster and faster and faster, until I reached a sprint at the top of the hill. I had to get to Krista, to my friends. It wasn't until I saw the weather vane creaking overhead that I froze, a new wave of terror crashing over me.

How stupid an idea was this, going to the mayor's house right now? All night I'd been waiting for the ambush. What if it was waiting behind Tristan's front door?

Suddenly, Krista walked around the side of the house, her face creased with concern. She was wearing a lavender sundress and her hair was pulled back at the sides. There was a streak of flour on her cheek and when she saw me, her eyes brightened.

"There you are!" she said, reaching for one of my hands with both of hers. "I was just about to go down to your house to check on you."

"Why?" I felt lightheaded.

"You're late," she replied. "And Joaquin said something about keeping an eye on you. He seemed like he was worried."

"Um . . . yeah. I guess I'm just a little freaked out about everything that's been going on around here lately," I said, glancing one last time over my shoulder. "Is Tristan inside?"

"No, he left a little while ago," Krista replied. "Nadia came by, and I think they went out surfing or something."

My stomach fell into my toes. "What?"

"Oh. Right. Sorry." Krista made an apologetic face. "I'm sure it's nothing."

I tasted bile in the back of my throat. It *wasn't* nothing. If the two of them were out somewhere alone together, Nadia was definitely trying to convince him of my guilt. Trying to make him believe he was just letting another girl pull the wool over his eyes. And considering that the last time I saw Tristan we'd yelled at each other, I couldn't trust that he would take my side.

"Come on," Krista said, tugging me toward the house.

We were just passing the dead garden in front of the porch when a shout sounded from inside, followed by a door slamming. A bevy of crows took off from the roof of the house, cawing angrily.

"Um, maybe we should just sit out here for a while," Krista suggested, clutching my hand so hard it hurt.

"What about Bea and Lauren?" I asked, clutching her right back.

"They'll live."

We looked at each other and shared a strained laugh over her choice of words. Cautiously keeping an eye on the front door, Krista led me up the porch steps and over to a wicker bench facing the bluff and the wide-open ocean beyond. As soon as she sat down, Krista deflated, hunching back against the puffy cushions in a very un-Krista-like way.

"What's the matter?" I asked.

"I've been thinking about what Joaquin said yesterday," she told me, picking at a broken piece of wicker on the arm of the bench. "You know . . . why are we even here if every-thing can go so wrong?"

I nodded. "Yeah."

Krista sighed and crossed her slim arms over her stomach. "Do you ever miss it? Your life?"

My life. Considering everything that had gone on in my new life the last few days, I hadn't had much time to think about my old one. And it was almost impossible to focus on it now, knowing that Tristan and Nadia were out there somewhere, talking.

But after a moment, I realized that unless I counted school, there wasn't all that much to miss. I'd had friends, but no extremely close ones. I'd already been missing my mom for years, so that hadn't changed, and Darcy and my dad were still with me. My mind flashed on an image of Christopher, but I could hardly remember what he looked like. When I thought of him, I felt a pleasant hum inside my chest, but nothing more.

"Not really," I told her. She gave me this doe-eyed look that was sad, like she'd been expecting another answer. "But I guess I haven't been here long enough to really miss it."

"That's true," she said with another sigh.

I gazed at her petite frame. She seemed so fragile in that moment, so breakable. "Krista," I started gently, "do you want to tell me . . . I mean, do you want to talk about how you . . ."

"Died?" she asked, her voice breaking. "I killed myself."

"Just like Joaquin," I said.

She laughed harshly. "Not exactly. *I* didn't mean to do it."

"What?" I gasped, startled.

Krista turned her hands over and over in her lap. "I just . . . my boyfriend, Andreas . . . he broke up with me, and I only took the pills because I figured I'd pass out and then he'd find me. And when he found me he would realize how much he loved me. It was a whole Romeo and Juliet thing. We were supposed to go to prom together, and I had a dress, and I just wanted him to want to take me. But instead, I ended up here. It was all supposed to be perfect, and I ended up here. Without him."

She pressed her face against my shoulder, dissolving into tears. I wrapped one arm around her and let her cry, thinking how awful it must have been for her, knowing she could've just gone to prom with someone else and gotten on with her life. If only she hadn't taken too many pills.

It was kind of how I'd felt about taking the shortcut through the woods that day. If only I'd gotten a ride, if only I'd taken the long way around, Mr. Nell would never have had the opportunity to attack me. My sister, my father, and I would all be alive back in Princeton. Back in "the other world." I wouldn't have to worry about the angry mob or the mayor or the Shadowlands or Oblivion or where Tristan was right now and what I would say to him when I had the chance.

Maybe I did miss my life.

"I'm sorry," she said, sniffling. "I'm really sorry. I've just been thinking about this a lot lately, with the one-year anniversary coming up and everything . . . but for some reason it just feels worse today."

"It's okay, Krista," I told her, rubbing her back. "Hey, what was your selfless act?" I asked, hoping that might cheer her up.

"Oh. That." She laughed and looked down at her fingers in her lap. "It was so lame. Not like saving a life or ridding the world of an evil maniac, like some people."

I smirked. "Tell me."

"I saved a doll."

"What?"

She rolled her eyes slightly, but smiled. "I'd been here for three days and I was down at the beach with a couple other people who moved on ages ago, and there was this family there. A mom, a dad, and two little kids. I found out later they died in a car accident."

"Wow," I said, the wind knocked out of me.

"Anyway, the little girl left her favorite doll near the shoreline and it got swept out to sea," Krista continued. "She completely lost it, crying, screaming, and her dad was basically like, 'Too bad. You have to learn to take care of your things.' I mean, the girl was, like, three years old."

"Are you serious?" I asked.

"Yeah. Real nice," Krista agreed. "All I could do was watch this soggy pink doll bobbing out on the ocean and the little girl crying, and it reminded me so much of me when I was little. I had this Raggedy Ann that I would take with me everywhere. By the time I gave it up in fourth grade it was falling apart and probably totally diseased."

She smiled again, looking nostalgic. "So even though I was never a great swimmer, I dove into the ocean and swam out there and saved the doll for her. I thought I was gonna die by the time I got back to the beach. I was panting so hard I was seeing stars. But she got her doll back."

"That's awesome," I said. "What did her dad do?"

"He basically grunted at me," Krista replied. "But the little girl was so happy . . . They moved on that night."

I swallowed hard, hoping that that family, even the grumpy dad, had made it into the Light. We both sighed at the same time, looking out at the sun glinting on the ocean.

"You know what this is, Krista?" I said finally. "It's just a bad day."

"What do you mean?" she asked. Her blue eyes were shot through with red.

"It's something my mom used to say. One day everything can look okay, and the next day everything looks so grim, even though nothing has really changed," I said. "On bad days you have to remember the okay days, and then you'll know that things will be okay again, eventually."

"But something *has* really changed," Krista protested, sitting up straight, pulling away from me. The bench groaned as she shifted her weight. "I liked how I had this important job, ushering people to their eternal destiny. But if that's getting all screwed up, then what else do I have? No one here even likes me."

"That's not true!" I replied emphatically. "Tristan loves you."

"No, he doesn't. He thinks I'm annoying," Krista said, looking at her lap. Her pert nose was red, and a tear rolled slowly down her cheek. "Imagine how you'd feel being an only child for two hundred fifty years and then suddenly getting stuck with a sister."

"Well, the girls adore you," I said.

"Please," she retorted, rolling her eyes.

"Um, two of them are inside right now, baking cupcakes for your anniversary party, while you've been MIA for at least fifteen minutes," I reminded her. "If that's not dedication, I don't know what is."

Krista bit her lip. "I bet Lauren is separating the sprinkles by color and driving Bea bonkers."

"Probably." I laughed. We both stared out over the ocean. "I think you just have to find your thing, your place, how you're going to fit in for the long run," I said, thinking of Tristan, of my odd new relationship with Joaquin, and of the very slowly blossoming friendship with Krista. "We all do. But it's going to take time."

"And we have nothing but that," Krista muttered.

A soft knock sounded behind us, and I glanced back at the mayor's office windows. Two clear blue eyes stared out at me through parted wooden slats. I caught my breath. The mayor held my gaze for a long, long moment before snapping the blinds shut.

I turned back to Krista, an awful feeling spreading through my gut that my time might be running out.

IMAGINED CRIME

Joaquin was silent as he walked me home from Krista's later that afternoon, beadily eyeing the Lifers at the center of town like he was my own personal bodyguard. He'd shown up out of nowhere as we'd finished the last batch of strawberry-scented cupcakes and had ever so casually offered to escort me back to Magnolia Street. Now I knew why. He thought I needed protection.

I wasn't sure if that made me feel safer, or a lot more terrified.

"So . . ." I said finally, as we reached the far side of the square and the ever-present shadows on Freesia Lane. "How about those Yankees?"

"What?" Joaquin snapped.

I blushed, hard. "Sorry. It's just something . . . my dad always says that when there's an awkward pause in conversation. It's like a thing."

"Oh." It was his turn to blush. "I guess I'm a little tense."

We started down the hill, passing by the tall, imposing Victorian houses, their eaves decorated with intricate carvings, their porches lined with pretty potted flowers—although some of these had begun to wither and brown. The overgrown park at the center of the lane was as deserted as ever, and I averted my eyes from the eerily creaking swing.

"Did you see Tristan at all today?" he asked suddenly.

I shook my head, my heart skipping a beat. Every time a door had closed or a floorboard settled inside Krista's house, I'd been sure it was the mayor coming for my head, but it was always nothing. Apparently, wherever he and Nadia were, they were having a good time together.

"Krista said something about him going surfing with Nadia," I replied.

Joaquin rolled his eyes. "Yeah, right," he said. "Tristan and Nadia are like . . . What two elements explode when they're mixed together?"

"Well, there's oxygen and phosphorus. . . . There's—"

"Then they're like that," he interjected, gazing at the

241

ocean in the distance. "If they'd spent any kind of time together, we'd know, because the island would have been obliterated."

I smirked, feeling a little better. Joaquin, after all, knew Tristan better than anyone.

"He's probably just off on one of his thinks."

"His thinks?" I asked.

We emerged onto Magnolia and turned toward my house. Overhead, the sky was just beginning to darken, the lowering sun shading the clouds violet and pink. Joaquin sighed.

"Every once in a while Tristan . . . He just disappears," Joaquin explained, glancing down at a dying sunflower that drooped all the way to the sidewalk. He stepped over it with a wide stride, like it might suddenly come to life and bite him. "Doesn't tell anyone where he's going. Just vanishes for a day or two, and when he gets back he won't talk about it. One time I finally got him to tell me what he'd been up to, and he said, 'I was thinking.' That was it. So now we call them his thinks."

Something inside of me sank. All along, Tristan had been bent on protecting me. Postponing telling me the truth about my new existence, making sure I didn't hear about things dying for the first time ever, not telling me about Jessica and Oblivion. But now, when I really needed protection, it was Joaquin walking me home from the mayor's, not him. He was off alone somewhere, thinking. But I supposed it was better than the alternative.

"Well, here we are," Joaquin said as we arrived at my front gate. "Home sweet home."

"Yeah." I paused with my hand on the latch. "Thanks, Joaquin," I said, looking him in the eye. "I appreciate you going out of your way."

"Eh, I was gonna go for an evening swim anyway," he said, shrugging me off. Then he smiled. "I'll come down and get you for the meeting tonight."

"You don't have to do that," I said, even as my blood ran cold, remembering the looks on the faces of Nadia's crew that afternoon.

"Just for now," he said. "Until we figure it all out. Which we *will* do."

I nodded, trying to feel as confident as he seemed. "Okay."

I went to push the gate open, but he didn't move. When I looked up at him, I could have sworn he caught his breath. "You sure you're all right?"

My palms began to itch, and there was a slight hitch in my pulse, but I ignored it. This was Joaquin. He was a player. He'd screwed over my sister. And I was with Tristan. Wherever *he* was. I heard a loud caw and saw them coming, five dark splotches against the purple sky. The crows swooped in and landed on the apex of our roof, one, two, three, four, five. Overhead, the seagull circled and bleated, but it was clearly outnumbered. It finally turned and soared out to sea.

"Yeah," I said. "I'm fine. I'll see you later."

I shoved the gate open, forcing him to take a step back, and strode inside without a second glance. As soon as I inhaled the familiar, musty scent of the house, I started to relax. I was home. I was safe.

Then I spotted Darcy at the kitchen table, and my heart froze. Maybe I wasn't so safe.

"Hey, Darcy," I said casually, hoping that if I acted like nothing was wrong, she'd follow suit.

But Darcy just made a grunting, scoffing sound in the back of her throat and pushed her chair back.

"Darcy," I implored her.

"Leave me alone," she said, one foot already on the bottom step.

My pulse started to race in that sickly way it did whenever Darcy was mad at me, but there was no way I was going to let a misunderstanding about a guy get between us. Not again. Not now, when Nadia was busy turning everyone on this island against me. I caught up with Darcy just as she was about to slam the door to her room. I flattened my hand against it and stopped her, jamming my wrist.

"Darcy, if this is about Fisher, there's nothing going on," I said.

She groaned again and walked farther into her room, tossing a book onto the bed. It flapped closed, and I saw the ancient silver writing, faded, on the cloth cover. *Wuthering Heights.* Impressive.

"Did you or did you not sneak out of the house to have breakfast with both the guys I like?" Darcy demanded.

I paled. She'd seen Joaquin, too? "It's not like I—"

"Answer the question!" she fumed.

"Okay, yes," I stated. "Yes. I did. But do you really think I'm going to go after Joaquin? Or Fisher?"

She flopped down on her window seat, turning her palms up atop her thighs.

"No, I don't think you're interested in either one of them. Not really," she said. "But do you have any idea how this feels? It's like you're *trying* to hurt me. You. My own sister."

She drew her legs up, facing away from me with forced casualness, as if she were fine and not vibrating with 5,000 megahertz of anger and sorrow. My chest heaved, desperate to just tell her the truth. Desperate to fix things between us however possible.

But I couldn't. Because if I told her the truth, I would damn her to the Shadowlands. I so wished she'd just perform a selfless act already, so this would all be a done deal. What

I wouldn't give to slap a Lifer bracelet on her wrist and tell her everything. But all I could do was keep my mouth shut and hope that it would happen. And soon.

"I'm sorry," I said finally, quietly. "I guess I'll just go."

"Fine," she spat. "Go!"

I turned on my heel but paused at the door, my fingers curling around the beveled trim.

"But, Darcy, there is one thing you should know," I said, looking halfway over my shoulder.

She sighed. "What?"

"I would never intentionally do anything to hurt you," I said. "Never."

Then I slipped into the hallway, closing the door behind me.

FIVE SOULS

I stared at the Scrabble board in the center of the kitchen table, but the letters might as well have been hieroglyphics. My vision blurred in and out. Nothing made sense. Darcy hated me. Joaquin, quite possibly, liked me. But worst of all was Nadia. Clearly, she was determined to turn the town, and especially the mayor, against me. And now she might even be working on Tristan. What if she convinced him? What if she and her angry mob stopped glowering from safe distances and came after me?

"Bam!" my father shouted suddenly, nearly knocking me off my chair. "Quixotic! *Q* on a triple-letter, *X* on a triple-word; that's one hundred and eighty-eight points! Read it and weep."

I stared at him, trying to pull myself into his present. A present where he was alive and well, devouring ice cream, playing Scrabble with his daughter, and kicking her sorry ass. He licked a drop of chocolate sauce off his lip and smiled.

"Sorry," he said when he saw my face. "That was a tad over the top. But you gotta admit . . ."

He gestured at the board, waiting for me to give him his props.

"Yes, Dad. You are a genius," I said in a jokingly toneless voice. "Get over yourself."

I looked down at the makeshift score sheet he'd drawn out for us, two columns labeled *R* for Rory and *D* for Dad, and it reminded me of the tally I'd found down at the cave. I wondered what Pete had done with it, where it was now, whether the mayor had seen it.

"Do you want to take a break?" my father asked. "I'm not really sure your head is in this tonight."

A survey of the board proved him right. My words were stellar little pieces of brilliance like *dog, from*, and *mat*. With one word he'd pretty much annihilated my score.

"I guess not," I told him, leaning back in my chair, feeling impossibly heavy. Outside the window screens, the waves sloshed against the shore, the low tide marking a steady, low rhythm.

"Everything okay, Rory?" my dad asked, his brow creasing with concern. "You look like you've got the weight of the world on your shoulders."

Not the other world. Just this one, I thought. I gazed across the kitchen table at him, hesitating. Over the past few years I had barely spoken to my father, other than to inform him when I'd be home, that I had a doctor's appointment, that I needed money for a haircut. It had been forever since my dad had offered to talk.

"Have you ever felt like you could trust someone one day and felt completely opposite the next?" I asked, toying with my tiles on their wooden rack.

He narrowed his brown eyes. "Is this about a boy?"

"Dad!" I said, blushing slightly. "Just answer the question."

He leaned back as well, mimicking my pose, and thought. "Yes. Yes, I have," he said at last.

"And? What did you do?" I asked.

"Well, Rory, things aren't always exactly what they seem," he said. "So I gave the person a chance to explain and then decided whether or not it was enough for me to trust them again."

"And? Was it?" I asked hopefully.

He frowned and picked up his spoon, swirling it in the melted remains of his sundae.

"In my case, no," he said, causing my heart to drop. "But that doesn't necessarily mean it'll be the same for you."

"I know," I replied.

I balled my hands into fists on the table, stacked them one on top of the other, and brought my chin down on top of them. The seven playable letters in front of me spelled out SPITBLA. My father sighed, gazing out the window to his right.

"Your mother was always so much better at these things," he said wistfully.

"You're doing fine, Dad," I assured him, just as Darcy padded into the room on bare feet, her pajama pants sitting low on her hips. She dumped her own sundae dish into the sink without looking at us.

"Yeah?" my dad asked.

I gave him a small but genuine smile. "Yeah. You're great."

He sighed and nodded, as if pondering whether or not *he* could trust *me*. Then he sat up straight and dropped his spoon back into his dish.

"Fog's coming in again."

I stood up, knocking my chair back, my eyeballs suddenly throbbing. The thick gray mist already covered all the windows, blocking our view of the house next door, squelching all the light. I went to the back door to look out, but all I could see was the swirling cloud. It had moved in faster than I'd ever seen before. My mouth went dry as unadulterated panic seized my heart.

This couldn't be happening. Not now. Not when we hadn't told everyone yet—not when we hadn't come up with a plan.

Darcy stepped up next to my dad, who was now on his feet. "Could it be any creepier?"

A sudden crash, like metal trash cans colliding, made all three of us jump. It was followed by a quick, but very real, shout of pain.

"What was that?" my father said, already reaching for the door.

I grabbed his arm and squeezed. "No, Dad! Don't!"

He ignored me. He yanked open the door, and a few fingers of fog licked at his shoes. Darcy and I looked at each other, and I could tell she was as terrified as I was.

"Hello?" my dad called out. "Is someone out there? Are you all right?"

The reply was a soft, mewling whimper. Like a hurt kitten. Except I'd never seen a cat or kitten on this island.

"Girls, I'll be right back," my dad said, fumbling for a flashlight from the nearest drawer. "You stay here."

"Dad, no. You're not gonna be able to help. You can't see anything," I protested.

"Seriously, Dad," Darcy added. "You can't—"

"Just stay here," he repeated. And then he vanished.

For a long moment we stood there on the threshold between crisp kitchen air and moist, warm mist. I heard my father barrel down the steps, shouting out, but after that, nothing. The mewling sound had stopped, and all I could hear was the incessant, menacing hiss of the fog, the pounding of my own heart, the sound of Darcy's broken breath.

"Where is he?" Darcy's voice was shrill.

"I'm sure he's fine," I said automatically.

"What if Steven Nell's out there?"

I froze. "What?"

"What if he followed us?" Darcy asked, her eyes desperate. "What if he's just been watching us? Waiting for a chance to lure one of us out? What if he's out there right now, stalking Dad?"

"Darcy, he's not," I said, trying for a soothing voice, wishing I could tell her why I knew this to be true. "Trust me. There's no way he—"

"Dad!" Darcy shouted into the swirling mist. There was no reply. "Dad! Answer me!"

Nothing. I looked at Darcy. Darcy looked at me. Then

something changed in her face. Something hardened. "Screw this."

Before I could even blink, she'd turned and dived into the fog. "Dad!" Already, her voice sounded distant. "Daddy! Where are you?"

I cursed under my breath and followed, my heart slamming against my ribs as I groped for the stairs and the handrail.

"Darcy!" I cried. "Dad!"

Someone laughed. The exact same laugh I'd heard coming through the phone line in Aaron's room. A mocking voice echoed back my plea: *"Dad!"*

I stumbled down the steps, clinging to the railing for dear life. I misjudged how far I'd come, and where I'd thought there'd be one more step, there was nothing. My stomach swooped as I tipped forward and fell face-first into the sand. Pain radiated through my skull and down my spine, and zipped up my arms. Another laugh, but farther away this time.

"Dad!" I shouted, scrambling to my knees.

"Rory?" he sounded impossibly far off, his voice a mere croak.

"Dad? Are you hurt?" I asked, whirling around, blind. "Where's Darcy?"

A dry finger grazed my cheek. I reached up and

slapped at it, my skin burning from the violence of my own hand.

"Stop it!" I shouted as loud as I could. "Stop screwing with me! Where's my family?"

Another sound behind me. "What are you—?" my dad said.

There was the unmistakable sound of a punch hitting home. A cry of pain. "Dad?" I cried, terrified, desperate. I felt around in front of me blindly, looking for someone, anyone, in the mist.

There was a struggle. A tear. A crack. I whirled toward the sound, catching my breath again and again. Nothing but gray.

"Get off him!" Darcy shouted.

Another crack.

"Darcy!?" I wailed.

I turned and my foot jammed into something hard. I flew forward again, my arms flying out to brace myself. I flipped over and scrambled back on my hands like a crab, but it wasn't a body that had tripped me. Just a large piece of driftwood, rotted and riddled with holes. I started to crawl, tears now streaming down my face.

"Dad? Darcy?" I whispered. "Where are you?"

Silence. No laughter, no mocking, no cries. My fingers groped in the darkness, growing colder as they dug into the frigid sand, finding nothing but seaweed, shells, smaller shards of wood. The longer I searched, the more sure I was that someone had taken my family. That I was never going to see them again. The fog seemed to drag on for hours.

Whoever they are, fight them, I begged silently. *Don't let them take you to the Shadowlands.*

"Rory?" Darcy shouted suddenly. "Are you there?"

"Darcy!"

At that moment, my hand came down on a shoe. I screamed at the top of my lungs.

"Rory?"

"Dad!" I shouted, jumping up.

My sister threw her arms around me, and I flung my arms around my father. But the second I touched my dad, I had a sudden flash. I saw Mr. Nell grab him from behind and whip his head to the side, snapping his neck. I heard the sound of the bones splintering. I watched my father's limp body slump to the ground, stunned, his eyes open, his mouth hanging down on one side like he'd just been numbed at the dentist. I released him and staggered backward. Until that moment, my only memories of that night had been the things I'd actually seen, and I hadn't seen my father die—only his body after the fact. This was new, and it was horrifying. I clutched at my stomach, swallowing over and over to keep from heaving.

I knew what this meant. My father was never going to be a Lifer. He was going to move on. And I was supposed to usher him.

"Rory?" Darcy asked, her eyes concerned. "Are you okay?"

I turned away from her and fell to my knees in the sand. At that moment, I couldn't have been more grateful for the fog that enveloped me.

"Rory? Where are you?" my father asked.

"I'm here," I squeaked. "I . . . I tripped."

I breathed once. Then again. Struggled to stop the sobs from coming.

"Where?" he asked. His foot kicked the side of my leg. "Oh. Oops. Sorry. This fog is so thick. And my head . . ."

"Your head?"

"Some asshole tried to grab him," Darcy said.

"Yeah, but we fought them off," my dad replied, sounding proud.

"Yeah, we did," Darcy replied.

I pushed myself up off the ground at the exact moment the fog began to lift. It pulled back across the water, the last wisps curling teasingly around my ankles until it was gone. My father was holding the back of his skull. I shoved the image of his death—and his looming ushering—from my mind.

"Are you all right?" I asked, grabbing at his arm.

He pulled his hand down and held it in front of us. His fingers were bloody.

"It's okay," Darcy said, checking the cut. "He'll live."

"Did you see who it was?" I asked her.

"No. Probably just some idiot messing around." She leveled a look at me, and I knew it meant she didn't want me to bring up Steven Nell.

"Losers," I said, because I felt like I should say something as I stood there trembling from head to toe. "Come on, Dad. Let's get you inside and clean that up."

We fumbled our way up the stairs, him unsteady from his injury, me trembling from my desperation and fear. As soon as we got into the kitchen, I stopped cold. In all the relief of finding my family here and okay, I had forgotten what the fog really meant. Someone somewhere on this island had been ushered. Had they gone to the right destination?

"I have to go out for a sec," I said, leaving Darcy clutching my dad's arm. "Get that cleaned up, okay? I'll be back soon."

"Are you kidding me right now?" Darcy demanded.

I groaned in frustration. "I'm sorry! I'll be back as fast as I can."

Then, with Darcy shouting at me, I ran out the front

door. I didn't even care whether Nadia and her angry mob might be out there, waiting for me to run into their waiting claws. I tore up the hill as fast as I could, and as soon as I hit Main Street, I skidded to a stop and faced Tristan's house. I saw Fisher standing in the park with Bea and Lauren. Bea shot me a knowing look, then turned toward the bluff.

The weather vane spun crazily, so fast it was nothing but a blur. The movement was so unnatural it caught the attention of a few other passersby, people who knew nothing about the truth of Juniper Landing, people who'd talk about a phenomenon like this in the morning, wondering if they could have seen it right, if it had really happened. It spun and spun until I thought it was going to snap off and go flying into the night. But then, suddenly, it stopped. The arrow pointed due south, quivering against the dark sky.

I glanced at Bea and the others. Fisher looked back at me, grim. Then someone gasped. The vane was spinning again, same as before, but this time it stopped sooner.

Pointing south.

It spun again.

South.

And again.

South.

And once more.

South.

By the time it was done, Lauren had covered her mouth with both hands. Bea was red with anger. Fisher was visibly sweating. In that one fog, five souls had been taken. Five souls had been relegated to the Shadowlands.

NEW RULE

"I'm not going to usher him," I hissed to Joaquin as we followed Bea, Fisher, and Krista through the crowded Thirsty Swan toward the back hallway. "He's not going. Not now. Not when everyone's going to the Shadowlands."

"Don't worry about it," Joaquin whispered back, tugging me toward the wall. "No one will expect you to usher him. I can't even believe he's your charge. It's like the universe is trying to mess with you."

I scoffed. Like the universe gave a crap about me. But Joaquin fixed me with a stare that made me shrivel inside. *Could* the universe really be messing with me?

"You should have seen Darcy, though," I said, trying to think about anything else. "She was sure Steven Nell was out there, ready to grab my father, and she just ran out there to save him. It was intense."

Joaquin's eyebrows darted skyward. "Really?"

I laughed under my breath. "Yeah. I've never seen her do anything like that before. She was, like, Super Darcy."

"Interesting," Joaquin said, stepping sideways to let a visitor pass by with a mug of beer. "Sorry I missed that. I was busy serving chicken soup to my 'grandma.'"

"Right!" I brought my hand to my forehead. "How *is* Ursula?"

"She's . . . sick," Joaquin replied, sighing. "I'd say she'll be all right, since it doesn't look that bad, but with everything else going on around here, what the hell do I know?"

Bea, Fisher, and Krista were all waiting in the hall, eyeing us expectantly. Joaquin fumbled in his pocket for a set of keys, then opened the door to the stockroom and backed up against it, holding it for us. I stepped through first and slid aside to make way. The room was long and slim and cramped with boxes and barrels, old wooden things with iron clasps that looked like they'd been there for centuries. The air smelled of stale beer and sawdust, peanuts, and salt. The others filed in silently, their sneakers and sandals scraping on the wood floor. Krista hoisted herself up onto a barrel, and Bea leaned back next to her against a shelf full of condiment bottles and coffee mugs. Fisher took a spot by the back door, squaring his shoulders like a bouncer. A moment later Kevin appeared, and right away he began pacing and muttering to himself, as if hopped up on too much Red Bull. Then Lauren slipped through, shooting me an unreadable glance as she squeezed by me.

"What's up?" I asked.

Her eyes darted to the door. Joaquin had just started to let it shut when a hand stopped it. I held my breath, expecting to see Tristan, but it wasn't him. It was Pete. A moment later, Nadia and Cori joined him. They walked along the near wall until Pete's shoulder knocked into a stack of boxes taller than him, and they stopped. Nadia shot me a piercing look as she settled back against the shelves.

My stomach clenched, and the temperature in the room seemed to spike. Joaquin gave me a look that was somehow alarmed and soothing all at once. Like, *Yes, this is not good, but it will be fine.* I pressed my sweaty palms together and hoped he was right.

"Everyone here?" Joaquin asked.

"Not Tristan," Krista pointed out.

Joaquin glanced back toward the noisy bar. A loud cheer went up, as if the home team had just scored a goal on TV.

Except there were no TVs here. No home team to speak of.

"I don't think Tristan's coming," he said, closing the door.

Everyone looked around nervously.

"What the hell is going on?" Bea asked, cracking her knuckles.

"What's going on is, I just sent someone to the Shadowlands," Kevin blurted out vehemently. "Someone who was *not* supposed to go there."

"Me, too," Krista said quietly.

"Anyone else?" Joaquin asked, stepping farther into the room.

Nadia raised her hand, staring straight at me until I had to look away.

"Me, too," Cori said.

That made four.

"Who else? There were five," Joaquin said. His question was met with silence, apart from the laughter out in the bar. "Who else?" Joaquin shouted.

"Pete!" Cori said through her teeth.

"All right! I brought someone up there, but if he went to the Shadowlands, I got no beef with it," he said. "That guy deserved it."

"All right, fine," Joaquin said. "That's four out of five gone to the wrong place."

"And three of us had one, too," Fisher said. "Me, J., and Rory."

All eyes flicked to me.

"There's a shock," Nadia muttered.

"Nadia, don't even start," Bea said.

My legs trembled. My eyes darted to the door.

"Oh, please! Do you people really not see what's going on here?" Nadia said, gesturing at me with an open hand. "She's doing this! First the dying and the insects and the sickness, now this! All of it started when she got here, but somehow she's got all of you snowed! Even Tristan! It's just like Jessica all over again."

"Shut up about Jessica!" Joaquin shouted, his voice ringing loudly through the room. "You don't know anything about her!"

The room went silent. I held my breath, startled. Joaquin's chest heaved, his face a hardened mask of fury. He pressed his fist into his other hand and clenched his jaw. Suddenly I remembered what Nadia had said the other night at the cove, about a pissing match over a girl. Jessica. It had to have been.

"Were any of you here when the Jessica incident happened?" Joaquin asked. "No! You weren't. I was, and this is nothing like what Jessica did. What she did was the fault of one person, a result of an error in judgment."

Kevin scoffed.

"Okay, a *huge* error in judgment, but still . . ." Joaquin continued. "She made a choice and acted on it. This is *nothing* like that. This couldn't be perpetrated by one person and especially not by one person who just learned our ways five days ago."

"I don't know," Kevin said, looking me up and down. "She did kill someone in the other world."

My jaw dropped. "He was a serial killer!"

"She was only defending herself, Kevin," Krista put in. "And he killed her first." She cast me an apologetic look. "Sort of."

"Yeah, and you're hardly one to throw stones, Slimy, considering your life," Bea added.

"Screw you, Bea! Not all of us grew up in a perfect house with perfect parents and crazy athletic genes!" Kevin shouted, getting right in her face.

"Oh, will you stop using your drunk father as an excuse, already?" Bea replied. "People make their own choices!"

"You have no clue, *Beatrice*," Kevin sneered, looking her up and down.

Suddenly, she took a swing at him, and the situation crumbled. Pete grabbed Kevin, Fisher got between them, and Lauren and Krista did their best to hold back a seething Bea. I flattened myself against the wall as a wayward foot flew toward my face.

"That's enough!" Joaquin shouted, grabbing Kevin by his lapels and throwing him against the door. The crack brought everyone up short. They froze in the middle of a violent tableau, everyone grabbing everyone else, chests heaving for breath.

Kevin had hit the floor, and Joaquin now leaned down with his arm outstretched to help him up. Amazingly, Kevin took it. Everyone breathed a sigh of relief as he quietly stood, his sheepish gaze on the ground.

"Sorry, Bea," he said.

"Me, too," she replied, holding out her hand. After a beat, he shook it.

Joaquin took in a breath and let it out slowly. "Look, we can't let our emotions get the best of us right now," he said to the crowd. "What's really going on here is huge."

At that moment, the door swung open. Fisher made a move to block the intruder but then backed off. The mayor stepped in from the back alleyway wearing a black trench coat over a pressed white shirt, her blond hair pulled back from her face, as always. I shrank back at the sight of her, knowing in my gut that this was it. Her and Nadia in the same room. They were going to officially accuse me. They were going to send me to Oblivion.

As the door began to close behind the mayor, I stepped closer to Joaquin, closer to the door leading back to the bar.

Then a hand stopped the back door before it could shut, and Tristan slipped through.

I froze. His normally tanned skin looked pale under the fluorescent bulbs. His gaze darted around from face to face. I couldn't tell if he felt guilty, betrayed, or something else entirely, but when he looked into my eyes from across the room, I felt calmer. I felt safe. At least, relatively. Whatever suspicions my brain was entertaining about where he'd been today, my heart was glad to see him.

"Well," the mayor said, scrunching up her nose at the dusty top of a vodka box. "Isn't this cozy?"

She looked at Nadia, who lifted her chin and smiled. A shiver went through me. Joaquin took a step closer to me.

"What're you doing here?" Joaquin demanded.

"We came, Mr. Marquez, to apologize." The mayor sniffed. "It appears that you and your little friend here," she said, sneering at me, "were correct about the usherings."

My jaw dropped slightly. I hadn't known the mayor long, but she didn't strike me as the type of person who readily admitted her mistakes.

"So you admit it?" Joaquin said. "You admit that something's wrong?"

She tilted her head. "Five souls to the Shadowlands in one fog is . . ."

"It's unprecedented," Tristan cut in. "Nothing like that

has ever happened before. As long as I've been here, the good souls have always outnumbered the bad. Always. And five have never been taken at once." He looked at me. "Not only were some of those people certainly not destined for the Shadowlands, some of them weren't ready to go at all."

I glanced at Pete and Nadia, thinking of the tally from the cave. *The good souls have always outnumbered the bad.*

Whom did the tally really belong to? I looked around the room. Whoever it was could be here right now, watching. Itching to make five more marks on that page.

"How do we fix it?" Lauren asked.

"That's just it," Tristan said. "We don't know. Until we figure out how it's going wrong, we can't figure out how to make it right."

A disturbed murmur filled the room.

"But we *will* figure out what, or who, the problem is," the mayor said. Then she turned and looked directly at me. "You can trust me on that."

My face burned so hot I could have fainted. So she did still think it could be me. She just hadn't made her final decision yet. Realizing this, I somehow still managed to muster up enough courage to state the obvious.

"In the meantime, we have to stop ushering souls," I said.

The mayor looked me up and down coolly. "I agree."

Nadia's face went slack.

"We talked about it, and we both think that's the best plan," Tristan told the room. "Better this place get foggy and crowded than more innocent souls get sent to the Shadowlands."

"And what about the souls that are already there?" Joaquin asked. "Can we get them back?"

There was a long, heavy silence. No one moved. No one breathed.

"You already know the answer to that," Tristan said finally. "No one ever comes back from the Shadowlands. That's why it's imperative that we all understand what we need to do." The mayor took a step back as he commanded control of the room. "From this moment on, no matter how many coins we each have, no matter how strong the call, no one is to leave this island. Are we clear?"

"Yes," the room said as one.

"Good," Tristan said.

Then he looked me in the eye, his gaze so intense it took my breath away.

"Rory," he said firmly. "We need to talk."

ONE OF A KIND

Tristan and I were silent as we walked back to his house, Krista and the mayor trailing slightly behind us. Every now and then I would catch his gaze; the guarded look in his eyes made me hold my tongue. He held the front door open for me, and together we moved up the creaky stairs and into his dusky room, the only light the full moon glowing through the window. He closed the door behind us, and I turned to look at him. His expression was filled with sorrow and sympathy, apology and regret.

"I'm so sorry, Rory," he said. "About your dad. You must be—"

"How?" My voice cracked. "How did you know?"

"It's a special . . . awareness I have," he said, taking a step toward me. "When a Lifer's charge is first revealed to them, it's revealed to me as well."

"So that's how you knew about Aaron," I said, tears flooding my eyes.

He nodded. "Are you all right?"

"No," I replied, shaking my head as the tears spilled over. "How can I be all right? He's moving on. He's . . . he's going to leave me."

Tristan closed the distance between us then, pulling me into his arms. I inhaled the scent of him, so like the calming, floral scent of the island itself, and released all the misery, confusion, and anger I'd been feeling since the moment I'd had that flash.

Tristan stroked my hair back from my face, clinging to my shoulder with his other hand. He kissed the top of my head and whispered in my ear, "It's okay. I'm here."

Gradually, my tears began to slow, my breathing returning to normal, until finally I was quiet.

"Where were you today?" I muttered, looking him in the eye. "Where were you when you found out about me ushering my dad?

"I was at the cove," he said.

"With Nadia?"

Tristan knitted his brow. "What? No. Not with Nadia. I mean, she did come by here earlier today, but I didn't go anywhere with her. I was at the cove, reading."

"Reading?" I repeated dumbly.

Tristan released me slowly, as if afraid I might crumble at any sudden movement, and went to his desk. For the first time, I noticed that piled on top were dozens of leather-bound journals, some with yellowed pages, others with crisp white ones. He grabbed one from the top of a pile and brought it to me, sitting down on the edge of his bed. I sat next to him.

"What's that?" I asked, dragging my hands over my face to try to dry the tears.

"I've never shown this to anyone," he said, tilting the spine up. "It's my daily log. The most recent one. I've been keeping them since I got here, so there are actually quite a few by now, but this is the one that matters."

"Why?" I asked.

He blinked and looked at me like it was so obvious. "Because you're in it." Tristan held the journal out to me, gazing directly into my eyes. "Take it."

"What?"

"I want you to have it," he said firmly, placing it in my hands. "I want you to see what I wrote tonight before I came back to town—how you've changed everything for me."

I stared down at the plain leather cover of the journal. "Changed everything?"

Tristan was silent for a moment, then let out a sigh. "I'm sorry I didn't listen to you," he said quietly. "What you and Joaquin were saying . . . It just didn't make sense to me. It was like you coming to me and insisting that the sky isn't blue or that the other world isn't round. It made no sense."

"Until . . . ?"

"I spent the whole day today going through these," he said. "The guy in these journals, he's so . . . idealistic." He chuckled. "He really believes in this place. But then I thought about what you said about Jessica and what she did and what happened as a result, and I realized . . . believing in this place doesn't mean thinking it can do no wrong. That's when I knew I couldn't keep turning a blind eye to what was going on around here.

"I was on my way back to tell the mayor that when I saw the weather vane," he continued. "That was the final nail in the coffin."

"You saw it?" I asked, lifting my head. "You were there?"

He nodded. "I'd just gotten to the library when the fog came in, and I waited it out there. I saw you, when you ran up from your house. I saw your face—how devastated you were—and I went right to the mayor."

"We have to figure this out, Tristan," I said desperately.

"If I have to . . ." I paused and took a breath, ignoring the dart of pain in my chest. "If I have to usher my father, I have to be sure he's going to the right place."

"I know." He put his arms around me, and I rested my chin on his shoulder, closing my eyes and relishing the solidity of him. "We'll figure it out. I promise."

"That's all I want," I replied. "What happened to Aaron and Jennifer, and those other people tonight . . . it can't happen to anyone else."

Tristan pulled back so he could look me in the eye. "I've never met anyone like you, Rory, you know that?"

"Coming from someone who's been around as long as you have, that means a lot," I said lightly.

Tristan smiled and leaned in to kiss me. His lips tasted of salt and something sweet I couldn't name. I poured every inch of myself, every ounce of sadness and longing, of terror and despair, of hope and love, into that kiss.

He pulled back, his blue eyes searching mine for a long moment. "I love you, Rory Miller."

I curled my fingers through his, clinging to him. "I love you, Tristan Sevardes."

He sighed at the sound of his real name, pulling me to his chest like he would never let me go. In that moment I knew that whatever happened with my family, he would never leave me. We were in this together. Forever.

FINISH THE JOB

Sometimes it bothers me how easy it is to fool people. It's almost as if they want to be lied to. Like they find it comforting. Like they need so badly to believe in the facade that I've put forth, to believe in me and this place and everything it stands for, that they allow themselves to be blind to everything else.

Or maybe I'm just that good.

But soon, that's all going to change. They won't be able to deny it anymore. Soon they're going to see me for who I really am. They're going to know who really holds all the power.

I can hardly wait.

ONE GOLD COIN

The moment I woke up on Friday morning, I stopped breathing. The air crackled with an ominous chill. I stared at the ceiling, my fingers curling into the blanket at my sides, balling parts of it up inside my fists. I wasn't going to look at the nightstand. I was *not* going to look. I refused.

But after two minutes of wide-eyed protest, my eyeballs actually ached. Finally, I ever so slowly turned my head, and there it was, sitting in the center of my nightstand.

One. Gold. Coin.

"It looks like Barbie, Minnie Mouse, and Hello Kitty got together to plan Mardi Gras," I said to Bea that night. "While drunk."

We were standing under the huge white tent set up behind Tristan and Krista's house, surrounded by potted topiaries swathed in pink tulle, tables set with yellow and pink and magenta china, and waitresses dressed like prima ballerinas—tutus, ballet slippers, and all. Bea sipped peach-colored punch from a sparkling crystal glass and raised one eyebrow at me. Right. She *had* spent two hours on a ladder today carefully stringing beaded garlands and tulle from the rafters.

"But in a good way," I amended.

I was trying so hard to keep it light, to not think about that coin in my room and what it meant for my family. To not think about everything that was going wrong on Juniper Landing. To not obsess about Nadia and Jessica and the mayor and Oblivion. Most of all, I tried not to think about how the person who was sending people to the Shadowlands might be a guest at this party. Might be watching us right now, waiting for their chance to grab more innocent souls.

"Yeah, right," Bea said with a sigh. "We both know it's butt-ugly. But at least she's happy."

She gazed across the dozen round tables and the white tiled dance floor at Krista, who was chatting with a few visitors in her circle-skirted pink party dress. For the first time, I saw that Bea really did care about our "birthday" girl. The Lifers were all so different, but they were a family.

"Having fun?"

Tristan wrapped his arms around me from behind and nuzzled my neck. Bea gave us an annoyed sort of look and quickly glanced away.

"It's nice," I said as he kissed my cheek and moved to stand next to me. He was wearing a light blue polo shirt and white linen shorts, his blond hair grazing his eyebrows. "It's nice just to think about something else for a little while."

"Agreed," Bea said, downing the rest of her drink. "And what I'm thinking about is getting more punch. You guys want anything?"

"I'm good," Tristan said.

"Me, too," I added, leaning into him.

Bea rolled her eyes and walked off, tugging down on the hem of her denim miniskirt. On the dance floor in the center of the tent, Lauren was letting loose along with a crowd of visitors as Pete DJ'd from a booth set off to one side. The paper lanterns and swaths of garland swayed in the ocean breeze as the ballerinas delivered salads and champagne to the tables, then moved off, pirouetting with their free arms raised elegantly overhead. It was as if the whole service were a carefully choreographed dance. Officer Dorn shuffled slowly around the periphery of the tent, his hands clasped behind his back, keeping a surreptitious eye on the guests. He looked up and met my gaze. I stared at him until he looked away.

"What kind of party do you think you'll have for your anniversary?" Tristan asked, holding me closer.

"I don't know," I replied. "I haven't even thought about it. The whole idea of being here for a year . . . It seems impossible."

"Wait till you've been here for a hundred," he said, half joking, half grim.

It was the first time he'd even come close to approaching the truth about his time on the island.

"What's it like, being alive for that long?" I asked, turning to face him and wrapping my arms lightly around his neck. Dorn passed behind Tristan, and I ignored his glare, biting my tongue to keep from asking where his friend Nadia was tonight. "Don't you get bored? Do you ever want to just . . ."

"End it?" Tristan asked, a shadow flickering across his face. "I can't say I haven't thought about it on the darker days—trying to figure out a way to move on from here. But then I remember that I was meant to be here. That this place needs me. And I just . . . go on."

I lifted his other hand and laced all our fingers together. "You'll have to show me how to do that, once I start having darker days."

He gave me a confident smile. "I will," he said, kissing the bridge of my nose. "You know I will."

I melted into him, and we hugged for a long time. Then he spotted something over my shoulder and pulled away.

"What's this?"

I turned to find my father and the mayor walking into the party together. He was wearing a suit jacket unbuttoned over his shirt, and she had on a pretty black dress with lace at the neckline. Her hair was down for the first time since I'd met her and was so long it fell past her shoulders in a girlish way. My father had his hand on the small of her back as they weaved around the tables together. My stomach clenched at the intimate gesture.

"I don't even want to know," I said, swallowing hard.

Behind my father, Darcy and Fisher walked into the party, making a stunning couple, him in a stark white shirt that contrasted sharply with his dark skin, her in a slinky black dress and red heels. I saw a few heads turn as they sauntered by, and I could read the jealousy in the girls' glances. That was how people always looked at Darcy. Like they hated her and wanted to be her all at the same time. I was glad Fisher had brought her here. Darcy deserved a party.

"I guess everyone's coupled up for the night," Tristan said as a new song started and Lauren and her posse of visitors cheered.

"As long as we're coupled up, that's all I care about," I said, resting my head against his shoulder.

Suddenly, a series of explosions nearby killed all conversation. The music stopped abruptly, and Krista screamed.

"Krista?" Tristan shouted in alarm.

Out of nowhere, a bubbly, pop version of "Happy Birthday" blasted through the speakers. Tristan and I stared at each other, confused.

"What the hell?"

But Tristan's words were still hanging in the air when people around us began to gasp and smile. Bea pointed toward the back of the tent and cheered.

"What is it?" I asked.

"I don't know."

Tristan took my hand and led me around the outskirts of the tent. Set up near the back of the property, a safe distance from the guests, was a huge sign made out of crackling sparklers, the words HAPPY BIRTHDAY KRISTA! spelled out in bright white lights. Joaquin stood nearby, eyeing Krista with a cocky grin.

"Joaquin! I can't believe you did this!" Krista cried, jogging forward to give him a hug. She covered her mouth as she watched her name sparkle, and everyone began to applaud.

"Dude, you are out of your mind!" Tristan shouted to hoots and hollers. He moved forward to high-five Joaquin, and I trailed after him.

"Not bad, huh?" Joaquin asked, clearly proud of himself. He raised a hand toward the party, and I saw Pete, who'd put on the "Happy Birthday" song, signal back.

"I'm stunned," Krista said. "I thought you said this whole thing was lame."

Joaquin shrugged modestly. "Yeah, well, it was important to you, so . . ."

"Best birthday gift ever," Krista told him.

"This is going well, I think," Tristan said, gazing out over the party. "So far so good?"

"Yep," Krista said. "No fog equals good birthday."

I glanced back at the tent, where Fisher and Darcy broke from a kiss. She smiled happily.

"Yeah. Not bad at all."

The four of us started back toward the crowd. Bea, Cori, and Kevin were already digging in to their salads. I spotted my dad pulling out a chair for the mayor, and suddenly felt a tingling sensation that started in my toes. My whole body went cold, and I stopped so abruptly it took Tristan a moment to realize I wasn't next to him.

"No," I said, pressing my hand to my heart as my eyes filled with tears.

But the effervescent sensation didn't stop. It just came on stronger, swirling through me, bubbling from my toes all the way up through my torso and into my head.

"What?" Tristan said, the remnants of a smile still lighting his face. "What's wrong?"

My throat completely closed. I stared at Tristan, desperate, until realization washed over his face. Then, all of a sudden, a hush came over the bluff. Bea dropped her fork and stared at us. Lauren stopped dancing. Slowly, everyone else on the dance floor stilled as well.

That was when I felt it, creeping up my legs and over my shoulders. The cold wetness of it. The first fingers of fog curled around my feet and my knees went weak. The sparklers started to hiss and smoke, dying out one by one.

"Sonofa—" Joaquin said, turning around to face it.

The fog rolled in over the bluff, rushing toward us over the grass. Tristan, Krista, and Joaquin all stared at me grimly until the mist consumed them.

"It's my dad," I croaked finally, the fog hissing in my ears. "I'm supposed to take my dad."

BROKEN

A clear path to my father opened up in the fog. I could see him plain as day, looking wonderingly, blindly, into the mist. I was supposed to walk along that path, take his arm, and usher him over the bridge to his eternal life.

"No," I shouted. "No! I won't do it. I can't." I turned around and ran, the fog engulfing me from all sides.

"Rory, no!" Tristan shouted.

I could practically feel him coming after me and turned on the speed.

"Don't!" Joaquin yelled. It sounded like he was somewhere to my left, but it was impossible to tell. Still, I turned right and barreled ahead, tears streaming from my eyes, trailing across my face, and dripping onto my shoulders.

My father was going to die. He was going to die for real. That's what this really was, wasn't it? This moving on? He was going to leave, and I was going to be left here. Alone.

"Rory! Stop now!"

Something in Joaquin's voice made me freeze. I gasped for breath, the ragged effort scratching my lungs.

"Don't. Move," Tristan instructed. "You're right on the edge of the bluff."

I gasped, my head going weightless. Suddenly I could feel it, the emptiness in front of me. My toe twitched, and a rock popped over the edge, clicking along the wall into the endless nothing. I had almost fallen. I could have been killed. Except . . .

"So what?" I cried, my voice cracking as I turned around. I couldn't see them. There was nothing but fog. "I can't die, right?" I shouted into the nothingness, my fingers curling at my sides. "Who cares if I fall?"

"No," Tristan said, appearing in a swirl of mist, his hand outstretched. "You can't die."

"But you can break every bone in your body," Joaquin added, stepping up next to Tristan. "And believe me, that hurts."

I let Tristan close the gap between us and pull me away

from the edge. Down below, the surf crashed louder.

"It's okay, Rory," Tristan assured me, holding me at arm's length. "No one expects you to take him."

"Of course not," Joaquin added. "We made a pact."

"It's not that," I said, sniffling as I shook my head. "I may not take him tonight, but I'll have to eventually. I'm going to have to say good-bye to my father. I had to say good-bye to my mother, and next it'll be my father, and then Darcy . . ." I felt as if my chest were splitting open. As if it would never be mended. "I don't know how I'm supposed to do this, Tristan," I gasped. "It's not fair. It's not . . . fair."

"I know," he said, pulling me to him and letting me cry all over his pristine blue shirt. "I know it's not fair."

"This is so intense," Joaquin said. "We've never had a Lifer have to sit here and watch their family go, one by one."

I let out a loud sob.

"Dude. Just stop talking," Tristan said.

Joaquin blanched. "Sorry."

Somewhere in the depths of the mist, a car door thunked shut, and an engine revved. A shiver went through me. No one should be driving in this mess, which made me wonder what sort of person would try, and for what reason.

"Listen, we're not going to figure out what's going on or how to fix it tonight, and no one is taking your dad," Tristan said, releasing me. "So why don't you just go home with your family? Spend some time with them tonight. That's what you should be doing."

"Yeah?" I asked, glancing back in what I thought was the direction of the house. "How do I get them to leave? Darcy hates me, and my dad is clearly on a date."

"Tell your dad you're gonna blow chunks," Joaquin said. "He'll go home with you."

I shot him a disgusted look, but he just shrugged.

"And he'll make Darcy come because he won't want to leave her behind in this," Tristan added.

"Great. Then she'll really hate me," I muttered. "She'll think I'm lying just to ruin her night or something."

"So stick your finger down your throat and puke if you have to," Joaquin said. "That'll get the job done."

I laughed in disbelief, but they said nothing, and I knew then how urgent the situation was. This was no joke. It was time for me and my family to go home and spend some time together. We didn't have any to spare.

MOVIE NIGHT

"This movie's stupid," Darcy grumbled, snuggling further into the couch cushions.

"Bite your tongue," my dad shot back, his arm slung around my shoulders. "This is one of the greatest films of all time."

We were watching *Superman*—the original one from the 1970s—on his laptop, which glowed brightly in the center of the coffee table. It was ridiculously cheesy, but it was one of my father's favorites, so at the moment, I didn't care.

"Fine, but we're watching *Footloose* next," Darcy muttered.

"Kevin Bacon?" Dad said hopefully.

Darcy gave him a look as if she was embarrassed to share the same air with him. "Please. Do I look like I'm forty?"

"Okay, fine. We'll watch *your* version. What about you, Rory?" my dad asked. "What's your pick for this little all-nighter you've got planned?"

"I don't care," I said honestly, tugging the musty afghan up over my shoulders. "I'll watch whatever."

"*The Natural* it is, then," he announced.

Darcy groaned, and I stifled a laugh. Dad could have whatever he wanted as far as I was concerned. I hadn't been forced to fake illness to make him leave the party. The mayor had mysteriously disappeared on him, and he said he was more than ready to "blow this popsicle stand," as he put it. Darcy had been the harder sell, but my dad put his foot down. Joaquin was right. He didn't want her walking home alone in the fog.

So now here we were, ensconced in our little house, the fog still clouding the windows as we indulged in a family movie marathon. As Superman struggled with his kryptonite necklace on the screen, I rested my head against my father's chest and listened to his improbable heartbeat. I hadn't done this in so long—cuddled with my dad on the couch—not since I was a little girl. Now it was the only place I wanted to be. He was still warm, still breathing, still here. And that was all that mattered.

I gazed through the living room window at the grayness outside, and a pair of sinister, glittering eyes stared back at me.

"Dad!" I shouted, jumping up.

"What?" he asked, startled to his feet. "What is it?"

"Outside! I saw—"

But when I looked at the window again, the eyes had vanished. I walked to the front door, shaking, and yanked it open, met with a swirling wall of wet gray air. In the distance a crow cawed.

"Who's out there?" I demanded, as my father and Darcy walked up behind me. "Who's there?"

Silence. Nothing but the hissing of the fog.

"It was probably just a bird or something," Darcy said, trudging back to her seat.

"This fog can really mess with your imagination," my dad added, putting his hands on my shoulders. "Come on. Let's get back to the movie."

He waited for me to close the door, then walked me back to the couch. We settled back in together, but this time I found I couldn't relax. While my dad and Darcy watched Superman save the planet, I kept my eyes trained on the window and the swirling fog outside.

Someone had been out there, watching us. I was sure of it. And whoever it was was out for blood.

ANOTHER BEAUTIFUL DAY

A merry morning birdsong tugged me from my sleepy state on Saturday. The first thing I noticed was that my face was not on my pillow, but stuck to something grooved—soft but grooved. I blinked open my eyes and looked around, disoriented. The living room. Right. I'd passed out somewhere between Ren getting his butt kicked and . . . whatever happens after Ren gets his butt kicked. I glanced at the end of the couch. No Darcy. I pulled the corduroy pillow I'd been sleeping on into my lap, then stretched my arms over my head, yawning as I gazed out the window.

It was another beautiful morning in Juniper Landing. Light breeze, sun shining, waves crashing in the distance . . .

Suddenly, I was sucked backward through the couch and thrown against the wall, all the air knocked out of my lungs.

Sun shining. The sun was shining.

I threw myself off the couch cushions, screaming, "Dad!"

I tripped over an ottoman as I raced for the stairs, and my big toe exploded in pain. Tears burned my eyes as I stumbled forward, shaking, trembling, gasping for air. He wasn't gone. He couldn't be gone.

"Dad! Daddy!" I screeched, fumbling up the staircase. I threw open the door to his room.

His bed was made. There were no slippers on the throw rug next to it. No worn novels on the nightstand. No glasses, no coffee mug, no piles of dog-eared manuscript pages. Tears spilling over onto my cheeks, I staggered to the closet and tore it open. Two dozen empty hangers stared back at me. Everything was gone. Everything.

"No!" I shouted, whirling around. "No!"

I ran over to Darcy's door and reached for the knob, when it suddenly turned and the door swung open. Darcy, wearing a black nightgown, stood before me, her hair in a tangle.

"*What* are you shouting about?" she demanded through her teeth, her eyes at half-mast.

"Where's Dad?" I yelled.

There was a long, silent moment as Darcy's face slowly screwed up in confusion. "Dad?"

She pronounced the word as if she'd never heard it spoken before. Her eyes were a total blank.

My sister had forgotten our father.

"Omigod," I said under my breath, turning around on knees so weak they buckled. I forced myself to breathe. How could this be happening? I was the one who was supposed to take him. And they'd all promised. No one else was to leave the island. They'd made a pact.

And just like that, it hit me. The pact. Nadia. Nadia had looked so betrayed when the mayor had agreed to my plan. She hadn't wanted to stop ushering souls. Why? Because if we stopped ushering souls, there would be nothing else to frame me for. It was her all along. She was the one doing all this and trying to pin it on me.

That was why she'd been the only Lifer who hadn't attended Krista's party last night. She'd probably been off somewhere, plotting this—planning her ultimate revenge. She wanted Tristan so badly she was willing to betray the Lifers, usher my father before his time, and get me sent to Oblivion in the process.

Suddenly I remembered the pair of sinister eyes watching us through the window last night. The pair of dark, glittering eyes.

"Omigod," I said again. "Omigodomigodomigod."

"What the hell is the matter with you?" Darcy demanded.

I shoved myself up to my feet and ran, barreling down the steps. I stopped short when I saw the table by the door, bare. She'd taken the family picture. The only one I had of my mother, my father, Darcy, and me all together.

I was going to kill her.

Slamming the front door behind me, I ran for town. On Freesia, the guy on the bike with his surfboard swerved around me and crashed, but I didn't care. I threw myself out onto Main Street and almost collided with someone's chest.

"Rory!"

It was Joaquin. He held both my arms in a death grip as I bent toward him, heaving, gasping for air. At my toes, a long line of ants marched toward the curb.

"Where's my father?" I begged. "Where's my father, Joaquin? Where is he?"

I leaned past his shoulder, trying to get a look at the mayor's house, needing to see.

"Rory," he said, tugging me around in a circle, trying to put my back to the bluff. "Don't. Just calm down. Just—"

"Get off me!" I screeched, shoving him so hard he fell to the sidewalk. For a split second, we both stared at each other, stunned. Then I turned to look.

There was the weather vane, gold and gleaming against the bright blue sky, sitting up with its proud swan, like its message was unimpeachable, like it had all the authority in the world.

And it was pointing south.

EVIDENCE

"Where're you going?" Joaquin asked as I sprinted away from him and started across town, my eyes so blurry I could barely see straight.

"It was Nadia," I spat, keeping my eye on Tristan's house. "I know it was. I'm going to tell Tristan and the mayor."

"Rory, stop!" Joaquin shouted. He grabbed my arm as I reached the curb, and a car jammed on its brakes. "You're going to hurt yourself. Just take a breath."

"Take a breath?" I screamed, my heart splintering in my chest. "My father is in the Shadowlands! I can't take a breath!"

Bea jogged up next to us. Her face was all red, and her hair was darker at the hairline, soaked with sweat. Fisher and Kevin were close behind, their jaws set, looking grim.

"What happened?" Bea demanded, gasping for air. "Where's the fog?"

"Her dad was taken," Joaquin told them, still holding on to my arm.

"*What?*" Kevin's eyes were wide. "Who?"

"Nadia," I said, gnashing my teeth.

"You're kidding," Bea replied.

"We don't know that for sure," Joaquin said placatingly.

"No. *You* don't know that for sure." I lowered my voice as two visitors strolled by, carefree, holding hands. "I know what I saw. She was at my window last night, watching us. Just waiting for us to fall asleep so she could take him."

Tears welled up behind my eyes as I remembered the feeling of my father's arm around me, my cheek resting against his chest. I fought as hard as I could to keep them at bay. I couldn't break down right now. I had to help my father.

"Rory, I know you don't like Nadia and she doesn't like you," Bea said. "But she would never do something like this. She lives for the rules almost as much as Tristan does."

"It was her, Bea. I swear to you." I looked up at Fisher's mirrored sunglasses and he removed them, as if he sensed this was too important not to look me in the eye. For the first time all week, I knew exactly how I felt about him—I felt he could be useful. "Where does Nadia live?"

"What?" Fisher asked, glancing over at Joaquin. "Uh . . . down by the docks. Why?"

"Get her," I said. "Go by yourself, take someone, whatever you want to do. Just get her."

Fisher laughed nervously. "Um, okay. I don't know what you're thinking right now, but I don't take orders from—"

"Get her," Joaquin grunted. Fisher stared at him. "Just go, Fish. The sooner we let her tell her side, the better off we'll all be."

"I'm on it," Fisher said, and he ran off toward the bay.

"We'll be at Tristan's!" I shouted after him. Then I turned and speed-walked up the hill. Joaquin, Bea, and Kevin were rght on my heels. I stared blearily at the weather vane.

My dad is in the Shadowlands. She sent him to the Shadowlands.

One sob burst from my lips, and I bit it back. I couldn't think about that. Not now. If I thought about that, I would go down in a swirling black cloud of despair, and I couldn't let that happen. I was my father's only hope. Nadia was the key. If she'd sent him there, she had to know how to get him back. And if anyone could make her talk, it was the mayor.

The moment I crested the hill, I saw Cori and Pete sitting on the bench at the fork in the path, one trail leading back down the hill toward the beach, the other to the house. Two dirt bikes lay in the grass next to them. They both stood up as I approached.

"Stay away from me!" I shouted, veering toward the house.

"Where's she going?" Cori asked behind me.

"She's lost it," Joaquin replied. "She thinks Nadia took her dad."

"What?" Cori blurted.

"Where is she, anyway?" Bea asked as they all jogged to keep up with me.

"I don't know," Pete replied. "I haven't seen her since the Swan on Thursday."

I pressed my lips together, triumphant. I knew it. She'd even steered clear of her friends yesterday? It was her. It *had* to be her.

"Tristan! Mayor Parrish!" I hurried to the porch. I stumbled up the steps, and Krista opened the door.

"Rory! Are you okay?" she asked, stepping toward me.

"Where's your mother?" I demanded. "Where's Tristan?"

"Oh . . . uh . . . the mayor's not here. But Tristan's up in his room, I think," she said hesitantly. "Why don't you—"

I shoved past her and barreled up the stairs. I had to get to him. I needed him. I needed him to tell me he would help me fix this. That everything would be all right.

"Tristan!" I cried, my voice breaking. "Tristan!"

The door to his room was wide open. He wasn't there, but sitting in the middle of his bed was a red drawstring bag, bottom heavy and bulbous. The sight of it, so odd and out of place, stopped me cold. I took in a deep, shaky breath as I heard the rest of the Lifers scramble up the stairs. Joaquin looked over my shoulder into the room.

"What is that?" he said.

"I don't know," Krista responded.

With the confidence of a person who'd been in this room ten million times before, Joaquin pushed between us and opened the bag. His face lost color so fast I thought he was going to faint. He looked up at me, his eyes wide with terror.

Everyone else froze. Bea and Kevin took two steps past me into the room, while Krista stayed rooted with me at the door. Cori and Pete hovered at the top of the stairs.

"What?" I breathed. "What's wrong?"

Joaquin overturned the bag. Dozens upon dozens of fat gold coins rained out onto the bedspread, tinkling a happy song as they slid this way and that, forming a messy pile. Krista covered her mouth with both hands. Nadia leaned into the wall.

"Ho-ly. Shit," Kevin said.

Then we all heard a footstep in the hallway.

"Rory?" Tristan's voice said.

"Tristan, don't," Krista said.

But he'd already stepped into the room. His eyes focused on the pile of coins, and his face went slack.

"Tristan?" I said blearily.

"What the hell is going on?" Joaquin demanded.

Slowly, Tristan tilted up his chin. He gave me a long look. The depths of his beautiful blue eyes swirled with shock, with pain, with fear—and with guilt.

A fissure sliced a jagged line through my heart, and I felt my knees start to buckle.

Then he turned around and ran.

MAKE THEM PAY

I stood at the very back of the cave, a flashlight stuck into the ground at my feet, shining up at his name.

TRISTAN SEVARDES (PARRISH) 1766.

He'd made me believe that he loved me, that he was willing to change everything for me, but it had all been a ruse to throw me off the scent. He and Nadia had been together all along. That confrontation between them on the night we first kissed had been for show. He'd been lying to me from day one. Setting me up to take the fall.

I was so stupid. So very, very stupid.

The wind outside shifted, howling through the mouth of the cave. I shivered inside my heavy sweatshirt and hugged it closer to my sides. I was never going to trust anyone ever again. I was never going to allow myself to love. Clearly, I had no sense of people, no ability to judge character, no clue what was going on in anyone else's mind.

"Rory?"

Joaquin's voice echoed through the cave, surrounding me, filling me with a whisper of hope.

"Back here," I called out.

His flashlight beam darted across the wall, illuminating colorful snatches of names, a riot of letters and numbers. I wondered if Tristan had been here that night, when I'd come here to find his name. If he'd hidden from me in the shadows. If he'd left that tally behind in his haste to get away from me. Bile rose up in my throat at the millionth realization of how stupid I'd been.

Never again. Never.

After a moment, Joaquin and Krista appeared. I'd left them just over an hour ago, but they both looked as if they'd been marooned somewhere for days. Krista's white T-shirt had a streak of dirt across the front, and Joaquin's forehead had gone red with sunburn. They were out of breath as they stopped behind me.

"What're you doing?" Krista asked, eyeing the open can

of red paint at my feet, the paintbrush handle sticking out the top.

"I realized I never added my name to the wall," I told her coolly. I wouldn't let my voice betray my emotions. Once I started letting my emotions pour out, they would drown me. My sharpened gaze flicked to Joaquin. "Did you find him? Nadia?"

"Not yet, but we will," Joaquin said, gasping for breath as I turned my back on them to face the wall. He reached out to grasp my shoulder. "Are you okay?"

"No. I'm an idiot," I said, glaring at Tristan's name. "There are all these things I'm remembering. The other morning I walked in on him locking something inside his desk—probably the coins." I looked at Krista. "Then you heard him and Nadia talking Thursday morning and they were both gone all day—the same day five souls got ushered? They must have been off somewhere, planning it. Making sure everything would go off like clockwork."

"I can't listen to this," Krista said, shaking her head and taking a few steps back toward the fire pit.

I pursed my lips as I looked over my shoulder at Joaquin, knowing how hard this must be for her.

"Remember that tally I found the other day? The one Pete took from me?" I said, and Joaquin nodded. "I think it was theirs. I think that's why Nadia immediately knew what it was and tried to pin it on me. I saw Tristan making those same kinds of marks in the sand the other day."

"This is insane," Joaquin said, rubbing his forehead. "This can't be happening."

"I just didn't put it together until today," I finished.

"Stop it," Krista snapped suddenly, storming over to us. Her skin had gone from white to red, and I'd never seen her eyes so angry. "Tristan is the best of all of us. There's no way he had anything to do with this."

"Krista . . . what other explanation is there?" I asked.

"He's had a lot going on," Krista said, looking at the ceiling. "He's been distracted. Maybe Nadia planted those coins in his room—did you ever think of that?"

"Then why did he run?" Joaquin asked. "Why is he hiding?"

Krista just stared at him. She didn't have an answer for that.

"And why did he have this?" I reached into the back pocket of my jeans and unfolded the photo of my family.

"Where did you get that?" Joaquin asked.

"When you guys went after Tristan, Fisher came back to tell us Nadia was gone, and he and Kevin searched Tristan's room," I told them. "They found this in the bottom of his shoe trunk."

I looked at it once, staring into my father's laughing eyes, before folding it and putting it back into my pocket.

"So what do we do now?" Krista asked.

"Simple." I reached down and picked up the paintbrush, scraping the excess paint from its bristles into the can. "We figure out how to get my father and Aaron and Jennifer and the others back."

I reached up and started to paint my name right above Tristan's, the tail of the R touching the top of the T. It took all my concentration to keep my arm from shaking, but I managed to work through it.

"But how?" Joaquin asked, watching the brush as if mesmerized. "No one has ever come back."

"There has to be a way," I said firmly, biting my tongue to keep from cracking as images of my father, Aaron, and Jennifer swirled through my mind. I dipped the brush into the paint again and methodically wrote my last name, Miller. "If people can be sent there erroneously, there has to be a way to bring them back. We have to believe that."

"And then what?" Krista asked. "If we do get them back. What happens then?"

I didn't reply. Not until I'd finished. Not until my name was fully inscribed on that wall for all eternity.

RORY MILLER (THAYER) 2013.

The bottom curl of the *3* dripped down the craggy rock wall, the bloodred paint marring the top of the white *h* in *Parrish*. Satisfied, I dropped the paintbrush back into the can and faced them.

"Then we find Tristan and Nadia," I said clearly. "And we make them pay."

ACKNOWLEDGMENTS

Every book I write is a journey, and this one in particular marked my path from a dark, devastating moment in my life back into the light. As such, it started out in a rocky place and seemed to take forever to be guided to where it needed to be. For their help along the way, I have to thank the following people, who always seem to be there to support me in ways large and small.

I owe the deepest gratitude to Lanie Davis, who worked as hard as I did on this book, if not harder. I couldn't have finished it without you. (But you knew that.) Thank you also to Josh Bank, Sara Shandler, Katie McGee, and Emily

Meehan for their input and insight at various stages of the manuscript. Thanks to Sarah Burnes for metaphorically holding my hand through my breakdown and to Matt for actually holding my hand and talking me out of my threats to drop everything and become a Realtor or a cupcake-baker or a cupcake-baking Realtor. Most of all, thank you to Brady and Will for always bringing a smile to my face and reminding me why I do what I do. I love you more than anything and always will.

Turn the page for a look at

ENDLESS,

the breathtaking conclusion to the Shadowlands series . . .

THE BELL TOLLS

"Rory, stop!"

I tried to freeze, but the muddy, rocky path beneath my left foot began to slip, crumbling into the deep roadside river below. Rain pounded on my useless vinyl hood as I grasped at the air with cold, wet fingers. I was finally able to grab the slippery fabric of Joaquin Marquez's sleeve, and he hoisted me back up onto solid ground, my heart pounding in my throat at a maddening rate. The muddy pathway we were traversing had been, until recently, wide enough for at least one car, if not two, to navigate safely. But now it was half its former width and eroding by the moment.

The rain had been nonstop since Saturday night. Now it was Wednesday, and half the island of Juniper Landing seemed to have turned to mush. The sand on the beaches had taken on the consistency of oatmeal in spots, and the grasses and reeds and flowers had been flattened to the ground, beaten into submission by the relentless weather.

"Are you okay?" Joaquin asked.

I nodded, clutching both his elbows for stability. His brown eyes were shaded by the brim of his own hood, and a few days' worth of dark stubble covered his sharp cheekbones and chin. This had become a habit of Joaquin's lately— saving me from serious injury. I wasn't sure how I felt about the fact that the boy my sister used to hook up with was now my protector, but I was grateful to have someone by my side. And it clearly wasn't going to be the boy *I* used to hook up with. He was no longer around.

Which was why we were out here in the first place— looking for Tristan Parrish. The guy I had been falling in love with, until a few days ago. The guy who had betrayed us all. According to Joaquin, there was a cave beneath the bridge where Tristan used to go to for his "big thinks"—the days he just wanted some space away from the other Lifers. Unfortunately, it was located in a part of the island Joaquin had always avoided unless he was ushering a visitor to the bridge, so we weren't entirely clear on where we were going.

That, plus the relentless rain, didn't make our mission any easier.

"Is this ever going to stop?" I asked.

As if in answer, a bolt of lightning cracked overhead and the whole world trembled with the accompanying thunder. Over Joaquin's shoulder I saw a shadow illuminated by the flash—someone standing on a rock ledge not fifty yards away, raincoat billowing in the wind. My fingernails dug into Joaquin's arm.

"Is that . . . ?"

Joaquin turned, but just like that, there was no one there. One blink, and the shadow had disappeared. The storm was playing tricks on my mind.

"What?" Joaquin asked.

"Nothing. Forget it." I didn't want to admit I was seeing things. "I just can't handle much more of this."

"Relax. Take a breather," Joaquin said. "Let me figure out where the hell we are."

As he moved off to peer into the grayness surrounding us, I tried to shake the jittery feeling that shadow had left behind and looked north toward the bridge. It was so encased in fog that I could see nothing but the pointless warning lights throbbing at the top of its four spires. The bridge had become—to me, anyway—the symbol of everything that was wrong on this island. Juniper Landing was an in-between—a place where souls came to reside between death and the afterlife, a place where they were given a chance to resolve any issues that might have plagued them during their lifetimes before moving on. Joaquin and I were both Lifers, a group of souls charged with helping others find their resolutions and ushering them to their final destinations. The bridge was the means of transport. When a soul was ready to go, we would take the person to the bridge and hand him or her a coin. As soon as he or she touched the coin, it just sort of knew whether that soul was destined for the Light or the Shadowlands, based on how good or evil the person had been in life. We would then usher that person across the bridge, where a portal would open, taking him or her to the proper place. This was a system that had been in place since the dawn of time and had always worked perfectly, maintaining the balance of the universe.

Until now. Recently the whole thing had gone haywire, with devastating consequences. We were pretty sure that the coins were somehow to blame, since Tristan had been hiding a whole bag of them—more than any Lifer had ever seen in one place at one time—and had fled the second the rest of us discovered his stash. We weren't clear on what exactly was wrong with the coins, how they had been tampered with, or where Tristan had even gotten them. All we knew was that last week, a few souls who were undeniably good had wound up in the Shadowlands. Souls like my friend Aaron and Joaquin's charge Jennifer. Souls like my father. They were good people, damned to hell, and soon after they had left, we caught Tristan with the coins.

Something lodged in my throat at the mere thought of my dad in the Shadowlands—alone, terrified, possibly tortured—and for a second, I couldn't breathe.

"I think it's this way," Joaquin said, nodding toward the bridge. "Let's keep moving."

I let him lead the way, allowing myself one glance back over my shoulder at the spot where the shadow had been. The outcropping was deserted. I breathed in and out deliberately, trying to calm the frantic beating of my heart. As we moved closer to the bridge, I could just make out two figures clad in black rain gear, their nebulous forms like dark ghosts, moving in and out of my waterlogged vision. Ever since we'd discovered the tainted coins, the Lifers had been taking turns guarding the bridge, to insure no one could cross over. I had no idea who was scheduled to be there now, and from this distance through the rain, I couldn't make out their faces. For some reason, their dark presence felt ominous instead of comforting.

It's going to be okay, I told myself. *You're going to fix this. You just have to find Tristan and Nadia and make them tell you how to fix it.*

Tristan. The image of him and his smiling, duplicitous face twisted my stomach into knots. I had believed in him. I had trusted him more than anyone. I had loved him. And he'd betrayed me. I had been suspected of ushering good souls to the Shadowlands, and then it was finally revealed that Tristan was the villain. Tristan, who had told me that the rules of this place couldn't be broken. That I had to trust in the system. That everything would be fine.

He'd said those things to me. He'd kissed me. He'd made me feel safe. And then he'd ushered my father straight to hell.

Joaquin and I turned up an even scrawnier, more circuitous path, leading toward the drop-off into the ocean, toward the very foot of the bridge. As a cold rivulet of water found its way under my collar and down my back, I couldn't help wondering, for the millionth time, *Why?* Why had Tristan done this to Aaron, to Jennifer, to my dad . . . to all of us? What did he stand to gain? And, most selfishly, why had he done this to me? Why suck me in and make me care? Why make me believe in him and everything this place was about, only to turn around and betray me and destroy his home?

Joaquin looked back at me and held out a hand. I grasped his fingers, half expecting them to slip away from me, but his grip was surprisingly solid. A few weeks ago I never would have believed that I would one day willingly hold Joaquin's hand. When I first met him, I had hated him. He was *that* guy. That guy who knew how hot he was and used that fact to toy with the heart of any girl who showed an interest in him. In this case, that girl had been my sister, Darcy.

But the more I got to know Joaquin, the more I respected him. He truly cared about his charges, about his friends, and about this place. And when things had started to go sideways, he'd basically become my personal bodyguard. And over the past few days, since we'd found out Tristan was the big bad around here, we bonded even more. No one wanted to find Tristan more than we did. Joaquin had been his best friend. I'd been Tristan's girlfriend. (Would-be-ex-girlfriend the second I saw him again.) We *needed* to find him. We needed to ask him that one burning question: *Why?*

It was what kept us going—the hope that we would one day get the answers we were looking for: why he had done what he'd done, how he could betray everyone he claimed to care about, and, most important, how to free my dad and Aaron and Jennifer and those other poor souls. What I didn't know was what we were going to do with Tristan and Nadia—another Lifer who'd disappeared with Tristan—once we'd found them. My brain didn't even want to go there.

"I think it's down there," Joaquin said, squinting downward, tiny droplets clinging to the ends of his thick eyelashes. "I noticed the pathway the other day. It's kind of like a series of steps cut into the rock."

I didn't see anything, but I shrugged. "You lead the way."

Together we started slowly and carefully down the side of the drop-off. My foot slipped on the very first step, and Joaquin's grip on me tightened. We both froze.

"You good?" Joaquin asked.

I nodded mutely.

"Okay. Stay behind me and be careful."

He didn't have to ask me twice.

We descended the steep stairway in silence, and I focused on the sound of my own breathing, the plop of raindrops on my hood, the crashing of the waves far below, and the cautious positioning of my feet. But I couldn't help thinking of the look on Tristan's face the day we'd found the bag of tainted coins in his room. The realization in his gorgeous blue eyes that he'd been caught.

I wasn't stupid. I knew what I'd seen. Tristan was guilty. I just wished my heart would catch up with my brain and start believing it.

After what seemed like a lifetime, Joaquin jumped the last couple of feet to a foot-wide stretch of broken shells and sand that ran along the foot of the rocks. I leaped down after him, lifted my head, and saw it—the wide-open mouth of a cave.

"Score," Joaquin said.

Every inch of my skin flushed with heat, making me itch beneath my vinyl jacket. Tristan was in there. Maybe with Nadia, maybe not. Either way, we were about to get some answers.

And I was going to see him again.

I narrowed my eyes and clenched my teeth. Stupid heart.

Through the fog and the rain, I noticed a pile of something white and gray near the mouth of the cave. As we edged closer, I saw the blood. The glassy eyes, the twisted necks, the torn and shredded feathers. Dead seagulls. Dozens of them. Broken, deformed, and staring. Flies buzzed around their misshapen heads, and as I watched, one of them landed hungrily on the dome of a wide, glassy eye. Within seconds a swarm of them had engulfed the seagull's skull.

Then the wind shifted and the stench hit me like a brick in the face. I turned my nose away and covered my mouth with a hand.

"Just keep walking," Joaquin said, quickening his steps.

We passed by the carcasses and into the coverage of the cave. The sand near the opening was thick and sloppy, and my sneakers let out a sucking sound every time I lifted a foot. I nudged my hood from my head, relieved to be out of the rain even as my breath quickened. I could already smell the pungent scent of a recent fire.

Joaquin and I locked eyes. He tugged his flashlight from his jacket pocket but didn't turn it on, and he raised one finger to his mouth. I nodded. Moving in sync, we tiptoed forward. Joaquin paused for a moment at a corner and peeked around it. He visibly relaxed and flicked on his light.

"They're not here."

Deflated, I stepped out into an open area of the cave, the ceiling only five inches from the crown of my head. It was a wide space, and as Joaquin flashed his light to and fro, something caught my eye against the far wall.

"There!"

I grabbed his shoulder and pointed. Joaquin swung the beam back around, and it caught on something—a blue-and-white blanket. We raced for it. I got there first and dropped to my knees. The sand in this part of the cave was cold but dry. I whipped the blanket aside and stopped breathing. Underneath it was a crowbar, a first aid kit, and a hammer, with a few balled-up, bloody bandages tossed alongside. There were also two small piles of folded clothes—his and hers—several granola bars still in their wrappers, and three full bottles of water.

"So they were here," I whispered, irritated at the flash of jealousy I felt at the sight of Tristan's clothes folded next to Nadia's in such a cozy-couple way. Outside, thunder rumbled, but it was muted by the miles of rock over our heads.

"What were they doing with a crowbar?" Joaquin asked, crouching. He tentatively picked up one of the bandages by the clean end. "And whose blood is this?"

I shivered. "I don't want to know."

Joaquin dropped the scrap back into the sand and stood up, dusting off his hands. He was tense. I grabbed the light and flashed it along the floor, finding the remnants of their fire. It was still smoldering. Joaquin cursed under his breath.

"We just missed them," he said. "They were right here."

"Well, this is good, right? They can't have gotten far." I shoved myself up, the adrenaline pumping. "We can track them."

"How?" Joaquin demanded, whirling on me. "It's not like they're leaving footprints out there! The rain'll make sure of that!"

"You don't have to yell at me," I shot back. "What do you want to do? Just stand here? Let them get away?"

I turned toward the mouth of the cave, and Joaquin followed, his flashlight beam dancing ahead of us.

"You're about to go out on a wild-goose chase," Joaquin muttered. "And it's going to start getting dark."

"This whole thing is a wild-goose chase!" I cried, throwing my arms wide. "But this is the best lead we've had in three days. We can't just go home."

Joaquin grabbed my arm, turning me roughly toward him as I tried to lift my hood.

"But how are you even going to—"

His question was cut off by the distant clanging of a bell. It sounded like one of those old church bells they used to ring at the chapel near my house in Princeton whenever someone got married. Except this wasn't a merry, celebratory song. It was a frantic, uneven plea. Joaquin went white.

"What is that?" I asked.

"The bell." He turned away, facing south toward town, which wasn't visible from the foot of this cliff.

"Yes, I know it's a bell," I said. "What does it mean?"

"It means there's an emergency." He scrambled back toward the rocky stairway, past the pile of seagull carcasses, and over the broken shells.

"What kind of emergency?" I asked, sliding and slipping after him.

He paused with one foot on the third step, stretching his long legs as far as they would go, and looked back over his shoulder. I'd never seen him so terrified.

"I don't know," he said. "That bell hasn't been rung since Jessica got those innocent people damned to the Shadowlands, Rory. It hasn't been rung in a hundred years."

DESTRUCTION

The rain stung my face as we sprinted toward town, my feet slipping on fallen leaves, my lungs burning from the effort. My nostrils prickled with the ominous scent of dank, billowing smoke. Over the constant thrum of the rain and whooshing of the wind, I caught an errant scream, echoed by a dozen more. Joaquin's eyes were wild as they met mine, and we ran even harder.

When we finally arrived at the point overlooking the town square and the docks below, I was so stunned by what I saw I almost skidded right over the rocky ledge. Somehow

I managed to stop myself in time and doubled over next to Joaquin, heaving for breath.

The ferry that had always brought new souls to Juniper Landing was on fire and sinking—fast. The entire back of the vessel had gone up in flames. The air was torn with shouts and screams, and I could see several prone figures lined up on the bay's meager shore. Dozens of others clung to jagged shards of wood in the choppy, roiling surf or desperately swam for land, while Lifers dove in from the docks to help.

"Holy shit," Joaquin said between gasps.

We sprinted down the hill, skidding by the library and along the west side of town toward the docks. The air here was thick with smoke. We passed a few dazed Lifers in the shopping district, each of them frozen, their eyes shot through with confusion and fear as they watched the disaster unfold before them. It was an eerie sort of stillness to pass through before reaching the chaos of the docks. The long walkway was flanked on either side by slick, steep outcroppings of rocks. Bodies of the injured were laid out on the shore, while the more mobile survivors made their way to the rocky slope or up the stairs to the docks. Everywhere I looked, my friends and fellow Lifers were helping however they could.

Darcy's current boyfriend, Fisher Morton, tossed a person onto his broad shoulders and carried him to the sand before turning right back around and swimming out again. Bea McHenry was towing three people toward shore as they clung to a large chunk of the boat's prow. Farther down the dock, Krista Parrish and Lauren Caldwell helped patch up scrapes and bruises and burns, while a few strangers wandered aimlessly, shouting names or pleading for help. I yanked off my jacket and ran for the water. Joaquin was right behind me.

"Stop right there."

The sound of the mayor's commanding voice froze me in my tracks. I turned to find her standing on the rocks near the water's edge beneath a huge black umbrella, her blond hair slicked back in a low bun, her black raincoat cinched at the waist. Her ice-blue eyes flicked over me.

"They need help!" I shouted.

"Let them handle it," she said, nodding at the swimmers, who included my sister. "We need more hands out here cataloging the injuries."

Cataloging the injuries? Who the hell talked like that? But as I looked around at the wounded visitors huddled or lying on the slim stretch of sand, I saw that she was right. These people couldn't die, of course, but we had to find the ones in critical pain and separate them from those with simple bumps and bruises.

"Joaquin! Rory! I need some help over here."

Krista—Tristan's "sister" in the world of Juniper Landing, and as of the last few weeks, my friend—waved us down. She stood next to a man whose arm hung limply, the bone jutting at an unnatural angle. She had on a white raincoat over her jeans, but her blond hair was lifeless, and her skin was as pale as ice. Joaquin raced to her side just as Kevin Calandro and Officer Dorn sped up on a flatbed truck loaded with boxes, stopping in the parking lot at the top of the hill.

"We have the supplies!" Kevin shouted, swinging down from the cab. His normally shaggy black hair was slicked back from his face, and he wore a black tank top that exposed the colorful tattoo of flames that danced over his arm. His pointy chin rose in determination as he yanked open the back of the truck.

"Get us a splint!" Joaquin shouted at me. "And a sling!"

I ran to Kevin and helped him unload, tearing boxes open at random. The containers were full of first aid supplies, from ointments and creams to bandages, scissors, and stitching kits. In the third crate I found a dozen blue-and-white slings and flat plastic splints. I grabbed a set and stood.

"Here. You'll need this." Kevin tossed me a roll of medical tape, which I caught in my free hand.

"Thanks," I said, then sprinted for Joaquin and Krista,

checking the chaos for Darcy along the way. Where was she? Was she okay?

"I need help. I need help," a mocking voice passing very close behind me mimicked the victims.

My shoulder muscles coiled and my blood turned cold as Ray Wagner, one of my charges, stomped by in his dirty brown coat, his wispy hair sticking up on one side, even in the relentless rain. I ignored him and jumped down to the beach, but he leaned into the dock's railing above my head and laughed, exposing his yellow teeth and a tongue that had been blackened by chewing tobacco. With the rain running freely down his face, he spat in the sand and smiled, as if settling in to watch a ball game.

"What should I do?" I asked Joaquin, who was holding a man's arm as gently as possible. The man's face was purple with pain, and the wrinkles on his forehead deepened whenever he moved. Krista had stepped back, watching the proceedings with wide blue eyes. She looked as if she was hanging on by a thread.

"Put the sling over his head, gently. And hand me the splint," Joaquin ordered.

"You'll be okay," I told the man, slipping the white band over his head. "Don't worry. We've got you."

"Don't worry. Don't worry. Blah, blah, blah," Ray mocked me, tilting his head from side to side.

I shot him a look of death, but he simply laughed.

Ray Wagner had slaughtered four people in a one-night killing spree in Richmond, Virginia, before getting shot dead in a convenience store parking lot while trying to take out his fifth victim. Normally, I would have done my best to usher him as soon as possible, but since things were all out of whack and the no-ushering policy was in place, he was still here. As were a few other unsavory characters my friends had yet to usher. Lauren had been charged with a white-collar criminal named Piper Molloy, who had swindled dozens of families out of their life savings and rendered them homeless. Bea had a woman who had stepped off the ferry two days ago looking as if she'd come right out of the Stone Age with her scraggly hair, dirty fingernails, and gnarly teeth. Her name was Tess Crowe and she'd murdered her own parents, brother, and sister before being relegated to an insane asylum. Bea currently had her locked up in the attic of the home she shared with two older Lifers. Supposedly Tess kept her hosts up at night screeching and trying to claw her way out.

There had been some talk of locking up the visitors meant for the Shadowlands in the jail beneath the police station, but it was comprised of only two tiny cells and wasn't equipped to hold them all, so for now, we were each tasked with babysitting them as best we could—making sure they didn't cause any trouble. Ray was the only one, however, whose sadistic heart had been drawn to today's devastation. Lucky me.

"Oh god! That hurts!" the man cried out as Joaquin taped his arm to the splint.

"Almost done," I said as Joaquin used his teeth to rip the tape.

Once he'd secured the arm with four tight circles of tape, we gently maneuvered it into the sling. Then I carefully helped the man sit down on one of the dock's pylons.

"Thank you," he said, slumping slightly.

"Just hang out here while we figure out where to take you," Joaquin said.

"Thanks, you guys," Krista said, stepping between us with her knees wobbling. "I had no idea what to do."

"It's okay," Joaquin said. "The question is: what next?"

We scanned the water and the beach. Nearby a woman was sobbing next to her bleeding husband. A man staggered past us and collapsed onto the sand, his chest heaving for breath. Joaquin had nailed it. Where were we supposed to start? Then I saw a flash out of the corner of my eye: my sister's dark hair as she ran for the water. She was wearing nothing but shorts and a tank top and was soaked to the bone. Clearly this was not her first time diving into the bay.

"Darcy!" I shouted. But she didn't hear me. She plunged

beneath the choppy waves, reemerged, and swam straight for a little girl whose arms flailed as she went under, choking. My hands flew up to cover my mouth as Darcy plunged after her. I watched the whitecaps where they'd disappeared, scanning for any sign of them. But I could only see the spot where my sister and the girl had gone under.

Where are they? I thought, clenching my jaw.

"There!" Joaquin shouted, startling me. He pointed a good ten feet to the left of where I'd been looking, and there was Darcy, gamely swimming for shore with one arm locked around the little girl's chest. "She's okay." He gave my shoulder a quick squeeze. "They're both fine."

"Who's *that?*" Krista asked.

A sinewy, strong guy about our age was swimming toward the shore, holding a middle-aged woman tight around her chest, her chin tilted up toward the sky so she could breathe. He placed her on the shore, then raced right back out to the ferry to grab a man who still clung to the doomed ship's guardrail. Quickly, he pried the panicked man's fingers from the railing and brought him back to safety, then went out again, cutting through the water like it was nothing to him.

"Where did he come from?" I asked.

"I have no idea," Joaquin said.

Darcy had just gotten back to the shore and pulled the

little girl to safety. I ran to her side, slipping over the rocks until I reached the sand.

"Darcy! Are you guys okay?" I asked, dropping to my knees next to her.

Darcy flung her wet dark hair over her shoulder. She was winded but otherwise seemed fine. The girl, however, was wailing.

"She may have broken her leg, and look at her skin. She's so pale. I think we should get her to the hospital. Where the hell are the EMTs, already? Or the Coast Guard?"

I swallowed hard. Darcy had no clue about the realities of where we were. As far as she knew, we were still alive, enrolled in the witness protection program thanks to Steven Nell, and about to get a call any day saying he'd been apprehended and we could return to Princeton, to our home and our friends. She didn't know that a place like Juniper Landing didn't need any personnel dedicated to saving lives, because no one here had a life to save.

"Um . . . maybe the weather is screwing things up?"

"Well, we have to get her to a hospital," Darcy insisted.

Joaquin, who was now tending to a woman nearby, glanced over at me. "We don't exactly have a hospital," he said reluctantly.

"No hospital?" We looked up to find Super Swimmer Boy hovering over us, heaving for breath, his jet-black hair dripping water down his square cheekbones. "What do you mean, there's no hospital?"

His skin was a healthy tan, and he had one blue eye and one brown eye. The whole package was so handsome and startling I found myself staring. Darcy rose to her feet next to me, as speechless and transfixed as me.

"Yes, they're different colors. No, I don't know how or why," he stated, not amused, but not angry, either. Then he focused on Joaquin. "What do you do, then? Go to one on the mainland?"

"How would we even get everyone there without the ferry?" Darcy said, gesturing around wildly.

Now it was Joaquin's turn to be stumped. "Um . . . we . . . "

The seconds ticked by slowly. Strangers began to gather, having overheard our conversation, the injured cradling their arms or holding torn scraps of fabric against wounds. Everyone seemed to wait on whatever it was Joaquin would say next.

"Take them to the clinic."

An unpleasant shiver raced down my spine. I looked up at the plank walkway leading to the town and saw Mayor Parrish looking down at the rest of us.

"The clinic?" I asked.

"Of course," she said, rolling her eyes. "The clinic."

Then she gestured oh-so-elegantly up at the bluff, where her gorgeous, sprawling colonial mansion sat overlooking the town.

"Come now, everyone," she said loudly. "Let's help those who can't help themselves. Once we're settled inside and out of this rain, we can assess the situation."

For a long moment, no one moved. Not that anyone could have blamed us. This was not normal procedure for a disaster, following the snappish mayor up the hill with no EMTs or nurses, no ambulances, no nothing.

But this was Juniper Landing, and I'd long since learned that nothing around here was normal procedure. It wouldn't be long before everyone else here figured it out as well.

UNEXPECTED

People scream and cry and beg around me, but for the moment, I am still. I watch the prow of the ferry slowly sink beneath the surface of the water, and then it is gone. Completely gone. This, I was not expecting. Without the ferry, there will be no new souls. The pickings will begin to grow slim, and I haven't met my goal yet. I haven't completed my assignment. I still need five more.

But it's okay. I'll just have to focus. I have to make sure that only the good are taken, not the bad. Taking the bad is fine, but, for me, a waste of time. I must fulfill my destiny before they find me, before they figure me out.

I turn away as a hand reaches out to me, and watch Rory Miller help some poor, bloodied woman up the steps to a waiting truck. Soon, it will be up to her. She just doesn't know it yet.

THE CLINIC

"So, what's your name?"

Super Swimmer Boy stared straight ahead as he walked, the little girl Darcy had saved clinging to him with her tiny arms around his neck. Darcy had gone ahead with Krista to get into some dry clothes. The little girl's blond hair hung in wet hanks down her back, and she sniffled continuously, her cheek resting on his shoulder. The elderly-but-spry woman I was helping held fast to my waist, each step we took over the wind-flattened grass slow but steady. She had a deep gash on her forehead near her hairline and was holding a wad of gauze to it with her free hand, but she seemed otherwise unharmed. Out on the bay, the water slowly swallowed the bow of the ferry. I couldn't believe it was gone.

"Liam," he said. His tone was somehow mournful as he gazed steadily ahead. "Liam Murtry."

"I'm Rory Thayer," I offered.

He glanced at me so briefly I wasn't sure I hadn't imagined it. "Nice to meet you."

"And I'm Myra Schwartz," my patient offered, touching her chest. Droplets of rain dotted the lenses of her red-framed glasses. "What's your name, honey?" she asked, tilting her head to better see the little girl, her smile kind.

"I'm not supposed to talk to strangers," the girl said in a meek voice that broke my heart.

Myra nodded. "Good girl." Then she winked at me as if to say, *We're in this together.* I smiled gratefully in return.

"Behind you, Rory!" someone shouted.

Liam reached out and tugged me and Myra toward him as Kevin and Fisher passed, toting an old-school stretcher of canvas and wood between them. On it, a heavyset man in a suit groaned, his arm flung over his head to ward off the rain. They raced by as Liam and I watched, his strong fingers still gripping my biceps. I looked down at his hand and waited.

"Sorry," he said, recovering himself. He released me and grimaced. "It's just . . . this is some scene."

I took a breath, really looking around me for the first time since we'd started for the mayor's house. Officer Dorn had set up a makeshift command post near the bottom of the hill, handing out the stretchers he and Kevin had retrieved from the police station's basement along with the other supplies. There were only a few, so he was busy assessing injuries to decide who needed one and who didn't, his buzz-cut blond hair covered by the hood of a huge army-green poncho. Pete Sweeney and Cori Morrison passed by, supporting a limping man between them. Pete was stooping to try to even out the marked height difference between him and Cori. Bea and Ursula, the older Lifer whom Joaquin shared a home with as pseudo grandmother and grandson, carried a woman on a stretcher whose skin looked waxy and green. There were new arrivals everywhere, wincing, groaning, crying—doing the best they could to make it up the steep hill as Lifers darted around trying to help. The girl in Liam's arms shifted her head to look at me.

"Where's my mom?"

Liam's eyes met mine. "We'll find her," he assured her, running his hand down the back of her head. "Don't worry. We'll find her."

My throat constricted as we kept moving, Myra's fingers gripping my jacket. I knew in my heart that we probably wouldn't find her mother. Unless the girl had died along with her mom in an accident of some kind, she was here alone. Most children stayed on Juniper Landing for approximately five seconds before they were ushered to the Light, too young to have unresolved issues or to have done anything in life that would mark them for the Shadowlands. But since we'd stopped ushering people, the few kids who had shown up here these last, agonizing days were still here. One adorable boy named Oliver had wept nonstop for his parents upon arrival, until the mayor had taken him aside and worked her magic on his mind, basically making him forget he'd ever had parents. He'd jumped up and run off to the other brainwashed kids to start a game of tag. It was the first time I understood the real benefit of her powers.

"You were pretty impressive out there," I told Liam, trying to change the subject.

He lifted his shoulders as best he could. "I'm a lifeguard. It's what I do."

We were making our way up the path to the mayor's front door, the pavement lined with dead brown marigolds and piles of wet, withered leaves—things we wouldn't have seen in Juniper Landing when we first arrived here, when even the plants could never die. A sort of traffic jam had occurred near the front of the house, and people stood on their toes, angling for a look at the front of the line. Liam's charge started to whimper.

"This looks like it's going to take a while," Myra stated, her brown eyes full of concern as she looked at the girl.

"Come with me," I whispered.

Liam raised his raven eyebrows, intrigued, and our small party stepped away from the line. I led Liam and Myra toward the back of the house, where there was a patio with a door to the kitchen and great room. We slid open the glass door and finally stepped out of the rain.

The scene that greeted us inside the house was astounding. Every last stitch of cozy, beach-house furniture in the sprawling great room had been cleared away, and in its place were rows of cots, each covered with a plain white sheet. Krista and Lauren moved about, efficiently smoothing bedding and setting up gauze and bandages and bottles of antiseptic on tables. On the far side of the room, the injured streamed in through the front door, where they were checked in and assessed by Police Chief Grantz and the mayor herself. Pete and Cori helped their patient onto a bed nearby.

"Where should I take her?" Liam asked me.

"See the blond woman by the door?" I said, gently rubbing the girl's back. "She'll want to take a look at her."

"Got it," he said, and carried the little girl toward the mayor.

"Come on, Myra. Let's get you a bed," I said.

"I don't want to cut the line," she said a bit uncertainly as she glanced around.

I smiled. "I won't tell if you won't."

We took a step, and Myra listed to the side. Panic gripped me as her eyes rolled up, and I desperately tightened my grip on her, but it was impossible to hold her suddenly lifeless form. Pete noticed and rushed over to help, ducking under Myra's opposite arm.

"What do we do?" I said.

"Here. Get her to the bed." Pete nodded at the nearest cot. Together we staggered toward it and turned around, sitting down with Myra between us.

Myra groaned and her head lolled forward. Then her arm fluttered off my back and she touched her hand to her head.

"What happened?" she asked.

"You fainted. I think."

"You should lie down, but keep your head propped up," Pete said. I shot him a questioning glance. His green eyes were bloodshot and his nose was red. Sweat poured down his face. "My dad was a doctor," he explained to me under his breath. "If you're faint or dizzy, you're supposed to rest but keep your head over your heart."

"Good thing we ran into this nice young man," Myra joked.

I smiled at Pete, who sort of grimaced in return. "Yes.

A very good thing," I said. Pete and I were not the best of friends, considering that not so long ago he and his pal Nadia had accused me of ushering innocents to the Shadowlands. This was the first time I'd spoken to him since Tristan and Nadia had fled, thereby exonerating me and making themselves look guilty as sin. Maybe that was why he currently seemed unable to look me in the eyes.

Once Myra was propped up on a few pillows, she gave me a nod and patted my arm. "Thanks, Rory. You go see if someone else needs your help."

"I'll be back," I promised her. "Thanks, Pete," I added.

But he had already moved on to the next bed to help Cori with another patient.

I turned around to do the same and was immediately overwhelmed by the frenzy of activity. Darcy and Fisher were leading people to cots while some of the older Lifers tended to wounds and complaints. The stream of "survivors" coming through the door was never ending, and I wondered whether we'd even have enough room for all of them. That was when I spotted a pair of people so odd they momentarily took my breath away. Huddled together a few beds from where I was standing were a guy and a girl, about twenty years old, with white-blond hair in the exact same bowl-cut style, their bangs wet and scraggly over their foreheads. Their features were so similar—broad foreheads, straight noses, angular chins—that I might not have guessed their genders except for the fact that the girl was wearing a plain black dress while the boy wore dark pants and a white shirt. They both had light blue eyes and their skin was an olive hue. Their temples were pressed together as they whispered to each other, but their gazes darted around the room, taking everything in. It was eerie—their awkward pose, the way they were communicating so intensely without looking at each other. An eerie, bloodcurdling sort of fear moved slowly through me, the way the fog had engulfed the beach my first night here. Something wasn't right about them. I could feel it.